Berkley Prime Crime titles by Julia Buckley

Writer's Apprentice Mysteries
A DARK AND STORMY MURDER
DEATH IN DARK BLUE
A DARK AND TWISTING PATH
DEATH WAITS IN THE DARK

Undercover Dish Mysteries
THE BIG CHILI
CHEDDAR OFF DEAD
PUDDING UP WITH MURDER

Death Waits
in the Dark

Julia Buckley

BERKLEY PRIME CRIME
New York

BERKLEY PRIME CRIME
Published by Berkley
An imprint of Penguin Random House LLC
1745 Broadway, New York, NY 10019

ISBN: 9780451491916

First Edition: April 2019

Printed in the United States of America
1   3   5   7   9   10   8   6   4   2

Cover art by Bob Kayhanich
Cover design by Alana Colucci

For Daphne du Maurier

Acknowledgments

Thank you first and foremost to Michelle Vega, who has championed this series from day one, and without whom Lena and Camilla would not be finding their way onto bookshelves across the country and beyond. Michelle, I am grateful for your wisdom, grace, and enthusiasm. Thank you for loving the books as much as I do!!

Thanks to Kim Lionetti, fellow Phyllis A. Whitney and Mary Stewart fan. Your insights are always spot-on, and I am grateful to have you as my agent.

Thanks to Karina Thibodeau for lending her name to one of the characters.

Thank you to Nicole Carino Garafolo, Suzi Litwin, Celia Warren Fowler, Kory Bull, Amanda Ciolek, Connie Glad Speters, Nicole Dawson Vickers, Becky Prazak, Barb Louthan, Catherine Lawry, Ann O'Neill Foster, Teresita Valadez, and Chris McCarthy for joining the dialogue about Camilla's eye color. You will find that the majority won.

Thanks to two Nashville readers, Katie Connolly and Jane Day-Tiller.

Thanks to all of these people for their friendship and support: The entire Rohaly clan—especially my dad, Bill; and my brothers and sisters, Bill, Claudia, Chris, and Linda; and my in-law siblings Ann, Cindy, and Kevin—for reading, coming to signings, and sharing the books around. Thanks to Cashie Rohaly, Evan Yszenga, Billy Rohaly, Erica Ewen, Joey Rohaly, and Pam Connolly for your book launch support. To Karen Kenyon, Karen Owen, Lisa Kelley, and Linda Langford. To Lydia Brauer, Pam Costello, Quinley Costello, Patti Williams, Rachel Jendras Meiner, Kathy O'Brien Gentile and Vivian O'Brien, David Chaudoir, Mark and Ann Marie Andersen, Mia Manansala, Lori Rader-Day, Alli Bax, and Augie and Tracy Aleksy.

Thank you to Jeff, Graham, and Ian Buckley.
Thank you to the great Gothic suspense writers to whom I have been dedicating these books; this novel is dedicated to Daphne du Maurier. My wonderful seventh-grade teacher, Cynthia Barnett, used to read us a chapter of *Jamaica Inn* every day after recess. I think I might have been the only student who merely endured recess so she could get back in to the real fun: a spooky novel about smuggling set on the rocky Cornwall coast. After that first experience, I graduated to other du Maurier books, and by the time I read *Rebecca*, I knew I was dealing with a storytelling genius.

Bestselling Books by Camilla Graham:

The Lost Child (1972)
Castle of Disquiet (1973)
Snow in Eden (1974)
Winds of Treachery (1975)
They Came from Calais (1976)
In Spite of Thunder (1978)
Whispers of the Wicked (1979)
Twilight in Daventry (1980)
Stars, Hide Your Fires (1981)
The Torches Burn Bright (1982)
For the Love of Jane (1983)
River of Silence (1985)
A Fine Deceit (1987)
Fall of a Sparrow (1988)
Absent Thee from Felicity (1989)
The Thorny Path (1990)
Betraying Eve (1991)
On London Bridge (1992)
The Silver Birch (1994)
The Tide Rises (1995)
What Dreams May Come (1996)
The Villainous Smile (1998)
Gone by Midnight (1999)
Sapphire Sea (2000)
Beautiful Mankind (2001)
Frost and Fire (2002)
Savage Storm (2003)
The Pen and the Sword (2005)
The Tenth Muse (2006)
Death at Seaside (2008)
Mist of Time (2009)
He Kindly Stopped for Me (2010)

(a four-year hiatus)

Bereft (2015)
The Salzburg Train (2016)
Death on the Danube (2017)
Death at Delphi (in progress)

*At the risk of appearing melodramatic, I must
tell you this: When I met you, I realized there
were no other women in the world. Not for me.*
        —From the correspondence of
   James Graham and Camilla Easton, 1971

GRAHAM HOUSE WAS a respite from the late-June heat, especially in the air-conditioned office of my collaborator and hero, Camilla Graham. I was there now, sitting on the floor and telling an amused Camilla the story of my first date, which had involved much awkward conversation and an even more awkward attempt at a kiss, and I had reduced Camilla to a giggling fit more than once as the story progressed. It was amusing to both of us to contemplate my fifteen-year-old self, pretending to be a sophisticated woman while being scared to death. Camilla's German shepherds, pleased to see me at floor level, had immediately demanded petting, and Heathcliff was starting to lean on me as he relaxed into my massage. "Heathcliff, get off! You giant rug. You're making me hot. You, too, Rochester." They smiled at me with open, panting mouths, remaining exactly where they were.

Camilla laughed. "You've spoiled them, Lena. They get much more attention now that there are two of us in the house—double the walks and the petting. And now that I hired this little local girl to take them out sometimes, they have three devoted mistresses. Clearly they are smug about it."

I sniffed and looked into the brown eyes of each dog. "What's in it for me, you guys?"

They had no suggestions. A crash sounded from above us, followed by some loud swearing. "Oh no," I said. "That doesn't sound good."

Camilla stared up at the ceiling, as if trying to see through it. "I hope no one is hurt."

"I hope the air conditioners are still intact," I said, perhaps selfishly. Camilla had central air, but somehow it only cooled the ground floor of her big old house. When the heat wave began, Adam Rayburn, Camilla's steady boyfriend, enlisted the help of a group he called the "Three Amigos," namely Doug Heller, Sam West, and Cliff Blake, to install window units in the bedrooms upstairs. The younger men had spent a great deal of time together in the last month, and they did in fact seem to function well as a group of three—at least when they were doing "guy" things. At other times they invited me to join them, along with Doug's girlfriend, Belinda.

"It will be nice to have those window units," Camilla said. "They should make for better sleeping. Adam assured me that the machines are not loud."

"It will be wonderful. Up until this last week I never had a problem with the temperature. I slept with the window open and enjoyed the nice breeze. But now the air is just—stagnant. I thought it was always cooler by the lake."

Camilla nodded. "We mostly have mild summers, but we've been prone to heat waves in early July, which begins in just a few days, can you believe it?" She shook her head, apparently marveling at the rapid passage of time. "You're more of a fall person, aren't you? You do look a bit like a wilted flower there on the floor."

"I'll perk up now that I'm in here. But walking to town this morning wasn't a good idea. It's incredibly humid out there."

We heard loud footsteps descending the stairs, and Doug Heller's blond head poked into the room. "Camilla, where might I find a toolbox?"

Camilla pointed. "The closet in the kitchen hallway. Bottom shelf."

"Great, thanks!" he said, darting into the next room.

"Everything okay up there?" Camilla asked.

"Fine," Doug said. "A minor emergency, but we handled it."

"You taught me some new swear words," I called to him, winking at Camilla.

Doug appeared in the doorway, looking slightly guilty. "You heard that? It wasn't me, anyway, it was Cliff. Something fell on his toe."

"Oh my gosh! Is he okay?" I asked. The dogs became alert at my tone; their ears stood at attention.

"He's fine. He's looking forward to the cold beer Camilla promised."

"I'm chilling the glasses as we speak," Camilla

said. She stood up behind her desk and moved toward the kitchen. She wore a light summer dress of pale pink and a pair of white sandals. "I'll go check on them."

Doug went in with her, and I was left alone with the dogs. "I mean it, you guys, that's enough petting. I'm too hot to be surrounded by fur." I gave them each a last pat and then pushed slightly on their flanks. They got the message and ambled over to Camilla's desk, under which they liked to sleep during the day.

The doorbell rang. I managed to pull myself upright, feeling languid still, and to walk to the entrance hall. I peered through the window to see an elderly woman on the steps, looking like a mirage in the hazy heat; I did not recognize her.

I opened the door. "Hello," I said.

She studied me for a moment. She was tall and thin, with a halo of white hair. She wore a black cotton dress that draped down to her ankles; it looked severe, almost punishing, considering the temperature. Her hazel eyes were narrowed with a quizzical expression. "I'm here to see Camilla," she said.

"May I ask your name?" I said. I had no idea if this woman were a friend or a determined fan—Camilla did get unwelcome visitors now and again.

She jutted out her chin. "Tell her it's Jane Wyland. She knows who I am. But it's been a long, long time." She didn't smile when she said this.

I knew it would be polite to invite her in, but I didn't want to admit anyone to Camilla's house unless I knew Camilla wanted them there. "Excuse me for just a moment," I said. I left the door slightly ajar, so it didn't seem as if I were closing it in her face, and then I jogged to the kitchen.

Camilla was peering into the freezer, where the glasses were nicely chilled and waiting to be filled with beer. Doug had apparently gone back upstairs. "Lena, can you call up to the boys and ask when they think they'll be down?"

The boys. This made me smile, but something about the woman at the door distracted me from my amusement. "Yes, I'll do that. I don't know if you heard the doorbell, but there's a woman here to see you."

She closed the freezer and turned, brows raised. "Oh? Who is it?"

"I don't know her. She said her name is Jane Wyland."

Camilla blinked at me. "Jane *Wyland*? I—my goodness. I haven't seen that woman in more than forty years."

"Should I—?"

"I'll talk to her. Thank you, Lena."

I lingered near the doorway and heard Camilla greet the visitor in a rather stiff voice. The woman said something, and Camilla said, "Why don't you come in? We can talk in my study." And then, in response to a question, "That was Lena. She is my friend and writing collaborator. She lives here with me, actually."

They were closer now, and I heard the woman named Jane Wyland say, "You probably didn't think you'd ever hear from me again, did you, Camilla?"

Camilla's voice was smooth, unruffled. "I confess

I didn't imagine our paths would cross, but then again, life has a way of bringing us back to our origins."

They moved into Camilla's office, and Camilla closed the door.

A shadow moved on the wall, and I jumped when a pair of hands touched my shoulders. "Hey," said Sam West.

I turned and whispered, "Hey."

He leaned in to give me a warm kiss. "*Hey*," I said again, appreciatively.

"Why are you whispering?" he asked, smiling at me.

I spoke a bit louder, though still quietly. "Camilla has some woman in there. She hasn't seen her in decades, and they went in the office and closed the door."

"Do you think we should call the police?"

I poked him in the chest. "Very funny. But I got a weird vibe. And it's not like ominous things haven't happened around here before."

"That's for sure." He looked around the kitchen. "I'm supposed to make sure that beer is in the offing."

"Oh, right. I'll help you pour." We retrieved the chilled glasses from the freezer and I pulled three bottles of Corona from the fridge. As we worked, I asked, "Everything okay up there?"

He was pouring carefully, trying to avoid too much foam. "Your chamber shall be cool and pleasant, my queen."

"Oh, thank goodness. I just cannot sleep when it's that hot."

He took a sip of his drink. "If you were awake, you

should have walked down the hill to your boyfriend's house and told him of your insomnia. He has all sorts of ideas for night activities."

I laughed. "I spend plenty of nights at Sam House, so I know *all* about your night activities, and I approve. But when I'm working and staying here, I need the kind of cool you have over there in your gorgeous modern marvel of a house." Sam had jokingly started referring to his place, right down the bluff from Graham House, as "Sam House," and those two buildings had become my two residences.

Doug and Cliff came in and practically dove on the refreshments. Sam said, "Do you guys have time to sit for a while?" They nodded, and our group of four moved to Camilla's sunroom.

I flopped into a chair near the window. "Thank you so much to all of you. I am not a creature who thrives in the heat. Camilla said I looked like a wilted flower, and I felt like one this past week."

"You need to go down and jump in the lake when it gets this hot," Doug said, shrugging. "Ned Purchase offered us full access to his private strip of beach—he's in New York until September. Belinda and I have been in the water constantly."

"You just want to see her in a bathing suit," I joked.

Doug grinned. "She has some great bathing suits, but we've also opted for the au naturel experience. She rocks that, too."

Sam's eyes met mine. "We should swim more, Lena."

Cliff sighed. "Have a heart. Some people at this table have no significant other."

I touched his arm. "Why is that? How does a handsome guy like you end up coming to Blue Lake all alone?"

Cliff took a swig of beer and sighed. "Sam has already heard this whole story. There was someone. Beth. We lived together for several years. It didn't work out, but we parted on good terms. I think she's married now." He looked out the window at the lake, which was still as glass on this windless day.

"Maybe she just wasn't the right one for you," I said.

Cliff shrugged. "I've always been a little too devoted to the job. And I was—kind of obsessing over Sam West in those years. Following up on every little thing I could learn about my little brother here. Beth told me to just contact him, but I was stubborn."

We thought about that for a while. Cliff had finally taken a job in Blue Lake just to be closer to Sam, who hadn't known he had a half brother.

Doug pointed at his fellow cop. "We've got to get this guy back into the dating pool. Lots of attractive women in this town."

I studied Cliff and had a sudden inspiration. "You know what, Cliff? I know someone I think you would really enjoy meeting. And I know she would like you. You meet several of her criteria for what makes a good man."

Sam laughed. "And how do you know this woman's criteria?"

"She went to high school with Allison and me. She graduated a couple years before we did; she pursued veterinary school, and she got a job at an animal hospital in Chicago, but they ended up reducing their staff. Allison's been trying to get her to Blue Lake—you know Allison. She wants all her friends to come here."

"It worked with you," Doug said. We exchanged a smile; we both recalled the day that I came to town, lured by a phone call from Allison Branch.

"Allison's been sending her clippings of job openings at animal hospitals in this area. Allie is hilarious in her enthusiasm, as always. But Isabelle really is considering coming out for some interviews."

"Isabelle," said Cliff appreciatively. "That's a pretty name."

"Yes." I studied him. "Isabelle's the whole package: smart, pretty, fun. Like you, she was with someone, but he ended up revealing his true character, and Isabelle dumped him."

"Good for her," Sam said.

Cliff shrugged. "Well, if she ever comes to town, I'd be happy to meet her. Meanwhile, I'm on duty in about an hour and I need to get home and put on the uniform."

Doug's face changed; he always looked serious when he thought about cop things. "I'm off today, and I have plans to take Belinda to Warrenville for a movie and dinner. But if you hear any more about our vandal, let me know."

"Blue Lake has a vandal?" I asked.

Doug and Cliff both took on that shuttered look that law enforcement people get when they can't share information. "Don't we always?" Doug said lightly. He stood up, and so did Cliff.

I turned to Sam. "I think your playmates are leaving."

Sam stood and joined the other two as they walked to the kitchen door. The men exchanged some of those hearty man-hugs and thumped one another loudly on the back. I darted in and hugged them all, too. "I appreciate your help, and I always love your company. Come back soon, and we'll play a board game in Camilla's nice cool house."

"Invite Isabelle, too," Cliff joked.

Doug put a hand on my shoulder. "Belinda wants to have a little get-together at her place soon. She's thinking maybe a Fourth of July party. She'll be contacting you."

"Okay! Sounds fun," I said.

I waved and watched from the kitchen doorway as Sam walked his friends to the front door and saw them out. He shut the door and turned to say something to me, but he was interrupted by a loud voice saying, "Of course you would protect him! You were in *love* with him!" Camilla's study door flew open and the woman named Jane Wyland came stalking out, her fists clenched at her sides. Camilla emerged as well, her face paler than I had ever seen it, her eyes desolate.

The Wyland woman moved to the front door without saying a word, but when she reached the place where Sam stood, she pointed at him and said, "The notorious Sam West. It figures *he* would be your friend. That says a lot about your family, doesn't it? The whole *Graham* family. I'll be back tomorrow, Camilla. So make your decision."

She scowled at me, and then at Sam, and then she swept out of the door.

Shocked, I turned to Camilla, who seemed on the verge of tears. "Camilla? What in the world—?"

She held up a hand. "Lena, would you call Adam and cancel my lunch date with him?"

"Yes, if you want, but Camilla, are you all right? That woman—"

She covered her face with her hands for a moment and then moved swiftly to the stairs. She spared me one quick glance; her eyes were full of tears. "I can't talk about this right now," she said, and she ran up toward her room.

Sam and I stared at each other across the space of the foyer, our mouths open in disbelief.

Finally he said, "Who *was* that woman?"

I narrowed my eyes. In the ten months I had known her, Camilla had never lost her composure, in any situation. And no one had ever dared to speak to her in that tone. Now this Wyland woman, this stranger, in her grim black attire, had waltzed in and upset my mentor, my friend—my family. "I don't know," I said. "But I'm going to find out."

I ran out the front door and saw that she was just reaching her car—a long, dark vehicle that seemed to emanate heat. I tore down the steps and met her as she was unlocking the door. "Miss Wyland," I said. "I think there's been a misunderstanding. Camilla is very upset . . ."

If I thought that confronting her would make her back down, I thought wrong. Her face looked almost triumphant when she heard about Camilla's distress. "Oh, did I upset her? Well, that is a shame, isn't it? For forty years this family hasn't faced justice, and now that I try to hold them accountable, you take her side. They'll *all* be on her side! That's why I am taking a different route. She'll want to keep the family pride intact, won't she? So now I have my chance. Now I can stand up for *my* family, and for once people will listen. You can count on it." She climbed into her car and slammed the door.

I was too shocked to do anything but watch her drive away.

I RETURNED TO the house, shaking my head at Sam to indicate that I had failed in my mission. Recalling that Camilla had asked me to cancel her luncheon, I dialed Adam's number. Adam sounded concerned, and a bit confused.

"Jane Wyland? Why in the world—?" He paused for a moment; I could almost hear him thinking. "That is very distressing," he finally said.

"You must know her too, right? She said she knew Camilla way back when—I guess around the time Camilla came to America."

"Yes. I know Jane." His voice was neutral, but I sensed some emotion, as well.

"In any case—Camilla needs some time to recover, I think. The woman was really unpleasant. So—she doesn't want you to come over until she feels better."

"I understand," Adam said. "I'll text her later, let

her talk to me that way first. She's a woman of the written word, as you know."

"Thanks, Adam." I ended the call, glad that Adam understood Camilla so well.

Sam gave me a bracing hug and then went home to work, promising to check in on me later. "Give her some space," he advised. "She'll open up eventually."

I did just that; I cleaned up the beer glasses and recycled the bottles; I went to the store and bought some ingredients for dinner salads (Camilla's chef, Rhonda, was in Italy for two weeks with her family, so we were in charge of our meals); I walked the dogs briefly, until I couldn't stand the heat anymore; I took a nice, cooling shower and donned a T-shirt and some shorts; I ruffled the fur of my cat, Lestrade, who lay stretched out to his full length on my bed, letting the new stream of chilled air cool his belly.

Then I went to see Camilla. Her room was a space I did not normally enter, although I'd ventured in once or twice if called there. It was a wide, airy room that looked down on the driveway and the start of the path to the bluff and the forest vista behind it. Her bedspread was a lovely European-looking blend of garden colors, and above it hung a framed reproduction of Pierre Bonnard's *Young Woman Writing*, given to her as a gift by her late husband, James. He told Camilla that it reminded him of her when they first met. On a table near the window sat a vase of flowers and an antique typewriter that had belonged to Camilla's grandmother. There was a blotter there, too, so that Camilla could write her correspondence or jot ideas for books if they came to her while she lounged.

She sat at this table now, looking out the two panes of the window that didn't hold the new air conditioner. I had already opened the door to peer in at her, but I knocked on it. "Camilla? I waited a few hours, but I wanted to check on you."

"Come in, Lena," she said.

I moved into the room, which felt cool and smelled subtly like Camilla's perfume. "Are you all right?" I asked, sitting on the edge of her bed.

"I'm better now, thank you."

"I—I don't understand what that woman wanted."

She turned to face me for the first time. Her eyes were dry now, and her color looked better, but she still looked distressed. "I don't understand, either. But I confess I am at a loss. I need to ask for your help."

"Of course! Anything, Camilla. You know that."

She nodded. "You are such a sweet girl." She got up and came to sit next to me. I put an arm around her.

"Tell me," I said.

"I only met Jane Wyland a few times, when James and I were first married. He was working near Blue Lake, and we came to live here. His mother had died, and his father was ailing, so James and I essentially ran the house. He had a brother, Allan, but he had moved to Philadelphia."

"You've mentioned Allan," I said, my tone encouraging.

"William Graham—that's James's father—was an influential man here in Blue Lake. His family, for generations, had owned businesses in the town. James's great-grandfather ran the sawmill, and his uncle had a stake in what is now Schuler's ice cream. His father was on the school board and had his own law practice in Blue Lake. It no longer exists."

"Ah."

"Back to Jane," she said. "When James and I first arrived, he gave me a tour of the town. He was a proud local boy; he loved Blue Lake and was happy to have me here. We ran across Jane at a pub in town called the Lumberjack. It's no longer there, either, but it was a favorite haunt of the locals. James introduced me to Jane, and everyone was very polite, but there was palpable tension. Jane taught at the local grade school—"

"She taught *children*?"

"She was very good, and very popular. The parents and children loved her, from what I heard. I thought, at the time, that my children might one day end up in her class, and I said something of the sort to her."

This made me sad. I knew that Camilla found out, not long after arriving in Blue Lake, that she could not have children. "So you were all—friends?"

She shook her head. "No—James was friendly, or at least polite. But there was something stiff about her even then. Something felt off with the encounter, and when I mentioned that she might one day teach my children, she stood up quite abruptly, although she'd been there dining with some friends, and said she had to go. And she left, to the surprise of her friends and the consternation of James. He was quite upset about the scene, as I recall."

"That must have been, what, 1971?"

"Yes, 1971. Just after our wedding, when I came to Blue Lake for the first time."

"What did James say after that?"

She shrugged. "I asked him about it when we returned home. Returned here," she said, gesturing around us. "He said he didn't know what would have caused her to react that way, but that he felt badly about it. He said she was a nice woman, and that they had always gotten on well. He had gone to school with her."

"How strange—the whole encounter."

"Yes. After that I saw her now and again in town, and she was polite, but rather—cold. Then a couple years later she moved out of Blue Lake, although I think she still taught at the grade school. I never ran across her again. Until today."

I squeezed her shoulder. "What did she want?"

"She said she wanted to 'finally make things right.' I had no idea what she meant, and I told her so. She said she felt sorry for me, because I was ignorant of the Graham family's biggest secret."

"Maybe she just always resented them. They were powerful, and rather wealthy, right? Living in this big house on the bluff. Maybe life disappointed her, and . . ."

"I don't think so. The Wylands were a nice family. Well respected, well educated, although James did say they had some unlucky investments and were always at a loss for money. In fact, Jane had a sister who once worked for James's family. James said she was very sweet and did a good job. She came every day to clean and cook; it was especially helpful because his father needed looking after, which took James's time when he wasn't working. He really didn't have anything bad to say about the Wylands."

"But this Jane is insisting that the family has a secret?"

Camilla nodded. "Yes. And normally I would dismiss it as nonsense, but she's given me a bit of an ultimatum."

"She *what*?"

"Yes. She said that I should tell the truth to the press about my husband, James, or she will."

"What truth is she referring to?"

Camilla looked into my eyes, and I saw the worry in hers. "I have no idea," she said.

The family bond is such a mystery, isn't it, my dear Camilla? There is no dissolving it, no matter how much time or distance or circumstance may test it. Invisible and permanent, it reminds us of the reality of blood.

—From the correspondence of James Graham and Camilla Easton, 1971

I PROMISED CAMILLA that we would come up with some solution to the problem—a solution which would probably take the form of reasoning with Jane Wyland. "Even if we have to bring in some sort of arbitrator or a therapist or something. She seemed genuinely disturbed," I said.

Camilla shrugged. "Life continues to surprise me. I thought I had gotten to an age at which I'd seen it all, but her behavior, her words, are simply inexplicable. She's essentially a stranger, but something drove her to come to my house, to speak about my poor late husband with such—rancor. About his whole family. James's father was such a sweet man; he was ill when I met him, and he never got better, but he was always kind and solicitous toward me. I was proud to be a Graham." She lifted her chin. "I still am proud."

"Of course you are. Don't let that woman give you a moment's pause about your family. Whatever is tormenting her clearly has nothing to do with you."

She smiled at me. "Oh, Lena—you really do always know what to say to lift my spirits. And now I realize I haven't eaten a bit since that Wyland woman came charging in here. Do you think if we rummaged through cabinets we could find ourselves some dinner?"

"I bought salad fixings, but I have a better idea," I said. I took her hand and persuaded her to stand up. "What do you want on your pizza?" I asked as we crossed her slightly creaky bedroom floor.

She giggled. "Oh, pizza! Like we're girls in a dormitory. All right, yes. I like pepperoni and red peppers."

"Ooh, yummy. I'll order it right now. Allison tells me that Pietro's is the best in town."

We descended the stairs, and, using Camilla's kitchen phone, I ordered a large pizza. Then we sat down at her kitchen table. "Do you want to work on the book?" I asked. Camilla and I were almost finished with a draft of a book based on one of my ideas—we planned to title it *Death at Delphi*—and we were still putting on the finishing touches.

She shrugged. "I must confess I feel a bit too unnerved to be creative right now. I might have to spend the evening distracting myself in some other way. Watching television, maybe, or playing a game."

"Allison is always begging to play a board game. Shall I invite her and John over? Or better yet, what if we went to their house? A change of scenery would be good, right?"

She thought about this. I was used to Camilla's thinking silences, so I wasn't offended when she didn't answer immediately. She liked to ponder her options before she made a decision. Finally, she said, "Do you think Allison would be willing to host? I don't think I've ever seen her house. And I'd love to have Doug and Belinda there, and Sam and Cliff. Cliff needs a girlfriend, doesn't he?"

I laughed. "We were just talking about that today. I have someone that I'd like to introduce to him. She lives in Chicago right now, but we'll see. Allison's trying to bring her here."

Camilla smiled. She knew of Allison's strong persuasive skills. "I look forward to meeting her."

"I assume we should also invite Adam?"

She nodded. "Yes, my poor Adam. I canceled my lunch with him, and he's probably feeling neglected."

"Great. Let me call Allison first." I picked up the phone again and dialed my friend's familiar number. During our brief conversation, even Camilla could hear Allison's enthusiasm. She would *love* to host a game night. She would be *happy* to have everyone at her house, and John would be happy, too! She had *plenty* of snacks to pass around if people were hungry. I laughed. "I'll call Sam and Cliff and Adam if you'll call Doug and Belinda."

"Perfect!" she almost yelled into my ear.

"Let's say eight o'clock," I said.

"See you then!" said Allison.

* * *

WHEN WE BEGAN our journey to the more suburban area of Blue Lake where Allison's subdivision was located, Camilla was in a much happier mood and newly enamored of pizza. "I had a fair amount of it when James and I were first married, but then we started cooking our own meals, and then we had a cook to do it for us. We never did much casual dining."

"I highly recommend it," I said. "Although Adam is probably always offering you more elegant food."

"Still. Everyone likes cheese," Camilla said, and I laughed.

I turned on Sabre Street and headed toward Green Glass Highway. We stopped at a light and I glanced at the front lawn of Darrow Middle School. I gasped. "Oh, Camilla! Look what someone has done." A statue of Clarence Darrow graced the center of the lawn; it was one of the few public sculptures in Blue Lake, and now it was marred by a jagged yellow line of spray paint.

"My goodness," Camilla said with a clucking sound. "I suppose I had fooled myself into thinking that sort of thing didn't happen in our little town."

"It doesn't, usually!" I said. "Oh, it's so ugly. Do you think they can remove that paint? It's such a beautiful statue."

"I'm sure they'll find a way. A shame, really. That anyone would desecrate a work of art. The work of someone else's hands!"

The light turned green, and I drove on, feeling sad. With a mildly mischievous expression Camilla tapped my arm. "Don't forget you're on cheering-me-up duty," she said.

I laughed. "So, pointing out graffiti would not qualify as something cheerful?"

"Probably not," she agreed. "Go back to that story about your first date. Did he really bring you flowers from your own yard?"

"I kid you not. And not nice ones—weeds, Camilla. Dandelions and such. I think he thought it was romantic."

"They must have looked dreadful."

"They died almost immediately," I said, laughing.

Camilla was giggling in a very un-Camilla-like way. "Oh my. And what was his name again?"

I sighed. "Hugo Le Jardin."

"A name like that, and yet weeds were all he could summon." Her eyes twinkled in the dim car.

"We were both fifteen. I don't think he had any money. But still."

"Perhaps you should contact him and say that you judged him too harshly."

"Stop. It's still painful in retrospect, but I'm glad it has amused you."

"Oh, it has—immeasurably!" She patted my arm, still chuckling.

"I did find him on Facebook a few years ago."

"No! And what is Hugo doing these days? Is he a florist?"

"Don't laugh. No, but that would be perfect. You won't believe what he's doing these days."

"I must know." She leaned toward me, expectant. I kept my eyes on the road.

"He runs an online matchmaking company."

Camilla giggled again, and my stomach twisted pleasantly with a feeling that I recognized as love.

WE CROSSED THE dry grass of Allison's lawn just before eight o'clock, and Allison met us at the door, where she practically dragged us across the threshold into her cool, cozy living room. "Oh, I'm so glad you're here! I dug out all our games, and John is ready to take your drink orders."

Her husband, John, waved to us from the kitchen, smiling wryly. He knew to stay in the background when Allison was in hostess mode.

"Thank you so much, my dear Allison," Camilla said. "I am more than ready for a nice evening with friends."

Allison gave Camilla one of her intense hugs and then pointed at John. "This lady needs a cocktail." Then, to Camilla, "He is so talented—he knows how to make just about every drink, and he can sort of read your mood and know what you'd like. Go see Dr. John, Camilla!"

Intrigued, Camilla walked over to John, who led her to his little bar. The doorbell rang and Allison lunged forward to admit Adam, Doug, and Belinda, who had apparently met on the doorstep. Adam was sent toward Camilla while the other two came to find me and Allison darted outside to see if Cliff or Sam were coming.

"She's a bit manic. She loves people," I said. "She and I were the yin-yang of our high school. She wanted parties and loud voices, and I wanted quiet rooms and books."

Belinda smiled. "You complement each other nicely." As always, she was beautifully dressed in a cool mint green romper and some beaded sandals. Doug's hand was in her blonde hair, which, despite the heat, was loose and hanging on her shoulders.

"As do the two of you," I said. They turned to look at each other; judging by what I saw in their eyes, things were more serious now between them than they had been a few months ago.

"I agree with Lena," Doug said.

I took out my phone and snapped a picture of Doug and Belinda. "I don't know if I have a good one of you two together," I said. "Something for my album." Then, to Doug, "I know you don't talk business at parties, but did you know someone vandalized the Clarence Darrow statue?"

He frowned. "Vandalized how?"

"Yellow spray paint."

Doug's eyebrows rose. "Could you two excuse me for a minute? I need to make a call."

He squeezed Belinda's shoulder and then walked briskly into Allison's kitchen.

I smiled at her. "On a scale of one to ten, how sexy do you find it when he goes into cop mode?"

She grinned back at me. "Ten."

"Perfect. I have a feeling he'll be doing it often." She laughed and followed me toward Allison's table, which my friend had managed to fill with a festive array of party food in about half an hour. We each took a tiny plate and sampled some of Allison's treats.

Camilla, clutching a drink, returned with Adam at her elbow.

I pointed at her glass, which contained a creamy-looking beverage. "So, what did John prescribe as your healing cocktail?"

She held it up. "A White Russian. I don't think I've ever had one, but I find it delightful. I think I will keep John on retainer."

I smiled at Adam, who stood at her side like a courtly admirer. "It looks like John thought *you* wanted a beer."

Adam's smile was charming. "He was absolutely right."

Allison burst back in, leading an amused Sam and Cliff. In that instant they looked more than ever like brothers; it amazed me to think that at one point none of us had known of the familial link between the men.

Sam wandered toward me while Cliff spied Doug in the kitchen and walked toward him after a general wave to the room. Allison clapped her hands and said, "Everyone, John is taking drink orders and there are snacks on the table. The board games are on this coffee table—let me know your vote for what we should play, or if you'd like to divide into groups."

"She is hilarious," Sam whispered in my ear.

"Her energy is infectious," I said, sliding my hand into his.

Within twenty minutes Allison had supplied us all with food and beverages and we had agreed to play Pictionary. Doug and Cliff appointed themselves captains, laughingly claiming the authority of the police.

Doug chose the teammates of Belinda, Adam, and John, while Cliff chose me, Sam, and Camilla. Allison had appointed herself scorekeeper so that she could occasionally run away to update refreshments.

The game was revealing in many ways. It was no surprise that we were almost all quite competitive, even the more reserved Adam and John, but what I had not known was that we had two truly good artists in our midst: Cliff and Sam. Sam's first word was "mystery," which had amused Camilla no end (possibly because she was on her second White Russian). Sam thought for a moment, then drew, with just a few lines, a very realistic-looking book with a question mark above it. Camilla had guessed it on the first try. Cliff was given the word "fanatic," and had sketched a sports fan with a screaming, distorted face. I, like Camilla, had guessed it instantly.

"No fair," John said. "You boys clearly have some sort of artistic gene in the family."

Cliff and Sam exchanged a pleased glance, then shrugged. "Can't hide this light under a bushel," Cliff said, and we laughed.

When Allison put out desserts we all took a break from the game, which was a relief to Adam, who had really sweated over how to draw the word "patriotism." He had sketched a circle, for some reason, and then pointed to it with various arrows, to the great frustration of his team.

Now I saw him handing a cup of coffee to Camilla, who looked downright sleepy after her experiment with cocktails, and tucking a strand of hair behind her right ear. It was a tender gesture and somehow a private one; I turned away and found myself facing Cliff, who was holding a plate full of treats.

"Hey, pal," I said. Cliff smiled at me. For the last month he'd worked on building a relationship with his half brother, but in the process he and I had become friends. "What looks good at the dessert table?"

He groaned. "What doesn't? Your friend should open a bakery."

"She really should."

"I guess I'm partial to this blueberry pie. I'd give you a bite, except I want it. Didn't you say this was a spur-of-the-moment party? How did she make all this food?"

I nodded. "Good question. The answer is that she's always baking. She likes to bring stuff to her colleagues at work, so we might have cheated them out of their fix tomorrow."

"Huh. Try the pie, but also those chunky little chocolate squares—those are amazing. I'm going to have to log about ten miles tomorrow. You want to go with?"

Sometimes Cliff and I ran together; Sam didn't enjoy that particular form of exercise.

"Not really. Not until the weather cools down. I'll be all over that offer when fall comes."

He grinned. I scanned the room while Cliff chatted to me; near the kitchen I saw Belinda. She had grabbed a bottle of water out of Allison's fridge and was chatting with Allison herself: my two pretty blonde friends, enjoying a festive occasion. Belinda laughed at something Allison said and pushed her glasses up on her nose.

Then Doug, who had taken a call in another room, was at her shoulder and whispering something in her ear. "Uh-oh," I said, and Cliff's head came up.

A moment later Doug was moving toward us. "Yeah, I think the party's over," Cliff murmured.

Doug joined us and pointed at Cliff. "Finish your pie," he said. "We've got to go."

Cliff nodded and started wolfing down the last of his food. Then he gave me a quick hug and said, "Tell Allison thanks for the invitation, and sorry."

"I talked to her," Doug said. "She understands."

"What's going on?" I asked Doug.

He shook his head. "I can't say anything just now. We'll know more soon."

He and Cliff moved swiftly to the door and out into the warm night.

I turned to check on Allison, who did deflate slightly at the sight of two people leaving, but who was still in hostess mode for the five who remained. I gave her a thumbs-up and started perusing the desserts.

Sam appeared at my side. "Is my brother trying to steal you away from me?"

"Yes. He finds me irresistible."

"You are. What's that? A brownie?"

"No. Allison calls it a rocky road fudge bar. It has a ridiculous amount of chocolate in it."

"Put one on a plate for me," he said. I grinned and did as he asked, then handed him the treat.

I waited until his blue eyes met mine. "Any idea why the police had to go rushing out of here?"

Sam's face was solemn. "Just that Doug got a call from the station and apparently the chief wanted both of them. Since Doug and Cliff are essentially the entire Blue Lake homicide department, I'm guessing it's something bad."

"Not another body," I breathed. "This place has had enough of those in the past year. I hope it's just about this vandal."

"What vandal?"

I told him what Camilla and I had seen, and he frowned. "Strange. Doesn't sound like the Blue Lake we know, does it?"

"No, you're right. It seems—foreign, like something that would happen somewhere else. But crime has no boundaries. I get that."

Sam took a bite of the fudge bar. "Oh wow. Why would a nurse make something that will so clearly fill my veins with sugar?"

"She's a paradox. Do you want me to get rid of it?"

He held his plate out of reach. "I didn't say that."

I laughed, and we found our way back into the living room. The rest of the evening passed very pleasantly, but a part of me had been on alert ever since I had seen the look on Doug's face across the room.

CAMILLA AND I finally prepared to leave, and Adam volunteered to drive Belinda home. Sam still had his car because Doug and Cliff had left in Doug's vehicle. Allison packed us all goodie bags and Camilla gave her a hug and thanked her for brightening her day.

Sam appeared at my shoulder to say good-bye. "Want to come by later?"

I wrapped my arms around him and pondered for

a moment. "Camilla was really fragile today, so I'll wait to see if she needs me, or if Adam is staying over, or what. I'll text you."

"Okay. I'm going to head home and do some work, but I'm there if you miss me." He gave me a quick kiss, waved to everyone, and left.

In the car with Camilla, I listened while she praised everything about the evening: Allison's kindness and her sweet relationship with John, the loveliness of their home, the great connection between Doug and Belinda, the wonderful resemblance between Sam and Cliff. "And, of course, my dear Lena, who arranged the whole thing. You looked lovely in that white blouse, and Sam couldn't stop looking at you, as always," she said.

"I would say the same thing about Adam and you. We are alluring women."

Camilla laughed. "Remind me to try a White Russian again someday. But definitely not two of them." She leaned back on the headrest and closed her eyes.

I put my left hand out the window and let the air hit it. "It's nice out now. There's even a tiny cool breeze. Maybe it will be more bearable tomorrow."

Camilla yawned. "One can hope."

I dreamily gazed out the windshield and breathed deeply . . . Blue Lake looked beautiful at night. It was far enough from any city that the stars were visible in large glittering clusters, a promise of beauty beyond human dreams, and realities beyond human comprehension.

"I can read your mind," Camilla said. Her eyes were open again.

"Yes? What am I thinking?"

"That the stars are beautiful and people are fools."

"Wow! That is unbelievably accurate."

She shrugged. "I think the same when I look at a night sky in Blue Lake."

A moment went by in which we heard only the occasional hum of traffic and the rushing of the air as the car sped toward home. "Camilla?"

"Yes, dear."

"I'm so glad you're my friend."

She absorbed this quietly, in her way. She was looking out her window, up at the sky, when she said, "That feeling is mutual, Lena."

·❖· · 3 · ·❖·

I miss you the most on days like this, when the Blue Lake wind blows cold, wintry as the wind on the night I met you. Do you remember? A gentle snow was falling, and through the window I saw you climbing the stairs, your dark hair loose on the shoulders of your silver-white coat, your hands deep in your pockets as you listened to your chatting companion.

I realized that I was leaning forward, hoping you would look up and see me through the glass. In that silent snow, you were a world away from me.

That's why my face was the first you saw when you entered the room, Camilla. Because I lunged out of my chair and raced to the door to be sure it was so. And when you smiled at me, I remembered a line from my high school Shakespeare—what Romeo says when he sees Juliet:

"Did my heart love till now? Forswear it, sight, for I ne'er saw true beauty till this night."

—From the correspondence of
James Graham and Camilla Easton, 1971

THE FOLLOWING MORNING Camilla smiled at me across the breakfast table. "Would you like any more tea?"

"No, thank you. I am content. That was a delicious sweet roll, too. Now I'd better walk a couple of miles."

Camilla was wearing her determined face. "I wonder if you'd accompany me on an errand."

"Of course! Where did you want to go? If we're going into town, I—"

"No, not into town. I'd like to drive to the Bayside Cottages. They're about a mile past the library, on that little inlet. You've probably seen them."

"Yes! They're quaint. Do you know someone who lives there?"

She sat up straighter. "Jane Wyland."

"Oh," I said.

"No, don't look like that. You know I'm not the type to brood over something. I want to get this resolved today. I intend to face her down and demand to know this secret she claims she has."

"I thought you said she moved out of Blue Lake?"

"Apparently she moved back when she retired, into the home where she grew up. She inherited it, I suppose."

I studied Camilla's face for a moment. She looked determined, but calm. "All right. I think—that's a good idea."

"Yes. I'll just get my purse. I let the dogs out when I made the tea, so they'll be fine for a while."

The dogs were not within eyeshot, and I was fairly certain that they were lying like dead things on the floor of Camilla's office. "I'm sure they will be. They're about as excited as Lestrade is to move around in the heat." Lestrade was a paradox; the heat seemed to pull all the life from his body, but he sought out every sunbeam and every hot place.

Camilla's face brightened. "Oh, but the air-conditioning does make things better, doesn't it?"

"It's wonderful. My room was quite pleasant last night."

She stood up and carried her cup to the sink. "Give me one moment. I'll meet you outside."

I brought my own dishes to the sink, scratched the ears of Lestrade, who sat sunning in the kitchen window, and went into the hallway. Now that I'd been at Graham House for several months, I wasn't as strict about stowing all my things away upstairs. I generally slung the strap of my purse over the handle of Camilla's linen closet, which I encountered on the way to the door. I grabbed the bag now and put it over my shoulder, then moved outside, where I was surprised by a huge gust of air.

"Ahhh!" I said aloud. I gazed around and saw that all of the trees were bending under the force of the wind, a warm wind, but not hot, and not at all unpleasant. I pushed against it, heading toward my car, laughing slightly.

Camilla joined me. "What's funny?" she asked.

"I love a windy day. Always have."

She looked at the sky, blinking as the air hit her face. "This one seems ominous, though. Look at those clouds."

"Just a touch of gray. I don't think they're rain clouds," I said, opening my door. A piece of paper fluttered out—some store receipt that I didn't remember leaving in the car. "Oh no! Oh, there it goes!" I shouted, then laughed again.

Camilla stared at me, mildly amused by my euphoria. "Let's go, Lena."

"Okay, okay." We got in the car and buckled in. A glance at Camilla told me that she was too distracted to enjoy the rare weather. Jane Wyland and her toxic anger weighed on my friend's mind. Camilla was right; this needed resolution.

I pulled out of the driveway and turned left onto the rocky road that led down the bluff, then right on Wentworth Street, heading toward Belinda's workplace. "We turn near the library, right?" I asked.

Camilla was looking for something in her purse. "Hmm? Yes. Two blocks past, on a street called Derby. Take a right and drive until you see a sign that says 'The Bayside Cottages.' Then left on Vista."

"Got it. It's really such a lovely area." I leaned forward to peer at the sky. "It doesn't seem as if it will storm. Remember how the sky looked, back when I moved to town? That day you could tell the rain was coming."

"Yes. And what a storm we had. I'm lucky you stayed in town, after the chaos of last October."

"I had plenty of reasons to stay."

I followed Camilla's directions, my eyes enjoying the effects of the wind: the traffic lights swaying on their ropes, a half-uprooted stop sign bowing to us like a dignified butler, the occasional burst of green leaves that hit our windshield after being wrested from trees.

When I turned on Derby, Camilla consulted some

notes. "Left on Vista, and her number is 57. That should be the fifth house down."

"Okay." I turned again. I saw a cluster of cars down the street, and as we came nearer we could see that they were emergency vehicles—an ambulance and three police cars. "What's going on?" I said aloud. "Do you think this is why Doug and Cliff got paged last night?"

Camilla stiffened. "It's her house. Look—that's number 57." Her eyes were wide. "What do you think she's done?"

I pulled up directly in front of a cream-colored cottage with brown window shutters and potted flowers on either side of the door. Camilla focused on a couple of paramedics who stood by the ambulance. I wasn't sure where to go; there wasn't any visible parking spot. Across from us, behind the even-numbered houses, one could view an inlet to Blue Lake. I gazed for a second at the little strip of blue that Jane Wyland would have seen every morning when she left her house . . .

Thumping sounds on my window made me jump and swivel my head back toward Jane's cottage. Doug Heller stood there in his police-issued khakis and Blue Lake polo. He was scowling, and his blond hair blew around in a chaotic cloud, making him look like an angry Norwegian god. I rolled down my window and got a blast of warm air along with his disapproval.

"Lena. Camilla. What are you two doing here?" he asked.

"We had an appointment," I said. "Or at least Camilla wanted to make one. We need to talk to the lady who lives there." I pointed at Jane's house. "Can I just—"

Doug's eyes widened. "What do you know about the woman who lives here?"

Camilla leaned toward my window. "Douglas, I'm not sure what's happening on this block, but if you could let me have a few moments with her, I'd be grateful. There's an issue I'd like to resolve."

Doug leaned in the window. "Are you talking about Jane Wyland?"

"Yes, Jane," Camilla said.

Doug shook his head, then climbed into the backseat of our car, slamming the door against the wind. He leaned forward so that his head was between us. "Camilla, I'm sorry. Jane is dead."

"What?" I said, shocked.

"What happened?" asked Camilla. Her posture had become straight and still, as if she feared a giant predator would detect her presence in the car.

Doug frowned. "No, you first. Why did you come here to see Jane?"

Camilla leaned back in her seat and closed her eyes. "Tell him, Lena."

"Hang on, I'm in the way." I piloted our vehicle behind one of the police cars, put the gear shift into park, and then turned to face our visitor. As succinctly as I could, I described Jane's visit. Her angry demeanor, her threat to Camilla and her family, her promise to expose a Graham family secret. "I brought Camilla to Allison's house as a diversion because she was so upset by Jane yesterday, her mean attitude and her cryptic comments."

Doug listened with growing interest and said, "Camilla, do you know what she meant?"

Camilla opened her eyes and turned her head. "I have no idea. That's why I came here today. I wanted to reason with her, talk it out, get her to confide in me. Something was eating away at her, and she was vengeful. But I can't imagine how it related to poor James or anyone in his family." She turned sadly toward the house. "What was it—a heart attack?"

Doug paused, and I felt a burst of guilt. We were always asking him for information he really wasn't supposed to give. Because Camilla and I had been very helpful in some of his previous investigations, though, he sometimes relented, as he did now. "No. She was murdered, Camilla. Shot." I gasped, and Camilla made a soft regretful sound. Doug's face was somber when he added, "And this new information tells me that she was killed just before she was going to take some sort of extreme action."

Camilla's demeanor was calm, but her eyes were wide. "And it also tells you that I had the best motive for killing her."

She and Doug exchanged a meaningful glance. He said, "No, because you had no idea what the secret was."

"You would have to consider that I might kill to save my husband's reputation," she said.

I put a hand on her shoulder and pointed at Doug. "But she didn't. She was at Graham House all evening with me. We left the party not long after you did, and then we sat around and talked about how nice it was and how tired we were, and we finally went off to bed.

Is that a good enough alibi, since Camilla seems interested in offering herself as a suspect?"

A tiny smile flickered across Doug's face as he got out his little computer tablet. "It's good for starters. But I need some more details about what the woman said when she came over. She spoke to Camilla only?"

Camilla nodded, and I said, "Uh—yes. But then I chased her to the driveway and tried to reason with her, which made her even more angry."

Camilla's large eyes found me, surprised. "What did she say?"

"She said something about how the Grahams hadn't faced justice for forty years, and she was going to stand up for her family, because no one else would, or something like that. I was just shocked by her demeanor, and the intensity of her words. That stays with me more than the words themselves."

Doug nodded and typed. "And to you, Camilla? What did she say in your office?"

"Similar things. She claimed my husband and his family were not what I believed them to be. That they hid a terrible secret and she felt the world needed to know about it. Then she said maybe I did know the secret, and I assured her I did not, because James would never have kept anything from me. She laughed in my face then and said that I hadn't known my husband very well."

"She was wrong about that," Doug said.

"Yes, she was." Camilla looked at me, her eyes clear but sad. "I am very sorry this happened. I had nothing against Jane, although I did consider her a mystery. It's always a surprise, isn't it, when people we barely know dislike us? We can't help but wonder at their reasons."

"She didn't like you?" Doug asked.

Camilla shrugged. "Back when we were young, the very first day I met her, she was cold. Polite, but cold, as though I had offended her terribly and she was still learning to forgive me. That was how it felt. I think I asked James about it once. I was twenty-four, and I wanted everyone to like me, especially because I was in a new town, a new country."

"Of course," I agreed.

"Did she ever say anything back then? Hint at any reasons?"

"No. She was quiet as the grave," Camilla said, and her troubled eyes drifted back toward the ambulance. Then she turned to Doug. "If you were called last night, why is the ambulance still here?"

Doug stopped typing to look up at her. "Our photographer was on another job in Daleville. She finally got out here at around five, so we're a bit behind."

Camilla's eyes were sad. "She's still in there, then?"

"Yes. And I need to get back," Doug said, but gently.

"Yes, of course," Camilla said. "Lena, I suppose we have no need of our errand now." She had switched from shock mode into thinking mode, and her gaze was far away.

I reached out to touch Doug's hand. "Sorry we interrupted you. We had no idea—well, you know. One of those strange coincidences."

"You two have an unerring ability to discover coincidences," he said. "See you later."

He held up his hand in a brief wave to both of us and climbed out of the car.

Camilla was turned away from me, looking out her window. I turned the radio to a classical station that was playing the "Overture" to *Candide*. I left it on at a low volume, appreciating the genius of Leonard Bernstein and giving space to the genius of Camilla Graham.

I drove back toward our house, watching everything dance in the chaotic wind, first the boats in the bay and then the wheat-colored grasses along the highway, which sighed and bowed to the inevitable. I loved windy days because they spoke of anarchy, of truthful disorder. We had control of nothing. Since moving to Graham House, I had become more and more convinced of this philosophy, and now the forceful air that shook our car reminded me of our frailty, our vulnerability. Why did I find that so invigorating?

"Lena, I've never seen you so enthralled with the weather," Camilla said drily.

"It's fascinating. Such energy, seemingly from nowhere."

"Yes."

"What are you thinking, Camilla? You can't feel guilty about Jane's death?"

She rustled in her seat. "Guilty? No. Curious? Very. She gave me an ultimatum, Lena. She said I had one day, and that tomorrow—now today—she was going to take action. To reveal some long-buried secret." She shrugged and then smiled. "If you had known James—you would know how silly it seemed, to think that he would keep any secret, much less a decades-old one. He could never even wait a few weeks to give Christmas presents. He was terrible at hiding things."

"I wish I had met him. And I wish I knew what Jane Wyland had been thinking."

Camilla nodded, and I grew suspicious.

"You're forming some sort of plan."

She shook her head. "Not a plan, no. But I do have one way of going back in time, and I've decided that I may just need to use it."

AT GRAHAM HOUSE we made a pot of tea; every window drew my gaze because the wind continued to put on a show. A little wren hovered in front of the dining room window, beating her wings as hard as she could, in vain, against the giant gusts. Finally she gave up and retreated to a nearby tree, where she clearly intended to wait out the intractable forces of nature.

Camilla joined me at the casement, teacup in hand. "It is rather dramatic. Almost Shakespearean."

"Yes. Presaging the death of a king."

"Certainly a death," Camilla said.

I turned at the tone of her voice. "Are you planning to tell me your method of time travel? Will it rival something from *Harry Potter*?"

She smiled. "No, although wouldn't that be fun? No, it's very simple. Come here, Lena." She walked toward her office, and I followed. She moved toward her desk, where I recognized a large blue box that had previously sat on a side table in her bedroom. It had been there the day that I sat on her bed to console her.

She touched the box. "When I was still in England but engaged to James, I was finishing a book I was working on—I had a contract for a series of nonfiction books about the Gothic era—and I needed to complete that and tie up all of my affairs before I could go out to join him."

"Those were the books you were promoting when you came to America the first time?"

"Yes. A few of us who wrote for my publishing company at the time had the opportunity to travel here on a press junket. I thought I was so impressive, a young author going to America for her very first book contract. It ended up being a life-changing trip."

"You met James at a Christmas party, right?"

Her face grew softer with the memory. "Yes. Just a chance thing; our American contact, Bridget, asked if we would like to attend a party that one of her friends was throwing. We were in Chicago at that time; we were stopping in four American cities. We were all young, we English authors, and we all wanted to go, to experience America. Most of the people at the party were going to be publishing types, but James was there because he was good friends with one of the hosts. He told me that he fell in love with me instantly when he saw me through the window."

I put my hands on my hips. "The Camilla I know would never believe a statement like that."

Camilla's laugh sounded refreshingly like her old self. "You are right. I thought it was nonsense. Of course, he didn't dare to tell me that night, but he did manage to extract my contact information from me."

She sighed. "This will not sound at all like the Camilla you know: I thought he was unbelievably handsome, like a man from a fairy tale."

"That's romantic."

She nodded, then patted the box briskly. "In here are all of the letters he wrote me when we were apart. He had ambitiously promised to write me every day, which he did not manage, but he wrote often. We were separated for six months, during which he made one visit to England, and I one to America. Other than that, we were in our respective countries. We missed each other." She lifted the lid from the box and I saw neatly filed, thin envelopes with red and blue borders. "Airmail," she said. "It was the norm back then."

"So what do you intend to do with these letters?"

"What *we* will do is read through them all. More than one hundred letters, Lena. All written around the time that Jane Wyland was friends with James. We're going to read the letters and make notes and try to see if there are any clues in my husband's history— any references that I wouldn't have understood then but which I might understand now."

"Wouldn't you know? I mean, don't you know all these letters by heart?"

She smiled at me. "You are sweet. I haven't read most of them for decades. It was enough to know they were there. Do you understand? To have my precious history in this box."

"I think I do," I said.

She sipped her tea and frowned. "I need to warm

this up. It may be hot out, but the sight of this wind makes me feel cold. Where shall we read?"

"How about the sunporch? You have a big table there, and a nice view of our Shakespearean weather."

"Perfect. See you there in a moment."

She left, bound for the kitchen, but I lingered at the window. The dogs loped up and joined me, and the three of us watched the punishing wind shake leaves from the elm tree in Camilla's backyard.

4

I often feel sad these days; I worry about my father and I miss you. How hard it is, sometimes, to accept life's sterner rules, especially after one has tasted happiness.

—From the correspondence of
James Graham and Camilla Easton, 1971

CAMILLA ASSURED ME that nothing in James's letters was so personal that I couldn't read it. "He was most circumspect," she said. "And he knew that my mother liked to read the letters, too."

She gave me a pile of envelopes that were all post-marked June of 1971. "That was just after we became engaged, and that was when we wrote the most. I'll take July. When you find lines of interest, either jot them down or run to the copy machine in my office. We can save them all for Doug, if need be."

I sighed. "It seems we are once again looking for a needle in a haystack."

"We've become quite good at it," she said, smiling.

"Sam thinks you and I have a psychic connection that makes it easier for us to work out puzzles."

She sipped her tea and removed a letter from a thin airmail envelope. "Sam is rather a romantic himself, given to whimsical notions. At least he is since he met you."

"Yes, I suppose so." For some reason my face felt hot, and Camilla smirked at me before she looked at her first letter.

I consulted my own. James had a neat, regular cursive that almost looked military in its precision. The letter was dated at the top (June 4, 1971), and a quick Google consultation told me that this had been a Friday. Perhaps he had sat down to write to his young, pretty Camilla at the end of his work week. In any case, I soon learned that he had an unerring devotion to his English fiancée.

"My dear, my sweet, my own Camilla," he began. "As I sat down to write this letter, thoughts of you opened up a vast compartment of memories in my brain, and now it's as though you're sitting beside me, so clearly can I see you in my mind's eye."

"He's quite formal," I said without thinking. "Loving and affectionate, but stately, like a suitor from the Romantic era."

Camilla paused, considering this. "I think one of the things that drew me to him was his courtly air. He looked and sounded like a knight to me. And yes, his letters retained that character. I suppose it stayed with him from his school days, when formality was a requirement."

"It's lovely, actually. So charming."

"Yes." She was concentrating on a letter in her hand and jotting things on a pad. I took this as a sign to get to business.

I read the whole letter, feeling like a voyeur but

also pleased to have this window into Camilla's past. James reminisced about some things they'd done together on his trip to England (where they had become engaged) and then talked to her about some of his daily tasks. He wrote of a terrier named Edmund who was his constant companion; apparently Edmund had been quite the character, with a smiling face, a high-stepping gait, and a comical bark. At night, James told her, Edmund slept across the top of his bed.

"Did you get to meet Edmund?" I said.

Camilla looked up, surprised. "Oh, Edmund! What a sweet little boy he was. Yes, we had him for five or six years before he died. One of those pets you just want to live forever."

She looked back at her letter, smiling at her memory of a dog from the past.

I went back to my letter, in which James spoke of an evening gathering with some of his local friends. I jotted down the names: Adam, of course, who was James's best friend in Blue Lake. Jane Wyland and her sister, Carrie. Rusty Baxter, who was now chief of police. That one had me pausing for a moment: James had been friends with Rusty Baxter, back when his hair had been truly red! The other people mentioned were Travis Pace, a woman named Karina Thibodeau, and someone named Marjorie Allan.

I studied my pad; I had met three of the people mentioned and knew who Carrie Wyland was, but three of the names were unfamiliar to me. I waited until Camilla seemed to have finished her letter and then held up my pad. "I've got some people here. Who is Travis Pace?"

Camilla took a sip of tea. "Travis was one of the locals back then. Still lives around here, but he travels a great deal. He owns a restaurant supply chain. He's quite wealthy, I think. Divorced now, has a few grown children. He too went to school with James, as did Adam and Rusty."

"Ah. Okay." I wrote this down. "And how about Karina Thibodeau?"

"Karina. I think I remember her." Camilla leaned back in her chair. "She was a tiny golden-haired thing, had a crush on Rusty Baxter. But Rusty ended up marrying Darlene Hill—remember Darlene? She's the president of that women's group who sponsored our book signing for *The Salzburg Train*."

"Oh yes, right. So is Karina still around?"

Camilla shook her head. "No, she married a few years later, to a farmer. He was from Daleville, but they ended up buying a bigger farm out in Bluefield. I see her in town every now and again, probably visiting family. I think there are still several Thibodeaus in Blue Lake."

"Huh." My eyes strayed to the window, where I could see a young sapling bending under the assault of the wind. Its branches lifted in protest, creating a weirdly human effect.

I dragged my eyes back to the pad. "And I don't suppose you know this Marjorie Allan?"

Camilla grinned. "Yes, and so do you. That's Marge Bick, dear. She and James grew up in the same neighborhood in Blue Lake. They once played together. Did I never tell you that? Lena, do close your mouth; it's gaping at me."

I snapped my mouth shut. Marge Bick, our town postmistress, wife of Horace Bick, owner of Bick's Hardware, town gossip but well-meaning friend, had grown up with James Graham. "So—were you and Marge friends?" I asked.

Camilla shrugged. "Not really. Back then James and I were living half the year in Blue Lake and half the year in England. I got to know people, but not as well as the regulars who were here year-round. And I think Marjorie always saw me as something of an interloper. Not from Blue Lake, not from Indiana, not even from America."

"Yes, I can see that. Were you lonely here, Camilla?"

Now it was her turn to look out at the wind. "Do you know, I don't think I ever was. I had James, and a lovely house, and the book I was starting to write. It absorbed me. Then I sold *The Lost Child*, and I never looked back. I had moved on to writing fiction."

I put the letter back in the envelope. "Well, what this letter told me was that he genuinely loved and missed you and that sometimes he got together with these friends at a pub called the Mill Wheel. Does that ring a bell?"

"Oh my, yes. That was a charming little place. It reminded me of little pubs back home. The proprietor died and they ended up revamping it into the building you know today as the Guardian Pub."

"Oh! Okay. Sam and I love their sandwiches."

"Yes. It's a nice enough place, but the Mill Wheel had real charm. It's a shame when little establishments like that die along with their owners. If only they could have kept the place running in honor of Bill. He was the owner—Bill Prentiss."

"You have an amazing memory," I said.

Camilla's mouth lifted on one side in an ironic smile. "Some things come back fresh and clear, as though they happened yesterday. Other things feel like a long, long time ago."

"What about James?"

Her eyes moved back to the window. "He's in the permanent file," she said.

WE BOTH READ several letters and took notes. I learned that James Graham had been a naturalist who loved to observe and detail the changing seasons in Blue Lake, and who was a member of the Indiana Audubon Society. Before his father's illness, the two of them had regularly hiked together, not just in Blue Lake but all over the United States and on a couple of overseas adventures. His favorite had been a walk they took in the Swiss Alps.

His letters to Camilla had been detailed, precise, and filled with an obvious love and longing for his young fiancée. They shared a penchant for mystery fiction, American hot dogs, and all things canine (Camilla had been enthralled with Edmund upon her first visit).

After three letters, Camilla put her pen away. "I think I must do this in small doses," she said.

"Oh, Camilla! Is it—making you sad?"

"Oh, a little bit. But it's not that so much as I think I'll be more effective processing his details a few at a time. Who knows which one will end up being relevant? We should think of these letters as chapters in a book we are writing. The clue lies within one of them—or so we hope. So we mustn't lose focus." She stood up and stretched. "You can go run errands and play in your beloved wind, if you like. We can work on the book tomorrow."

I had not expected free hours. Camilla laughed at what must have been my bright expression. "Have fun, Lena. I'm going to do some work at my desk and then perhaps take a lovely, luxurious nap." She put her three letters in a bin that was meant to hold the already-read pile. She seemed to be taking rather long at this task.

"Camilla? What's wrong?"

Her eyes met mine; they were clouded with something that looked like regret. "Oh, Lena. We do read each other's thoughts, don't we?"

"Yes, I think we do."

"I'm afraid I'm feeling guilty. Quite guilty, and sad."

I stood up and moved to her, slinging my arm around her. "Why? Do you miss James so very much?"

"No, sweet girl. The fact is that since I heard about poor Jane Wyland's death I've been—relieved. I must admit this: it was relief I felt, and that I still feel. I was so afraid, Lena, not that she had a secret but that she would tell some lie and drag my husband's name through the mud. I didn't know how to stop her, and now someone has. Something was tormenting that woman, though, and by all reports she was a *good* woman. So I feel guilty for my response, and sad that she has died."

"That someone *murdered* her, Camilla."

"Yes. It's all so hard to believe."

I squeezed her shoulder. "You and I have helped the police solve a number of crimes in the past few months. I think we've got intuition. We'll use it now to help find the truth for Jane Wyland and to help Doug catch her murderer."

"You are so right. This is the gift we can and will give. Thank you, Lena. Now go play in the wind."

ON THE WAY down the bluff I spied a dark-haired girl ascending, kicking at pine cones and looking like a heroine in a novel, framed as she was against the scenic backdrop. "Hello, Star!" I called loudly, hoping my voice would reach her.

She looked up and brightened; she was a pretty girl, with blue eyes and wavy black hair. "Hi, Lena! Camilla asked if I would walk the dogs. She knows I love them."

I moved closer, leaning into the wind. "They love you, too. Are you sure you can handle them? I can barely do it, and you're tinier than I am."

"I'm strong, though!" she said, making an impressive muscle. She wore a gray T-shirt and a pair of jean shorts. "And they know I mean business." She smiled at me, trying to keep her black hair out of her eyes, just as Doug had done with his hair at the Bayside Cottages.

"How's your dad settling in? And how's the law

office?" Luke Kelly, Star's father, had recently moved his law practice to Blue Lake, and Star, who had been living with her mother, had decided to live with him for the summer.

She shrugged, looking away. "It's okay. He unpacked all his books and stuff and he's already seeing clients. I don't have much to do yet, which is why it's good that Camilla offered me another way to make money." Camilla paid Star ten dollars to walk the dogs for half an hour.

"There are plenty of part-time jobs to be found in this town. People always want their lawns mowed or their leaves raked or their snow shoveled. Jobs for every season."

She clutched her stomach and stuck out her tongue. "Blech. I hate yard jobs. That's why I'm glad to be able to walk the dogs. Animals are so much fun."

"And I'm guessing working in your dad's law firm will be, too, assuming you want to be a lawyer someday."

She shook her head. "I don't. It doesn't interest me at all, even though I know Dad is great at it and everything. He's interviewing people this week to help him with his workload. I know kids in my class who think the law is really glamorous. I don't see it that way."

"Well, you have lots of time to decide on a career."

She studied me with her bright blue eyes. "Did you know what you wanted to be at sixteen?"

I nodded. "I knew I wanted to write, and to be a sort of modern-day Camilla Graham."

Her eyes grew wide. "Seriously? She was like— your role model?"

"Yes. And I never dreamed I would meet her in real life. She's quite famous, you know."

"I didn't. I mean, I heard she wrote books and stuff, but I didn't know she was like—known worldwide. I'm gonna have to Google her."

"You do that. You'll be amazed."

"Okay. Now I better go get the dogs so Camilla doesn't fire me."

"See you around, Star!"

She waved and headed up the bluff toward Graham House. I walked about twenty more feet down the bluff, then turned in at the curving driveway that led to Sam West's place. Sometimes I was lucky enough to see Sam standing there on the path, his blue eyes on me, just as they had been on the day we met.

Nowadays, though, Sam was usually busy, not just with his work as a private investment counselor (his clientele had increased since he had been publicly exonerated for a crime that had never happened—the killing of an ex-wife who was very much alive), but with his recently discovered half brother, Cliff.

I was thrilled for Sam; he had thought he was without family in the world, and Cliff had emerged as a wonderful surprise. Still, I sometimes missed the days when I had been the only person on Sam West's mind. For a time, I had been his entire universe.

I knocked on the door; there was no answer, but I could hear voices in Sam's backyard, so I walked around the house and found Sam and Cliff pulling up boards on Sam's back deck. They were both shirtless and sweating, wearing blue jeans and sturdy shoes. Sam paused to gulp down some bottled water and his eyes found me. He set the bottle down and offered me his slow smile. "Hey, beautiful," he called.

Cliff looked up and waved. "Hey, Lena."

"You guys look busy. I can come back later."

Sam shook his head. "Get up here and look at our job."

I climbed onto the part of the deck that remained in place and stared at the empty hole they had created. Sam pointed at the wood planks they'd yanked out. "See those? Look at the rot. Cliff showed it to me last month, and we picked this week to replace these boards because Cliff has a couple days off."

I turned to Cliff. "So you're not working with Doug on the Wyland case?"

Cliff looked regretful. "I requested these two days a week ago. Doug will work on it with Chip Johnson until I come back. And he'll keep me apprised."

"Anything you can tell me?" asked Sam, looking curious. He hated to be left out of the cop stuff that Cliff and Doug shared, especially since they had become a trio of friends.

Cliff began to pry up another board with a large crowbar. "Not much to tell yet. Except that it's murder. Doug's trying to determine people of interest."

I moved closer to Sam; his arm slid around my waist in a gesture so automatic he barely seemed to notice it. "Sam, remember yesterday when that woman yelled at Camilla? It was her. She's been murdered."

Sam's brows rose. "Didn't she basically threaten Camilla?"

"Yes. And said she knew some big Graham family

secret. Camilla was determined to tell Doug what a perfect suspect she herself was in this crime."

"But who would the other suspects *be*? Who else would need to cover up a Graham family secret?" he asked.

"I don't know. I guess we can't assume that's why she was murdered, but Camilla and I are reading some old letters James wrote, trying to get a sense of the past."

Cliff seemed interested in this. He met my gaze; in that moment he looked very much like Sam. "Let us know if anything looks interesting. Any little detail."

"You got it," I said lightly.

Sam took another drink of water, then kissed me. "We want to finish this section before we lose the light," he said.

"Okay." I had wanted to tell him about James's letters, how romantic and sweet they were, and to try to explain to him why I loved the wind so much, why it was like poetry to me. "I'll let you get back to work. I'm headed into town. Do you need anything?"

Cliff was already saying something to Sam about the nails they were using. "Hmm?" Sam asked.

"Nothing. See you later!" I said, waving to them.

I moved back to the path and turned right, marching toward the foot of the bluff.

The wind had lessened slightly.

It was inexplicably disappointing.

5

The people you grow up with, Camilla, are the ones you believe will be your anchors through life. They know you and love you well, as you do them. They are the ones you can trust. When you start to wonder who they are, the world holds no guarantees. The earth falls away and you are trying to stand firm on a bog of uncertainty.

—From the correspondence of James Graham
and Camilla Easton, 1971

THE BEAR IN the lobby of Bick's Hardware had been there for decades, and I had passed it untold times since my arrival in October, yet I almost bumped right into it when I moved swiftly through the doorway.

"Sorry, buddy," I said, straightening the "Bick's Is Best" sign in his stiff paws. I slowed my pace, but made a determined path to the back counter, where Marge Bick presided over the post office and had an excellent view of her entire store.

She saw me coming and waved. "Hello, Lena! Don't you look pretty today."

Marge always said this, and I was fairly certain I

looked less pretty than I did sweaty and irritated, but I smiled. "Thanks, Marge. Hey, are you super busy?"

She waved a hand at the nearly empty store. "Not so much," she said. "Too hot for even the tourists these days, although I heard it's not so bad out since the wind came."

"It's bearable. About eighty degrees, I think."

"What did you need to know, hon?"

I looked behind me. "Um—can I take you to the coffee shop or something? I wanted to ask some things about the old days."

Her brows rose, and her face brightened. "Well, guess how many cute young things come in here and ask me to reminisce about old times? Exactly none."

"Your lucky day," I said, smiling at her.

"I have a better idea than the coffee shop. Come on in the back. I have a little sitting room here, did you know?" She disappeared from her window and moments later opened a door in the wall. "Come on back, kiddo."

My phone buzzed in my pocket, and I peeked at my text as I walked. To my surprise it was from Victoria West, Sam's former wife. She had sent me a picture of her daughter, Athena, nine months old now, adorably plump and undeniably beautiful. *Look at my girl!* Victoria had written.

Touched by the image, and by the fact that Victoria had shared it with me, I texted back *She is amazing! Thank you for brightening my day!* as I followed Marge back through a cluttered room, as strange as the store itself and equally disordered, but not unpleasant. The Bicks' love of taxidermy was on display here, too, and various woodland creatures stared at me through strange button eyes. Marge took me to a wooden table at the end of the room, centered in front of a window. This was the biggest surprise of all: behind Bick's hardware was a little courtyard full of green grass and various types of bird feeders. With one quick glance at the grassy space I spied a wealth of nature's gentle creatures, sharing the seed that had fallen to the ground. I saw squirrels, a mother rabbit with three little babies, and about five birds with varying plumage. I turned my head to study a shelf next to my chair and met the gaze of a friendly stuffed raccoon.

"That's Biff," Marge said, following my gaze. "He used to visit us out there all the time. Not sure what happened, but one day Horace just found him out there, stiff as a board. We loved that little guy, so Horace did what he could." She gestured to the raccoon.

"Wait—you mean Horace does the taxidermy?"

"Oh yes. It's a hobby of his, as you can see. He's quite good now. Not so much at the beginning."

I thought about this as Marge went to a little refrigerator in the corner of the room. "Would you like a Dr Pepper, hon? Maybe a lemonade?"

"Lemonade is lovely, thanks."

She selected a Snapple for me and a Dr Pepper for herself, then came to sit across from me. "Oh—did you see that one? Goldfinch. We have a never-ending show here."

"Marge, I had no idea you were such a naturalist!"

"Well, this is the town for it, right? Horace and I

keep a chart, and we've seen two hundred seventeen varieties of birds. It's amazing, really. Like a jewel box."

A thought occurred to me as I screwed off the top of my drink. "Wait! Did Horace do the grizzly bear?"

"Oh no. But there's a story behind that fella, too. When he was alive, he was a fixture at the Riverton Zoo. Have you been? A really nice zoo, well kept and such. You and Sam should go. About a four-hour drive."

I nodded, taking a sip of the lemonade. "Sinfully sweet," I said.

"The bear's name was Wally, and everyone loved him. He got up in age—about eighteen years, I guess—and he got sick. The zookeeper who worked with him every day said he would like to keep his image alive when he passed, you know, to make it less heart wrenching for everyone. He got permission, I'm not sure who-all he had to ask, and he preserved Wally. They say he captured the bear's likeness and his personality and everything. But zoo officials didn't want to keep him at the zoo because they thought it would upset children to see Wally not moving. For a while he was in a local museum, and then he went up at a local auction. They would have given him to the keeper, but he had died by then. Horace got word of it and put a bid in. This was just a couple years into us starting the store. It wasn't that high a bid, even, but he got Wally. And now that grizzly is just a staple. It wouldn't be Bick's without Wally."

"No, it wouldn't. That's a wonderful story, Marge. I'm ashamed I didn't ask about Wally before. I talk with him just about every time I come in here." I took another sip of my drink. Marge's strange back room was surprisingly restful. "You know what? You should make a sign explaining Wally's story. Give him some context for the local people."

Marge pointed at the window. "Scarlet tanager! Now, that one you don't see every day!" She turned back to me. "That's a great idea about the sign. Horace could do a plaque, even. Lord knows he's got the materials in this giant barn of a place."

"Cool." My eyes drifted to the window, where birds vied for space at one of the large feeders, and a hummingbird flapped his frantic wings as he pulled honeyed water from a vial. The wind rattled the feeders and ruffled feathers, giving everything a slightly blurry look. "Marge, I don't know if you've heard about Jane Wyland."

I darted a look back at her and saw that she was pointing to the local newspaper. "She's in today's news. Page three."

"It's horrifying, I know."

Marge nodded. "She was a friend. Not so much lately, but back when." Her eyes were shrewd as they narrowed in on me. "Are you and Camilla investigating something? Is that why you want to talk about old times?"

"Sort of. Jane had visited Camilla just before she died. She was quite upset, but—she wouldn't say why," I hedged. "Camilla was mystified by it all. Then the next morning Jane was dead. Camilla can only imagine it has something to do with the distant past, because she hasn't spoken to Jane in more than forty years."

"It's true, Jane didn't appear in town much anymore. But the last few weeks I saw her several times. Her little sister, Carrie, had recently died, and Jane seemed really torn up about it. I'm not sure where it happened. Back when Carrie left Blue Lake I think word was she had gone to Chicago. Maybe she was still there." She shook her head. "Now both of them are gone. Makes a person feel old, you know? Like you have more friends under the ground than above it."

"Don't say that, Marge! You have friends all over this town."

She smiled. "Yes, yes. But your first friends are special, aren't they? The friends of your youth. I always think of that 'Auld Lang Syne' song. Drinking to the past." She shook her head and turned to look at her birds.

"Can you tell me about the old gang? And do you care if I take notes?"

"No, go ahead. What do you want to know?"

"Well—who were the major players? Who made up the base group?"

"I suppose it was the ones who had gone to school together at Blue Lake High. Graduated in the '60s, all of them. That was Horace, and Travis Pace, and Rusty Baxter. The police chief, you know? And of course Adam Rayburn and Camilla's James. He was a handsome one, that James Graham."

"Oh? Did you have a crush on him?"

Marge laughed and slapped her knee. "Oh no. Horace and I were high school sweethearts. He was the only boy for me, but I did admire James Graham. He seemed to come from another age, somehow. Had a very noble bearing. But some folks read that as stuck-up, like he thought he was better than others. You had to know James, though. He didn't feel superior to anyone. He was actually very kind." Her face grew slightly troubled, but she waved a thought away like a cobweb and sipped her soft drink.

"So those five were friends? And then it was you and Jane? Was Carrie a part of your group?"

"Sometimes she was. She was two years younger than Jane, so she wasn't always invited, but everyone loved Carrie. Very cute girl, blonde and pretty. Jane was dark and serious. They were like flip sides of each other. We saw Carrie as a kid. In fact, when she wasn't with us, she hung out with a girl even younger than she was, someone she knew from high school. I remember her talking about her now and then, like a best friend. Sandy was the girl's name. So sometimes Carrie was off with Sandy, being a kid, and sometimes she was with us, trying to act more sophisticated."

"And who did they have a crush on? Anyone?"

"Well, I think for a long time Jane liked Travis. They might have had a thing once, I can't recall. And Rusty was quite the ladies' man back then; girls went mad for his red hair."

"Like Karina?"

Marge's eyes widened. "How do you know about Karina?"

"I just spoke to Camilla about this same group."

She sighed. "Oh yes, my friend Karina was madly in love with Rusty Baxter. I think he led her on, to be honest. He loved the fact that girls loved him. But he really only had eyes for Darlene, who was so pretty she did modeling part-time." She sighed. "Karina finally realized she was barking up the wrong tree and starting seeing a farm boy named Ken Fields. She's Karina Fields now, as a matter of fact."

"Do you like Ken?"

"Oh yes. A very sweet and thoughtful man. They have four kids and five grandkids."

"And where do they live?"

"Bluefield, now. They started out with a little place in Daleville, but then Ken had the chance to buy out a farmer who was retiring. I visited once. Bluefield is a pretty place, but flat. Lots of sky. Blue Lake has a lot more trees." Her eyes flicked to her own trees rustling outside. "Karina called me this morning, as a matter of fact. She's going to come in for Jane's memorial service. So you can ask her questions, too."

"Did you have any sisters? Or were your girlfriends your closest confidants?"

"I had four brothers. Two are dead now, sad to say, and the other two are on the West Coast. They started a company together and it's doing real well. I'm the only one who stayed in Blue Lake. I never could imagine leaving this town. I don't know why anyone would."

Camilla had said something to me once, back when I first met her, about Blue Lake and the spell it cast over people, making it hard to leave.

Two cardinals got into a brief tussle over some seed and Marge watched them, smiling. "Those two. Always fighting over the food when there's plenty to go around."

"So let me see: there were five boys—Adam, Travis, James, Rusty, and Horace. Then we have you, Camilla—when she got to town—Jane, Karina, and sometimes Carrie."

"Yes. We were all close in age. Carrie was still like a sweet kid. She—well, like I said, everyone loved Carrie."

"Okay. So tell me about the guys. Did they all get along?"

Marge started counting on her fingers. "Well, James and Adam were two peas in a pod. Best friends since childhood. It's funny, Camilla ending up with Adam, but it makes sense, really. James would have wanted Adam looking after her."

"That's nice."

"Travis and Rusty were pals, too. And Horace kind of rounded out that group, but he was also my best friend, so we often did our own thing. Went on picnics, or hikes or things, just the two of us. They let us in and out of the group as we pleased, which was nice. No one gave us a hard time about being a couple. I guess because we always had been."

"And did Travis and Rusty get along with James and Adam?"

"For the most part. Until the end there."

"What end?"

"There was a big falling-out, right around the time Camilla got here. Maybe a few weeks or months after. I wasn't there when it happened, but we all heard there was a real yelling match down at the pub. The Lumberjack was the place we all used to gather, although there was another bar in town we liked sometimes."

"The Mill Wheel?"

"Yes. But that was a bit fancier. The Lumberjack was just for plain folks. That's where we young people hung out, once we were drinking age."

"And there was a big fight? Was Horace there for it?"

"I guess he came in at the end. He said everyone was red in the face—Jane, and the guys—Rusty, Travis, James, Adam. I can't remember if Karina was there. We can ask her. Camilla wasn't, I know that, because someone made the mistake of bringing her name into the argument."

"What?"

"I don't know what it was, and Horace didn't, either, but he just remembers the look on James's face when someone mentioned Camilla. He said James looked like he would kill, and Horace believed he would do it."

She stole a look at me. "I know that sounds gossipy, but it was a huge blowup. It ended friendships, I think. I don't believe the guys got together much after that. Horace and I got married and got busy with the store. None of us was a kid anymore, and we drifted apart. But it started from there. The big fight."

"And you have no idea what the fight was about?"

Marge closed her eyes. "I'll ask Horace if he recalls. I think Jane started it. I think Jane came in all hot about something and just started yelling at everyone."

This didn't surprise me, based on the one meeting I'd had with Jane Wyland. But what had made the woman so angry? And what grudge could she possibly have nurtured through four decades?

I sighed. "You said Carrie died. What did she die of, do you know?"

Marge shrugged. "I don't think Jane said. Sounded like natural causes. But it changed Jane, losing Carrie. It just opened up some old wound, and it was like it had never healed for her."

"Yes—I think you're right, Marge." I sighed. "This is a puzzle, and a very old one. I'm not sure we'll have access to all the information we need."

"Since so many of the players are dead," Marge said with grim finality.

I turned to the left and found Biff contemplating me with what seemed to be fuzzy sympathy.

"I know Adam. And I'm getting to know James through some letters Camilla showed me. And I know you and Horace. Tell me about Rusty and Travis."

"Rusty was handsome and red haired. Sometimes people don't find red hair attractive in a man, but Rusty had charisma. Still does. If he weren't still happily married I'll bet he'd be a real player in this town."

I thought about the police chief I had met—portly, gray haired, a bit sleepy-looking. It was hard to imagine him as the devil-may-care lady-killer that Marge described.

"Rusty also had a great sense of humor. He had us all in stitches all the time—maybe that's what the girls liked most," Marge said. "I liked to sit next to him at the pub because he always put me in the best mood."

"And Travis?"

"Travis was the smartest of us. At first he was looking to be a doctor, and he got top marks in all the math and science classes. We used to drill him on his terms at the pub, back when he was in college. But his dad got sick, and he ended up dropping out of school to help with the family business."

"Did his father die?"

"No, he got better, but by then Travis had taken a liking to sales. He was a quick talker and thinker, and he always found a way to make the sale. He increased productivity and his old man was thrilled. He still has the company, actually. It's a restaurant supply chain called Pacer. Named for Pace. He supplies Adam's restaurant. Easy to figure out how he got that customer."

"So not all of the old friends are at odds," I said.

"No—after all this time I think the bad feeling is dead and gone. Dead and gone," Marge repeated, looking sad.

"But not for Jane."

Marge sipped her soda and studied my face for a minute. "Poor Jane," she said.

I jotted down some notes, then said, "Marge, you said Carrie left town. When was that?"

Her eyes were on the birds again. "Carrie. It might have been Carrie that started it all."

"What do you mean?"

Marge turned to me. "I think the big fight happened right after she left Blue Lake."

6

I've learned today, Camilla, that a man can be pushed to the edge: of endurance, of trust, of civility, and of tolerance. I have reached the edge of all of those, along with my temper. You must think this does not sound like your mild-mannered James, but here in quiet Blue Lake I never had reason to stand up for what I believe in, or perhaps even to know my own heart in that respect. I know it now, and I know what I cannot forgive.

I've learned there is darkness in the human heart: a terrible darkness, and one that I wish I had never seen.

—From the correspondence of James Graham
and Camilla Easton, 1971

WHEN I LEFT Bick's, I gave Wally the bear a special pat on the arm. Who knew that Wally had been visited by so many people? Who knew that little children had found joy in his presence? Who knew that a caretaker had loved him enough to try to preserve his face, his fur, to let him somehow still feel the light?

"Lena?"

I looked up to see the pretty face of Belinda Fraley. "Hey," I said.

"Are you okay? You looked like you were crying."

I sighed. "I'm emotional today, and I don't know why. It might have to do with the wind, or the murder, or Camilla and James, or Wally." I pointed at the bear; we were still standing in front of him.

"Wally? Is that his name?"

"Yes. He—God, I am emotional!" I wiped at my eyes. "What's wrong with me?"

Belinda gave me a warm, spice-scented hug. "Poor thing. Come to my car; I have a present for you."

"Weren't you just going in?"

She waved her hand. "I can get it later. I'm running low on paper towels; no big deal."

She pushed her glasses up on her cute nose and tucked her arm into mine. "Now, come."

We moved down the sidewalk and I felt her studying my face. "Did you have a fight with Sam?"

"What? No. I never fight with Sam."

"Maybe you should. Work out some feelings."

I shook my head. "We're not that kind of couple. We're . . . peaceful." A gust of air blew my hair over my eyes, and I brushed it away.

"Anyway, did you know that weather like this can affect your mood?" Now she was wearing what I thought of as her librarian face. "Not for the better, sadly. But things like rain and wind have been proven to have a potentially negative effect on the spirit."

"I love the wind," I said in a small voice.

Belinda squinched up her eyes as we walked. "I'm trying to remember an article I read . . . some people have a particular sensitivity to weather. They can even anticipate coming storms." She peered at me.

"Maybe you're responding to weather that hasn't happened yet."

"Maybe it's just hormones," I said, shrugging.

"Here we are. Come sit inside for a minute and talk to me. I haven't seen you in a while. Did Doug tell you I want to throw a party?"

"Yes. He mentioned it yesterday," I said, climbing into her passenger seat. "But then all this happened with Jane Wyland."

"What's all this?" she asked.

I told her. About Jane's visit, and Camilla's distress, as the reason we had come to Allison's. "And the reason Doug and Cliff left turned out to be Jane's death. I assume you read about it in the paper, or maybe Doug has told you."

Belinda's green eyes widened with interest. "He just mentioned it in passing. He tries not to talk about cases. This is all rather neatly dovetailed, isn't it? How strange."

"Yes, everything is strange. Remember when Hamlet said, 'The time is out of joint'? That's how it feels. Out of joint. I think that's why I'm teary. I need someone to come and shove my life back into the socket."

"A tenuous analogy, but I get it."

"It's Shakespeare's analogy," I said. "I'm just borrowing it."

"In a weird way," Belinda said, grinning.

I giggled, then sighed. "Do you have any chocolate on you?"

Belinda made a show of patting herself down. "No. I can take you into Bick's and buy you a candy bar."

"That sounds great. But I should probably get back and see what Camilla would like me to do. She said we can work on our book tomorrow, but maybe I should do some chores or wash the dogs or something. She does pay me, you know. I'm spoiled, and it's the easiest job ever, but I try to be available for her."

"You can take a rain check on the candy bar. Now, do you remember I said I had a present for you?"

"Oh yes. What is it?"

"Stay here. It's in my trunk."

She got out, and I watched her long blonde hair windmill around her head as she walked in the tempestuous air. She came back with a box. "Camilla's publisher reissued all these titles with new covers, so we updated them and took these off the shelves. Old editions. They're yours, or Camilla's, if you want them."

I stared down at a box full of hardback Camilla Graham books, some dating back to the '70s and '80s. "Ohhh, they're beautiful! Look at this one. *The Torches Burn Bright*. Oh my gosh—I just read this line in a letter from Camilla's husband. He was so romantic. This is taken from *Romeo and Juliet*! I wonder if that's why Camilla gave the book that title. It *is* a romantic novel. Have you ever read it?"

Belinda shook her head. "No, but Doug tells me I need to get started. He's read three or four of them. At first, he was just being loyal to Camilla, but now he's hooked."

"Of course," I said, running my fingers lovingly over a copy of *The Silver Birch*. "Look at the cover art. Look at the way the light hits the birch trees. I was so in love with the hero in this one—Maximillian Brent."

"You should see your face," Belinda said with a little grin. "You know, you can tell a lot about a person by the books they read. Take it from a librarian; we are observers of human nature."

"Is that so?"

"Sure. What is Camilla reading right now?"

I thought of Camilla's living room, the cozy corner where she kept the knitting basket that she never used (although she did sometimes add a ball of yarn—I think she enjoyed the changing colors) and where her book of choice usually sat on a table beside her armchair. "*The Story of My Life*, by Helen Keller," I said.

"Perfect. Doesn't that just suit Camilla? I suppose she admires the woman's tenacity and genius."

"Yes, but also her philanthropy. Camilla's been reading me some parts—Keller was so focused on others, and on gratitude. Considering her disabilities, she could certainly have become hardened or bitter. But she chose joy and service."

"Interesting! Okay, that fits with Camilla. What's Sam reading?"

I thought of Sam's bedroom, where the two of us liked to occasionally cuddle together and read our respective books until we got distracted by each other. His bedside table generally held only his alarm clock, his watch, his *Far Side* coffee cup, and a small pile of books culled from a shelf in the corner, or newly received in the mail. I smiled. "He's got a pile of three that he's sort of rotating through. *To Kill a Mockingbird*, because I recommended it. He is in love with Scout."

"Good."

"Also a Bill Crider novel. Something about a sheriff in a small Texas town. He says I should read that one when he's done."

"Also good. He likes fiction, like you."

"But he's also reading a book about Crazy Horse and other great tribal leaders. He has great admiration for Native Americans."

"See? That gives me new insights into Sam."

"And what is Doug reading right now?"

Belinda smiled. "A book about Roosevelt, and a Sherlock Holmes novel. You know Doug—he likes his mysteries."

I smiled and stroked the cover of *The Silver Birch*. "That's right. He said something the day I met him, when he heard Lestrade's name. I should have guessed."

Belinda looked pleased. "I guess this was a good present, right?"

"Oh, it's amazing! I don't have all of these in hardback. I'm going to give you a kiss." I leaned over to embrace her and plant my lips sloppily on her cheek, and she laughed. "You did make my day, thank you. My blues are fading."

She waited while I tucked the books back into the box, then said, "So is it something with Sam?"

"No! I mean, I miss him a little. When I'm not busy with Camilla, he's busy with Cliff. But that's how it should be. He and Cliff have waited a lifetime to meet each other."

"And *you* waited a lifetime for *him*," Belinda said. "Reading romantic books and falling in love with fictional characters."

"Yes, that's true. And Sam is everything I need him to be."

She turned away slightly to watch a piece of paper blow down Wentworth Street. "Well, that's good. Shall I drive you home?"

"Don't be silly. It's just up the hill."

"But you have that big box now. And whatever you bought at Bick's."

"I didn't buy anything; I was just talking to Marge. Okay, my friend, I will take a ride, and while we drive I'll tell you about Wally the bear."

"Don't cry," Belinda warned with a sardonic lift of her lip.

"I'll try not to," I said.

I THANKED BELINDA again and invited her in for a cool drink, but she said she had to get home and make the most of her day off. She waved brightly as she shifted gears. "And we'll have chocolate soon!" she yelled out the window before she drove down the gravel drive.

Inside Graham House I found Camilla paying bills in her office. "I'll be finished in a moment, Lena, and then you and I can make a plan for the day," she said. The dogs were back under her desk; not even their tails moved at the sound of my voice. Star must have given them a good walk.

I waved my assent to Camilla and ran upstairs to deposit the precious bag of books in my room. Lestrade was not on the bed; I wondered if he had ventured to a warmer spot. He seemed to fluctuate between wanting cool air and wanting to be as hot as he possibly could. Sometimes he even stalked up to Camilla's attic, where he would lie in dusty sunbeams and bake in the hottest point of the house. At my dresser I combed my hair and then pulled it into a ponytail. Then I ran down to the kitchen, where I got some water at the tap and sat down to drink it. I checked my texts again; I had one from my father, asking how things were going. I texted back that things were fine and I missed him. I sent a hug emoji to go with it.

The emoji looked affectionate and comforting; I started to send one to Sam, but I got another text, this time from Allison. *Did you hear about Belinda's party? She's throwing it on the Fourth, before the fireworks.*

I wrote back that I planned to be there, and then I heard Camilla calling me. I returned to her office, where I spied Rochester stretching and yawning before rolling over and curling against his brother.

"Camilla, I meant to show you this," I said, crossing the room and summoning the picture of Baby Athena that Victoria West had sent me. It still felt odd, hearing from Victoria, perhaps because for so long she had been only an idea to me, and a world-famous missing person. Now she was just Sam's ex-wife, happily domesticated in a new relationship and clearly doting on her beautiful baby daughter.

Camilla looked at it, then clapped her hands. "Oh, she is so beautiful. I do hope they visit soon." She looked at me with one of her shrewd expressions. "Victoria liked you a great deal. Still does, obviously. She wants you as a friend."

"That's nice, I guess." I set the phone on Camilla's desk. "I'm not sure why."

Camilla raised her eyebrows. "You found her when no one else could. You *saved* her. And then you found her daughter. I think she idolizes you."

"Wow." I tended to feel guilty about Victoria, especially about the baby whose abduction I had witnessed without realizing it. Occasionally I was still haunted by the memory of Baby Athena's trusting dark eyes. I had been essentially spying on Sam and Victoria when a man I had thought was Victoria's assistant took the baby away.

"You don't view her as a rival, do you?"

"No, not at all. She told Sam and me, a month or so ago, that she is in love with Tim, the man who was her bodyguard in Blue Lake. They seem good for each other."

"It all worked out," Camilla said placidly. "Meanwhile, our fictional heroine is still pining for the man she thinks has betrayed her. I think we need to relieve her worries in this chapter, don't you?"

"Yes. We don't have to wait until tomorrow—let's do it now. And whatever revelation he brings must come as both a wonderful and a terrible surprise, because now she will realize that she has underestimated him."

"Fine. Shall we exchange notes or talk it out first?"

"Let's talk it out. Nothing like a good brainstorming session."

Camilla touched the gold rim of her teacup. "And afterward—I suppose we should read some more letters."

"All right. If it's not too difficult for you."

"I'll be fine. Meanwhile I'll ask Adam to come over soon. I want him to bring some old photo albums. Perhaps that will trigger some memories, in him or in me."

"Good idea! I told Cliff that we would be looking, and he said he wants to hear any little detail we think is relevant."

"Good."

"Camilla? I spoke with Marge Bick today."

"Ah?"

"She said that at one point there was a huge fight in James's old group of friends, and that they never really came together again. Do you know what the fight was about?"

She shook her head slowly. "Nooo, although I think it happened shortly after we were married. I only went to some gatherings at the pub a few times before James suggested that we didn't need to do it anymore. Whatever it was, he didn't want it to touch me."

"Marge said that the big fight happened right around the time Carrie left town."

Again, Camilla looked a bit uncertain. "I did not know Carrie. She worked for James and his father for a time, but she was gone by the time I got here. I never actually shared this house with another woman— until you."

"And look what a troublemaker I turned out to be," I said, my voice light.

Camilla smiled absently, then nodded a couple of times. "Carrie. Of course. She's a link to Jane and to the Grahams. She worked here; perhaps she's the one who found out whatever 'secret' her sister thought she knew."

I tried to picture it: Carrie dusting the shelves and finding a deep, dark Graham family secret in the form of—what? A letter? A document? A secret identity?

"I think I've read too many books," I said. "The only things I can think of seem fictional."

"I agree. If Jane Wyland hadn't come here and made a scene I would never have believed there could have been anything shocking in the past—not regarding my husband, anyway."

A thought occurred to me. "Did Carrie live here while she helped care for the house?"

Camilla narrowed her eyes and looked upward, as though focusing in on a memory. "I think she lived at her home, at that place we just visited. Where poor Jane died. But if I recall there was a time when James's father was in a bad way and James had to go out of town that Carrie stayed for a while."

"In my room, I'm guessing?"

She shook her head. "No. Mr. Graham lived down here because he had trouble taking the stairs. So that back library near the sunroom was his bedroom, and I think Carrie stayed in the little room beside it—the one where I keep my Christmas decorations now."

"Ah. Did James have to travel a lot?"

"Back then he worked at a law firm in Daleville. He never practiced law; he did legal research. He mostly worked from his office or from home, but sometimes they sent him to seminars and conferences. He had to write up these dry things explaining the letter of the law, but he was actually a delightful creative writer. He composed a poem for me every Christmas, about the year we had just spent together. I have those somewhere, too. I'll have to show you."

"I wish I had met him, Camilla."

"I do, too." She smiled ruefully, then pointed at the office. "Now let's get to work. We'll come back to this mystery later."

"Let me get a refill on my water and I'll be right there."

I went to the kitchen and filled my glass again at the tap, and then, out of curiosity, I moved down the hallway, past the sunroom to a small, square space where Camilla stored all sorts of seasonal decor. It was a nice enough room, with a small window that looked out on the lake, and slightly musty blue carpeting. I tried to imagine Carrie Wyland standing there, looking out at the view for a moment before returning to her chores, or to answer the call of poor old Mr. Graham. She had been so young then—what had she dreamed about? What had she wanted to do with the money she earned? And what was it about her young life that had infuriated her sister, had sent the older sibling running to the pub to confront all of her friends, to cause a rift that lasted for decades?

Blue Lake, unchanged for all that time, lay serene beneath the summer sun, keeping Carrie's secrets and its own.

7

My dear Camilla, I apologize that you were distressed by the tone of my last letter. Life here has become complicated, but I continue to think of you with the same affection. I am facing a difficult decision, and it's kind of you to say you want to help. The best way would be to go to that lovely church we visited, the one surrounded by lilac bushes, and say a heartfelt prayer for me. I know I'll feel your inspiration, even across the sea.

—From the correspondence of James Graham
and Camilla Easton, 1971

ON THE FIRST day of July, Camilla and I went to Wheat Grass for lunch; Adam had insisted that we leave the house and that the change of scenery would do us good, but I knew that he had an ulterior motive of wanting to see Camilla. She hadn't been inviting him over as much, and I feared that sensitive Adam was feeling neglected. Even I had wondered if reading James's lovely letters had cooled her affection for Adam, although I didn't see any obvious lessening of Camilla's fondness when she spoke of him.

We pulled up to the sophisticated building on the

edge of Green Glass Highway right around lunchtime, and I realized that I was quite hungry, which I mentioned to Camilla as we walked toward the door.

"I think Adam said he has some new menu items," she told me. "You must treat yourself to something delicious. My, the heat has come back today, hasn't it?"

It had; the temperature was already eighty-five degrees and still climbing, and I was glad to enter the cool elegance of Wheat Grass, where the new hostess, Yolanda, met us at the door and led us to a table near the back of the room. As usual the silverware gleamed brightly, and a yellow rose sat in the center of the table. "I love this place," I said. We sat down and Yolanda brought us a small loaf of bread. "Your waiter will be Thomas; he'll join you in just a moment."

"Thank you," I said, already sawing away at the bread, to Camilla's obvious amusement.

"All the waiters seem new in here," she said in a rather sad voice.

"I'm sure some of your favorites are still on the staff—just on a different shift. Adam would tell you if any of your friends had left, wouldn't he?"

"Probably." Her eyes scanned the room casually, then focused in on something that made her shoulders tense. "Oh."

"What is it?"

"No, don't turn around, Lena. Just some members of the very group we were discussing yesterday—the old gang from the pub."

"What do you think they're doing here?"

"I don't—oh, here comes Marge."

Marge Bick, dressed in a muted black pantsuit, appeared at our table. "Hello, Camilla. Hello, Lena."

"Marjorie," Camilla said.

"I don't know if you knew, but there was a little memorial service for Jane this morning. There aren't many Wylands left, that we know of, so Rusty just arranged something in town. Some of the old group came out for it. I thought you might want to talk to them. I know Lena said you had some questions. Maybe after you finish eating you'd like to join us? We're over by the window there."

"Is that Travis Pace?" Camilla said. "And Karina?"

"Yeah. And Rusty's stopping by later, and Adam said he'll sit with us for coffee. Horace had to work."

"Well, that's kind of you, Marjorie. We will do that," Camilla said, nodding toward her.

Marge waved at me and went back to her table. She looked different in her attractive pantsuit, her face not framed by the window of her little post office. I realized, with a burst of shame, that I had a tendency to put people into figurative boxes and found it jarring when they proved to be more than I had thought them.

"Marge looks different, doesn't she?" Camilla asked. "More like the girl she once was, actually. It doesn't seem that long ago. I can see all their young faces in my mind."

"What about the young faces you left behind? There must have been friends you were sorry to leave in England. Did they ever come to visit you?"

She pulled her napkin out of its ring. "Once or twice. Back then the separations came naturally—we all seemed to get engaged or married at the same time. We were all moving on. But I have a few dear friends with whom I correspond to this day. Two of them have visited me here. One of them you met when we went to England. Do you recall the white-haired woman named Prue?"

"Oh yes! She was lovely."

"She was my schoolfriend and confidant. Still is, sometimes. I call her now and then."

"Hmm. Okay, I'm looking in the menu because the bread didn't do much for me. Oh, look at the special! Some sort of shrimp pasta. I think I'll get that."

Camilla paged listlessly through the menu. "Just a salad for me, I think. Speaking of food, I heard from our dear Rhonda. They are loving Italy. She feels inspired by the Renaissance."

"Wonderful!"

Thomas, a tall red-haired man, appeared at our table with his pad, and Camilla and I gave him our orders. He nodded and promised us they would be out soon. I stole a glance behind me at the group of James's old friends: they seemed to be in a close and serious conversation, all leaning forward toward the center of the table.

The woman named Karina had shoulder-length gray hair pulled back with barrettes. She wore a black dress with a white collar. It was surprisingly elegant.

"She always was fashion-conscious," Camilla said, reading my mind. "That's what James said, anyway. They called her 'Key' sometimes as a nickname. He would say, '*Everyone showed up in jeans except for*

Key, who seemed to be ready for the runway.'" She smiled at the memory.

Thomas brought our lunches a few minutes later, and we ate, for the most part, in a companionable silence. Camilla and I, after months of cohabitation, often became lost in our thoughts together. Mine bounced around erratically, from Jane Wyland to Cliff and Doug to Sam and his deck to Belinda and Allison. I felt jumpy and unsettled, and, as a cloud passed over the sun and made the room significantly darker, I had a growing feeling of unease, as though something malignant had crossed our path. Startled by this sudden change in mood, I scanned the room for any sort of alteration; Wheat Grass was fairly crowded, but I noted few familiar faces aside from the people at the long central table who gathered to remember Jane. I did see Star Kelly and her father, Luke, sitting at a window table. Luke was texting, absorbed in some sort of exchange, and Star was looking listlessly out at the parking lot. She slouched in her seat, and when she dragged her eyes back to her plate she poked her French fry halfheartedly into some ketchup. Her seeming malaise made me think of Carrie Wyland. Had she, like Star, been lonely in Blue Lake? Had it been hard for her to work in a house with a sick old man and a serious, lovesick young one?

But Carrie had been much loved—that's what Marge Bick said. She was a part of the group that included James Graham and Jane Wyland. And she had a best friend named Sandy.

My gaze covered the rest of the room without any further recognition.

Camilla seemed to feel my restlessness, even to share it. I was about to ask her if she had felt the sudden tension in the room, but Adam appeared in the doorway of the kitchen. It took him only seconds to find Camilla and to walk swiftly to our table. He bent to kiss Camilla's cheek and to give my hand an affectionate pat. "Good, here you are. Are you enjoying your lunch?"

"It's delicious," I said.

Camilla nodded. "Adam, did you see your old friends there?" She indicated the group with a subtle dip of her head.

Adam studied her for a moment; he could read Camilla even better than I could, and his tone was apologetic. "I didn't know they were coming; apparently there was some sort of memorial service for Jane. I didn't attend."

Camilla shrugged. "You could have attended. I suppose I should have as well. But I'm curious to know what they all have to say about Jane. Lena and I will join them shortly. Will you come, too? You might have insights that I don't regarding some of their comments."

"Of course! I would have been out earlier, but our chef needed some help until his lunchtime assistant arrived."

Camilla was clearly ready to start her interrogations. "Wonderful. Lena, are you finished with your pasta?"

I was not, but I was also full. "For now, I think. Adam, can Thomas wrap this up for me?"

"Yes, of course." Adam lifted a finger to get

Thomas's attention, and the waiter glided to our table with a smile. He took my plate and promised to return; Camilla informed him that we would be moving to the large table, and he nodded.

I followed Camilla and Adam to Marge Bick's table, where she sat in close conversation with the woman named Karina. Travis Pace was talking to a man I didn't know; Adam shook his hand and said, "Hello, Paul."

Marge said, "Adam, Camilla, thanks for joining us. Soon we'll have the whole gang back together. Or what's left of it," she said. I don't think she meant to be morbid, but her comment made everyone briefly avert their eyes.

Adam, ever the gentleman, said, "Camilla, I think you remember Karina?" Camilla nodded at the gray-haired woman, who nodded back and murmured a greeting. "And of course you know Travis?"

Camilla nodded to Travis, who said, "Long time, no see, Cammy."

The man called Paul looked to be slightly younger than the rest; he had gray hair with dark strands and lively eyes. He was perhaps in his early sixties. His eyes were on Camilla. Adam said, "Camilla, I don't know if you remember Paul Graves? His father was David Graves, the owner of the Lumberjack. You'll recall him as the man who walked around wiping tables and wearing a red apron that said 'Timber!'"

"Oh—yes, I do remember. I think I saw you in the pub now and then. Weren't you studying for some sort of exam?"

Paul Graves smiled and nodded. "Yeah—while

you all were starting your careers and marriages, I was still in college, trying to get my MBA."

Camilla sat in a chair that Adam pulled up for her. He did the same for me, and I sat beside her. "So did you end up taking over the family business?" she asked.

Graves looked away. "No, I ended up selling it when my dad died. The new owner didn't maintain it the way my dad had, and it went under. I made a mistake there."

"What did you do instead?" I asked. Thomas approached in silence and handed me a plastic to-go bag. I thanked him, my eyes on Paul Graves.

He looked back at me with pale green eyes. "I left town for a while, started a business with a friend. That died after a couple of years, so I came back to Blue Lake and started a landscaping company. By then—I was ready to come back."

Camilla rustled in her seat; she was eager to talk about Jane. Marge seemed to notice this, and she lifted a hand. "Listen, while we have you all here for the first time in decades, I want to ask you all something. Oh, look—here's Rusty!"

The chief of police was indeed walking toward us at a brisk pace. He glanced at his watch before he greeted everyone and sat down. "Thanks to all of you for attending the service. Jane would have liked it, I know."

I studied Bill "Rusty" Baxter. Upon close examination, I could still see some red strands of hair beneath the gray, and in his weathered face, partially covered now by a large gray mustache, I saw traces of the handsome man he was said to have been. I made a mental note to look for him in Adam's photo albums.

Marge said, "We were just talking about her. Or we were about to. Do you all remember when Jane got everyone fighting at the Lumberjack? It was sometime in September. I've been trying to think of the timeline, because Carrie left at the end of summer, and then Camilla came to town in October, didn't you, Camilla?"

"Yes," Camilla said. "The end of September, actually. And I never met Carrie."

"Why does this matter?" Travis asked, spearing a piece of pie and shoving it into his mouth.

Camilla leaned forward. "Because Jane came to see me the day before she died. I hadn't seen her or spoken to her in decades. She was—highly agitated and talking of stirring up some memories from the past."

The people at the table exchanged glances. I watched them for any odd behavior, but they mostly seemed surprised. Paul Graves didn't look at anyone else, but down at a napkin that he was shredding on his plate. He said, "So? Jane was always melodramatic."

Camilla shook her head. "She was most insistent. She was going to bring something to light the following day. Her words were ominous and threatening. By the next morning she was dead. *Murdered*. I think that is more than a coincidence."

Karina looked at us with wide blue eyes. "You think someone killed her because of some old secret? Something to do with us?"

Marge leaned in. "Carrie died just a couple of

months ago. Jane told me so when she came to the post office last month. Jane wasn't taking it well; she was brooding over something. Whatever it was finally exploded out of her, and she ended up confronting poor Camilla there."

Everyone turned to stare at Camilla. Rusty Baxter looked up from his menu and frowned. "In any case, the police are looking into Jane Wyland's death. It does no one any good to speculate about it—we'll get to the bottom of it. We have our best detective on the case."

He meant Doug Heller; I had no doubt that he was right, and that Doug would find the person responsible, but it was a bit more complicated than that.

Camilla met Rusty's gaze and held it. "Chief Baxter, I have no intention of impeding a police investigation, but I am curious about Jane Wyland's verbal attack on me. It was quite upsetting, and I only met her three or four times in my life. I think this group would know better than anyone why she might have been so upset."

Marge leaned in again. "And I told Lena, I think this all goes back to Carrie. Right around the time she left there was that huge fight at the Lumberjack. I know you all remember. What was it about? Was it something to do with Carrie? Horace didn't say much about it later. I can't remember why, but I wasn't there when it all went down."

"This is ridiculous," said Travis. "It's all water under the bridge."

Adam sent him a cool glance. "It is not. A woman has been murdered—a woman who was a friend to us all. The police will have to examine that *water* very closely. So you had all better start dredging up your memories. I also have a personal stake in this. Jane maligned the family of my best friend, and she had no right to do so. Obviously, somewhere along the line, she was told lies."

Camilla sent him a look of love and gratitude—the sort of thing the doting Adam normally longed for—but he barely looked her way. He said, "Marge, what did Horace tell you that night?"

Marge was obviously pleased to have been questioned. "I just remember he said Jane showed up and almost immediately got confrontational. She said her sister had left town because she hated Blue Lake and certain people in town had made it unbearable for her."

Karina sent an apologetic glance toward Camilla when she said, "I remember that. I think she said her sister didn't like working for the Grahams. That they made her life miserable, or something."

Rusty nodded. "I do recall her saying something of the sort, but I also remember that James told me Carrie had been very happy with them, had actually asked to expand her work hours, but then abruptly decided to leave."

Travis grew animated. "That's right. Jane said something about Camilla, didn't she? Like, *Wait until your pretty British fiancée is trapped in your Gothic nightmare*, or something like that. I always remembered that because I didn't know what 'Gothic' meant, and I had to look it up."

Marge said, "Yes, this matches what Horace told

me. That when Jane mentioned Camilla, James got angry."

Everyone turned to look at Camilla, who looked exasperated. "Does anyone remember what James said?"

Paul Graves said, "I do. I was there; I was always in the pub back then, trying to study in one of the booths, but their fight made a way better distraction. He told her that when people didn't know what they were talking about they should hold their tongues. I thought it was a great line."

"And what did Jane say?"

Paul Graves looked at me with his pale eyes. "She didn't have a chance to say anything, because James walked out. The way I remember it, he was angry at everyone. At all of you," he said, looking around the table. "He went home and, as I recall, he never really hung around at the Lumberjack again."

Adam looked stern, like a teacher who has caught the students cheating. "There was a lot of gossiping going on. I didn't hear much that night because I went chasing after James to make sure he was all right. But I know that you had all been making some snide comments about James . . . and Carrie."

Camilla, to her credit, changed not one thing in her expression, but I noted the sudden paleness of her skin.

Rusty cleared his throat. "There was some gossip, Camilla. But it was just that—gossip. Some of us probably talked about it at the bar."

Adam sat up straighter. "Any of you who were true friends of James Graham knew that he wouldn't have been interested in any woman other than Camilla, and certainly not someone who was barely more than a teenager and worked for his family."

Everyone nodded solemnly, but no one was looking at Adam. Finally, Karina slapped the table. "Oh, all right, I'm just going to say it. We all know what people were saying back then—not just our group but lots of people in Blue Lake. Carrie Wyland seemed to disappear overnight, and Jane told us she had gone to Chicago, where she didn't know a soul. Jane missed her; the two of them confided in each other all the time, and it was like Jane lost her best friend."

She waited for someone to take up the story, but no one did. She sighed and said, "So people around town said, *What would make a kid like that suddenly relocate? If she didn't like it at the Grahams', she could just quit.*" She took a sip of her water and cleared her throat. "So the gossip was, she must have been pregnant, and James Graham must have paid to send her out of town because he had a fiancée coming soon."

The table grew silent. The muted chatter and the clinking of silverware from other tables were all we heard for a time. Adam wisely did not try to hug Camilla or draw any attention to her. Camilla studied her hands, obviously thinking through the information. Finally she said, "And how many of you, I wonder, stood up for James at the time? How many of you said, *James Graham would never mistreat a young woman in that way, and even if he had made her pregnant he certainly wouldn't have hidden it and pushed her out of town like a coward?*"

No one spoke. Camilla said, "I know Adam

defended him, because he was a loyal friend. And you, Rusty? Did you stand up for James?"

Rusty looked uncomfortable. "It was just gossip, Camilla. No one actually believed it."

"Did Jane believe it?" she asked.

Travis was almost sneering. "Let's not forget we're talking about the Wyland girls. They were always grasping around for money and men. If Carrie got pregnant, James would make a great scapegoat."

Marge Bick glared at him. "That's an awfully uncharitable thing to say!"

The table erupted in defenses and recriminations; people were almost hissing in their attempt to keep their voices low.

Camilla sighed. "And does anyone know if Carrie actually did have a child after she went to Chicago?"

The table grew silent. Camilla stood up. "That would certainly be a place to start, wouldn't it, Chief? Meanwhile, Lena and I will do all we can to find out what really happened to Carrie Wyland and to clear her name and James Graham's."

The restaurant, too, had become quiet. I looked up to find that both Luke and Star Kelly were staring over, openmouthed, apparently having heard the last part of the conversation.

Camilla picked up her purse and nodded to the assembled group. "Thank you all for sharing your memories." She walked to the door, regal as a queen, and I followed. Adam caught me in the doorway, when Camilla was already outside.

"Do you think I should come over?" he asked.

"Give it half an hour. I'll text you," I said. We both

knew that Camilla sometimes needed silence, especially after a draining experience.

I joined Camilla on the steps; we walked to the parking lot and I opened the passenger door of my car so that she could climb in. I ran around to the driver's side and started the motor, flipping on the air conditioner. I tossed my purse and my leftovers in the backseat and turned back to study the sky through the windshield. The gray cloud that had obscured the sun had grown into many gray clouds, and the sky seemed to be descending into evening rather than early afternoon. Camilla and I sat in silence for a time; I let the cool air fill the car. In the rearview mirror I saw that the party had broken up and the various members of the old group were all moving back toward their own vehicles. Moments later Luke and Star came out, too. He was looking at his phone again, and Star was saying something, trying to get his attention.

"Camilla?" I finally said. "Are you okay?"

Her voice was strong. "Of course. Why wouldn't I be? This gives us something concrete to look for in James's letters. Any reference to Carrie, or how he might have helped her."

"Yes. Good idea." I pulled my seat belt across my chest and tucked the metal into the plastic sleeve. It seemed more difficult to get it in than usual. I put the gearshift in reverse and said, "Adam seems a little worried about you."

"He worries too much," she said.

"He loves you."

"I know." Her face was averted; she seemed to be

watching the scudding clouds in the sky across Green Glass Highway.

"I love you, too."

"I know," she said. "I'm glad of you both."

I adjusted my seat, then scanned the sky. "It looks like there will be a storm. Yesterday Belinda told me that some people can sense storms before they come. I was feeling so out of sorts. I still do today, actually."

I pulled out of the parking lot and back onto the road that would take us home. "Lena," Camilla said.

"Hmm?"

"Don't you find it interesting that everyone at the table claimed to not remember anything about those days, or about the night that Jane confronted them? But by the end of our meeting they all shared some very specific details."

"Huh." I did find that interesting. I looked both ways before turning left onto Juniper Road and accelerating.

"I don't care for this street," Camilla said idly. "Too twisty, and the speed limit is too high. I sound negative, don't I? Perhaps I'm out of sorts, too."

"It's because the restaurant felt surreal, like there was a malevolent ghost watching over us. And the day went from sunny to—this—in a matter of minutes."

"Belinda is quite right; it does affect the mood," Camilla said.

I turned my wheel to accommodate the curve in front of St. Elizabeth's, a small church nestled into a green meadow along Juniper, and I looked in my rearview. "Oh! Where did he come from? It's—Aaggghhh!"

I think Camilla turned when I cried out, just before the impact, and then confusion: an explosion of my air bag, a flash of white and green and gray. Motion and sound, screaming—mine? Camilla's?—and a jarring thud.

Then pain, and blackness.

8

When you come, Camilla, things will be different. I know that things will be better if I can just touch your hair, hold your hand, look into your clear and honest eyes.

—From the correspondence of James Graham
and Camilla Easton, 1971

I OPENED MY eyes and then squinted them shut again, misty with pain. Vaguely I knew we had been in an accident. My foggy thoughts finally went to Camilla. I tried to call her name, but only a strange croaking came out of my mouth.

Her voice: "Lena? Oh, my dear girl, you're hurt! Where is your phone? I have to call someone, quickly, before he comes back."

"What?"

"Here it is. I'm dialing—oh God. Doug? It's Camilla. We've been in a wreck on Juniper. By the church. Lena is hurt, badly, I think. Yes, I think I'm all right." She said a few more things but I drifted away, perhaps into sleep.

I came back to awareness what seemed to be seconds later and looked into the gold-brown eyes of

Doug Heller. "Lena, we have to get you out of there. Can you hear me?"

"Yes." Again, my voice was unlike itself.

There were other voices, hands pulling. I screamed; it was terrible to hear the sound and know that it emanated from me. I thought I might be crying, but I realized the moisture on my skin was a light rain that had begun to fall.

"Hang in there, Lena," Doug said.

"Lena!" a voice cried; it was distant, urgent, but other voices intervened, a confusion of sounds.

I heard Camilla, near tears, angry, shaken. Then she seemed to be in conference with people unknown, and the assembled saints and angels who hovered in the air around St. Elizabeth's. I was on a stretcher, staring at the gray, misting sky through a cloud of pain, but I could see their faces, those saints and angels, weeping for me and warning, with gestures from their long, graceful hands, that I should not return to the road.

A demon waited there, his expression full of hate in my rearview mirror . . .

"The road," I croaked. "The driver!" but no one heard me.

I opened my eyes again to watery, fluorescent light and a constant wailing sound. People in white sat with me, their faces benevolent.

"Angels," I whispered.

A voice I knew. "Lena. Are you in pain?"

"Yes," I said. The angels looked remorseful, and the rain outside seemed to come in, running in rivulets down their faces, and before I closed my eyes I saw that one final face, a face wet with rain or tears, belonged to Sam West.

WHEN I WOKE again I was lying flat, moving down a narrow hallway in a hospital, past other stretchers and poles with dangling IVs. A woman in pale pink scrubs ran toward me: it was Allison. "Lena," she said, her voice unnaturally calm. "You're okay." I would have expected Allison to weep, to scream, to throw herself on me, but I had forgotten that she was very good at her job, and she must have seen that I was afraid.

"What's happening?" I rasped.

"You've got a badly broken arm. I know it hurts. Soon we'll have you stabilized in a room, with some lovely ice around that injury. But I need you to be brave a little longer, because we have to take some X-rays."

"I don't want to," I said without thinking.

"I know." She leaned close to me and kissed my cheek. "They'll be very careful, but it will hurt. They have to position your arm a certain way to get a good look at the break. Oh, my poor Lena."

She could see that I was trembling. It wasn't a conscious response; my body was doing it without my permission.

I tried to reach out with my good hand. "Will you stay with me?"

She nodded. "I think I can arrange that."

"Is Sam here?" I asked.

"Yes. Furious with me because I wouldn't let him in. It's hospital policy."

My face must have been pathetic. "Can he come in, Allie?"

She hesitated, then nodded once. "I'll be right back."

A minute later she was at my side, along with Sam, whose face was as white as the sheet that covered me. "What can I do?" he said.

"Just give her moral support," Allison said. "Okay, Lena, we're going to wheel you to X-ray now."

I closed my eyes as the cart moved along, but it felt good to hear Allison's light footfalls beside the stretcher, to feel Sam's warm hand on my good shoulder. Allison spoke briefly to someone in the X-ray room, and she stood beside me as a nameless man in blue scrubs helped me off the stretcher and lifted the broken thing that hung from my side. I had planned to be brave and not to scream, but the sounds I made were entirely out of my control, and I saw my pain reflected in the faces of Sam and Allison.

"Make him stop," Sam shouted to Allison, but she put a hand on his arm and whispered in his ear, and he was quiet, his wide eyes on me.

Finally, the man in blue left me alone, and Allison and Sam helped me into a wheelchair; she tucked a supportive pillow beneath my dangling arm. Allison murmured to me as though I were an infant, and I heard nothing but the word "surgeon."

"Surgeon," I protested, though I knew there was no other way to repair my broken bones.

"Don't panic. She's the best there is—Dr. Salinger will take good care of you, and of course I will. I'll be right here whenever you need me, and so will Sam."

"Okay."

A man appeared in the doorway, and Allison said, "This is Dan. He's going to wheel you to a room and get you set up in bed, okay? And when you're all set the surgeon will come and see you."

Pain is its own dimension; I was there by myself, but sometimes I would emerge to hear bits of conversation or see a face that came close to mine.

My foggy thoughts cleared for a moment as we traveled down a hallway. "Is Camilla all right? Where is she?"

Allison's voice. "She's fine. She'll be in your room soon to hear what the surgeon has to say."

"Okay."

"Lena? You're in shock right now. That's why everything seems a little bit weird."

"It hurts, Allie. I can barely concentrate."

"I know. We'll take care of that pain very soon. I love you, sweetie. You know I'm going to take good care of you."

"Yes." My teeth began to chatter, echoing in my head like castanets.

TWENTY MINUTES LATER I did feel slightly better; my arm had been stabilized and packed in ice, and the pain had receded slightly. I had an IV attached to my good arm, and a nurse had put in some painkiller that she told me would be working soon. Doug Heller sat next to my bed, looking grim. "Several people are waiting impatiently at your door, but we need to talk alone for a minute," he said.

"Okay."

"Lena. Can you tell me anything about the car that hit you?"

"I think it was blue. Maybe gray. It came up so fast, and I was so surprised—"

"And did you have any indication that they weren't paying attention? Someone texting and driving?"

I thought back. "I don't know. I was telling Camilla that he came out of nowhere, going fast. I know I screamed. He plowed right into us, on the curve, and I think we rolled over."

His mouth became one straight line. "You did. Camilla somehow came out of it unscathed. We think your seat belt wasn't properly latched, because you slammed against the door when you rolled."

"I can't remember much."

"Did you see anything? How many people were in the car?"

"One. That much I remember. Just one. I guess he was just going too fast. An accident, right?"

He shook his head. "If so, it's a hit-and-run. The guy who hit you didn't stick around."

"Oh."

"Any chance you recognized a face?"

"I didn't see a face that I can recall—" A fragile memory—something I had noted just before impact— but it was gone. "Sorry, Doug."

He burst out of his chair and came to stand beside me. "You have nothing to be sorry for." He bent to kiss my cheek. "I'll let your fans in now. You'll be okay, Lena. But you gave me a real scare."

"Me too." I managed a tiny smile.

He nodded. "If you remember anything else, you let me know."

"I will."

He opened the door and several people rushed in: Sam, Camilla, Belinda, Adam, and Allison. I almost laughed.

Sam was at the side of my bed in an instant, holding my good hand. "Hi," he said, still looking pale and rather sick himself.

"Are you okay?" I asked him.

"I will be, when you're out of here. What do you need?"

"Just you. And I guess whatever surgery will put my arm back together. Did anyone call my dad?" I puffed out my cheeks, trying to breathe evenly through the ache.

Sam nodded. "I did. He wanted to come out, but I told him to wait. I said we would take good care of you. He's going to call tomorrow." He managed a smile. "He's already texted me three times. I'll keep him in the loop."

"Good." I looked at the others. "You didn't all have to come here." But of course I was glad that they had.

Sam pointed at my damaged arm and murmured to Allison. "The bruise gets worse and worse," he said softly, perhaps thinking I wouldn't hear.

Allison patted his arm. "She's bleeding in there. It's not unusual. I know it looks frightening, but that's what happens when bones break. Belinda, would you grab that little brush and run it through Lena's hair? I find it can be very relaxing to patients."

Belinda did it, smiling at me, and once again I felt that I was in a play, or a surreal painting called *Soothing a Friend on Her Sickbed*.

While they stood beside me, saying gentle words and touching the edge of my blanket, I saw Camilla had detained Doug and was having a quiet conversation in the hall; I had never seen Camilla look so angry. She practically hissed something at Doug, and he nodded with a dark expression. I wanted to ask them what was happening, but the pain was making me woozy; for the first time I thought I would faint.

Allison was suddenly shooing everyone out of the room and ushering in the surgeon. Sam managed to remain, but he sat in the corner while the doctor came in, looked at the X-ray, and winced. "Oh my, Lena, is it? You've got a bad fracture of your humerus here, but in a day, you won't even believe that it was broken. I'll make it good as new—you'll just have a bit of a scar. Okay?"

"Okay," I said, closing my eyes. "Can we do it now?"

She made a clucking sound. "Well, someone named Camilla informed me that you had a meal at around one o'clock, so we won't want to anesthetize until that is fully digested. So we're going to aim for early tomorrow morning. Until then the nurses will keep you stabilized and give you some morphine for the pain. The super painful stuff is behind you."

"I'm glad," I said.

For some reason she laughed at this. She asked if I had questions, which I did not, but Sam followed her out, apparently with questions of his own.

When he returned he pulled the chair by the

window closer to the bed and sat slumped beside me like a man who has just heard his own death sentence. His skin was pale, his eyes clouded with anguish or desolation. "I'll be here all night. If you need anything."

"Maybe you can get some sleep."

"I doubt it." His face was solemn. "I can't believe this happened to you. Your poor arm—and the pain they put you through! I can't stop thinking about it."

"The worst is over, she said."

"Thank God."

I closed my eyes, then opened them. "What were Camilla and Doug talking about?"

He smoothed some imaginary wrinkles on the knee of his jeans. "We'll talk about that later."

I didn't argue. I fell asleep quickly.

I WOKE BEFORE dawn; my room was illuminated only by the light of the hallway. I could hear the muted beeps of machines and the occasional ringing of a phone. Distant voices of the nurses on call drifted in now and then. I almost fell back asleep, but the room became suddenly darker. I squinted and realized that a figure was in my doorway, blotting out most of the light. It moved forward slightly and I recognized blue hospital scrubs. I was not fully awake, but it seemed strange to me that this nurse or doctor just hovered there, not bustling in and taking action. I opened my mouth to speak; I wanted to ask for more of the pain-killer. I said, "Doctor?" and the figure stiffened. Whoever it was did not respond. Then, in the hall, one of the nurses said, "Roxanne, could you answer the call on Room Twelve? I just want to check on our car accident."

At this the figure turned and moved swiftly out of the room.

A nurse appeared ten seconds later and moved about, checking equipment. Then she came to stand beside my bed. "Oh, you're awake," she said.

"Yes—I was trying to tell the doctor that I need a little more painkiller."

"What doctor?" she said.

"He was just in here. A man in blue scrubs. Or it looked like scrubs. Definitely blue. Maybe a woman in scrubs. I didn't really see."

"There's no one else working this floor except for me—I'm Nurse Annie—and Nurse Roxanne. And she's all the way down the hall."

"Someone was just in my room. A doctor."

"I would have seen him, hon. There's no one else here but me. You were asleep, maybe."

I studied her as she took my pulse. "Where is Mr. West? He was on the cot there, and he's gone."

"Hmm? Oh, I think he said he was taking a quick walk. He couldn't sleep. He was texting or something."

"Can you stay here until I call him? And can you tell security that someone was in my room?"

She leaned in. She was taking me seriously now. "What description should I give?"

"I just—someone in blue scrubs."

She gave me a pitying glance. "Are you in a lot of pain?"

"I've been better."

"Okay, hon. I'll get you those meds, and I'll notify security to come check our floor."

"Thanks." I grabbed my phone with one hand and sent a voice text to Sam, asking him to come back.

I had already received a new dose of morphine when he returned a couple minutes later, looking rumpled and surprised. "Lena? I thought you were sleeping."

I waited until the nurse left, then beckoned him toward me. "I think someone was in the room. He was in the doorway, just standing there, and I spoke to him and the nurse called out from the hall, and he went scuttling away. But he was there in the doorway. I know it."

Sam studied my face. "I won't leave again. Don't worry; you can go back to sleep."

"Where did you go?"

He sighed. "I was restless, and sort of hot, so I went down to get some ice water, and then I took a quick walk outside. I was just coming back in when I got your text."

"Did you see anyone? Someone in blue scrubs, hurrying out of the building? Someone you recognized?"

He shook his head. "Not many people around right now, and I have to confess I wasn't really studying faces."

"Who could it have been?"

He shook his head. "I don't know. But no one's going to get in now. You can be sure of that." I studied Sam in the dark room; his rumpled hair, his worried face, the determined line of his mouth. "Are you in pain?" he asked.

"Yes, but she just gave me something. I think it's starting to help."

"Good. Go to sleep now. I'll watch over you."

"I know," I said.

Before I fell asleep I saw him standing by the window, typing rapidly into his phone.

LATER IN THE morning Allison and Camilla helped with the final paperwork that the hospital required, and Sam sat close to me, sipping a cup of coffee. His gaunt face and hollow eyes told me he hadn't slept.

"You need your strength, too, Sam. Go home and take a nap."

"I will, when you're home and comfortable. You had a nightmare last night."

"I did? How do you know?"

"You cried out. I was afraid you were experiencing the wreck again. I got up and touched your hair, and you calmed down."

"Did I say anything?"

"You said something about angels and saints, and an evil spirit."

"Wow. That was some good morphine, I guess."

Sam gave me the ghost of a smile, and a nurse came in to adjust my IV. She spoke briefly to Allison and then said, "All right, Lena, we're ready to wheel you down."

"How long will this take?" Sam asked.

The nurse patted his arm. "The doctor thinks about three hours, maybe less. Then Lena will be fixed up and on the mend."

"Let's go," I said.

Sam and Camilla each gave me a kiss, but only

Allison was allowed to walk with me down the hall and into the elevator that led to the surgery floor.

IT COMES BACK slowly, one's consciousness. I saw a blue wall with a calendar on it, then nothing. Then the blue wall again, for a bit longer this time. I heard someone shouting a name: "Carol! Carol!" I wondered, in a vague way, where Carol was. I saw the blue wall in more focus now and tried to make out the picture on the July page. It seemed to be an amorphous rock, but it eventually sharpened into the image of a puppy.

A nurse's face appeared before me. "How are you, Lena?"

Good question. "Okay."

"Do you feel nauseated?"

"Uh—no. Just tired."

"You're doing great. Let's just check your vitals; the doctor will come to speak with you shortly."

"Okay." I stretched my toes at the foot of the bed, my awareness returning in waves. It was over. I was mended. Was I? I glanced down at my left arm, currently swathed in a white bandage. "Why isn't it in a cast?"

"That comes later, hon. Right now you'll just have that bandage on."

"Okay."

"Are you in any pain?"

To my great relief, I was not. "No."

"Good, good."

"Who's Carol?" I asked vaguely.

She smiled and patted my arm. "People call out all

sorts of things here in the recovery bay. You heard Mr. Caldwell saying his wife's name. You said one, too."

"I did? Was it Sam?"

"No," she said. "I can't recall just now—sort of a strange name."

"Huh. I have no memory of it."

"People are still unconscious in recovery. It was coming from somewhere deep inside. You stay there and relax, and Dr. Salinger will come to speak with you."

I closed my eyes until I felt a presence standing beside me. Dr. Salinger, my healer, stood there looking casual in her surgical scrubs, her short blonde hair spiking around her head like a halo. "Hello, Lena. Do you feel all right?"

"Yes."

"The operation went well. It was an extreme break, a compound fracture, and I did insert some pins in there to be sure that the bone stays in place while it heals. We'll remove the pins in about a month. I'll cast the arm tomorrow; all you need to do today is relax, watch some TV, have a nice hospital meal—no, I swear, the food is really good here—and let your body start the healing process."

"Okay."

"I want to be clear: This was a severe shock to your system, and your body needs to recover physically and emotionally. You might experience depression, anxiety, bursts of emotion, or exhaustion."

"Sounds great," I said, and she laughed.

"Luckily, I saw that you have a whole army of

people to be certain that you receive the proper rest and care."

"Yes. I'm lucky."

"You are." She patted my good arm and said, "I'll leave my contact information with the nurse. If you have any problems or questions, call my office."

I thanked her effusively. She said that someone would wheel me back to my room and I could see my "fans," but that she didn't want them to stay long.

This made me feel like crying, and she said that was exactly the type of emotional symptom she had been talking about.

AN HOUR LATER I was in my room, sitting up in bed, and ready to eat lunch. Allison had washed my face, brushed my hair, and dabbed some ointment on my lips. The food on my bedside table smelled remarkably good, and Allison said it was a positive sign that I was so hungry.

She pushed the tray so that it jutted over my bed and took the lid off to reveal chicken nuggets and French fries. "A child's meal," I said. "But it looks delicious."

My left arm was in a sling and still felt rather alien to me, but I was pain free and euphoric.

"By the way," Allison said. "The only reason Sam isn't breathing down your throat right now is that I made him go home to take a shower. Frankly, I think he was bumming you out."

"He was afraid, Allie."

"I know. So was I. I can tell you now, Lena, you did *not* look good when they wheeled you in here. I almost had a heart attack."

"You hid it well."

She leaned close and stroked my hair. I had already devoured a chicken nugget, and a French fry protruded from my mouth. "I didn't want *you* to be afraid," she said.

I bit the fry in half. "I was, but it helped a million percent that you were here. I love you."

"I love you, too. And I can't tell you how happy it makes me to see you wolf down that food."

I laughed. Then I said, "Oh my gosh, my dad! Can you dial him for me, Allie?"

Allison did, then handed me the phone. I heard my father's voice, anxious and breathless. "Dad? It's me. I just got out of surgery a while ago. I'm fine. I feel a hundred times better."

My father bellowed his relief into my ear and assured me that he would be on the next plane whenever I felt up to having a visitor. Just hearing his voice was like powerful medicine in my bloodstream. I chatted with him for a few more minutes, finally assuring him that I would get several days of rest and then contact him again.

"Sounds like someone loves you a lot," said Allison when she hung up the phone.

"And I love him. He's my only parent, and I'm his only child."

The door to my room opened and Camilla walked in, holding a giant sheaf of roses. "Oh, Lena, you look wonderful!" she said.

"I feel good. The more I eat, the better I feel."

Allison found a vase in a closet, and she filled it with water for the roses. Camilla darted forward to give me a kiss, then started tucking the roses into the vase like a careful florist, her eyes studying me now and then.

"Adam plans to smuggle you some food from Wheat Grass very shortly."

I raised a finger in the air. "I shall eat it!"

Camilla and Allison giggled.

Then Allison sobered slightly. "Lena, last night you told Sam you saw someone in your room. Do you recall that?"

I squinted at the idea. Someone in the doorway, someone in scrubs . . . "Not really. Just a vague memory, like a dream."

"Well, Sam was very concerned, so we consulted Dr. Salinger. She said it is in fact possible, when someone has an extreme injury and is on morphine, to experience mild hallucinations. She said it's likely no one was there, especially since the nurse on duty saw nothing."

"Makes sense," I said groggily.

"That doesn't mean we won't be vigilant. No one's going to get anywhere near you."

"Good."

She patted my feet. "Now that Camilla's here I have to rush out. But you can page me if you need me. Love you." She blew me a kiss and speed-walked out of the room.

Camilla started to say something about my injury, but I held up a hand. "I just went through all of that with Allison, and I don't want to end up crying with each new person who enters. I have more pressing business with you."

She looked amused. "All right. May I sit on the bed?"

"Please. There, I made room. Oh, those roses are lovely. Thank you."

"What is our business?"

I stared until she met my gaze. "Last night when everyone was in the room, you were very angry, talking to Doug, practically spitting at him. What were you talking about? And don't say you don't remember."

She nodded. "All right. Now that you're feeling better I think you should know exactly what I said. I told Doug that he needed to get a list of everyone who was in Wheat Grass yesterday afternoon and check all of their cars, because one of them was going to show terrible damage to the front end."

"What?" I pointed a fry at her. "Why do you assume it was someone from Wheat Grass? I mean, a lot of us left at the same time, but—"

"Lena, before we left, I stood up and said that you and I wouldn't rest until we found the truth about Carrie Wyland and cleared James Graham's name. Twenty minutes later you and I were sent flying off the road in a terrible collision."

I thought about this. Hadn't I felt a malevolence in that room? What if it had been palpable emotion? After all, someone had been angry enough with Jane Wyland that he (or she) had killed the poor woman. And Jane, too, had promised to uncover secrets.

I dipped my fry in some ketchup. "I hate to think that someone could do something that violent and then just drive away."

"I hate to think it, too. And I hated to see you looking like a poor broken bird on that stretcher. It was horrible, Lena. For a moment I thought you—well, anyway." She looked out the window, and I couldn't see her face. Eventually, she said, "I'm afraid I came on a bit strong with Doug, but he was angry, too. We all were."

"So you don't think this accident could have just been a random case of road rage?"

"No, Lena," she said, her dark eyes meeting mine. "This was just rage."

9

Have you ever noticed, Camilla, that a tiny thing can make you think differently about a person? One small detail can shift your perspective, and after that, no matter how you might try, you can never see that person the same way again.

—From the correspondence of
James Graham and Camilla Easton, 1971

CAMILLA SAID SHE would return after checking on the dogs; I asked her to bring James's letters with her. Meanwhile I'd indulged in a brief nap and waked to ponder a rather boring cup of Jell-O until Adam smuggled in a piece of Wheat Grass chocolate cake. "Don't tell," he said as he bent to kiss my cheek. He told me he had to leave again, but that he'd left some other food in a bag on my side table. "Do you know what, Lena? I think of you as a daughter."

I was glad Dr. Salinger wasn't around to see my reaction to that statement. I clasped Adam's arm while he dabbed at my eyes with his handkerchief and promised to come back soon.

He passed another figure in the doorway and I said, "Sam, you should have gotten some sleep."

"Sorry to disappoint," said a familiar voice, and I saw that the visitor, though very like Sam, was not Sam.

"Cliff!" I said. "You didn't have to—"

"Of course I did," he said brusquely. "I would have last night, but I was on duty. And as we speak Doug Heller is turning this town upside down. I'll be joining him soon, but I had to see you."

"You're sweet."

"Let me help you with that. You're spilling all the good stuff." He took my fork from me and fed me a piece of my cake as though I were a child.

Because the cake was good, and because I was suddenly tired, I submitted. "Thank you for coming. I'm afraid I won't be able to go running with you for a long time."

He patted my hair with a big hand. "You don't know that. See how you feel in a couple of weeks. Hey, don't be sad."

I shook my head. "My emotions change approximately every thirty seconds. The doctor said to watch for that. I just had a weird burst of depression."

He patted my head again, and I laughed.

He said, "Take it from a guy who was shot in the chest not that long ago. The body heals at an amazingly rapid rate. You really won't believe it. Considering the severity of your wound."

"I still can't comprehend it. One minute I was talking to Camilla, and the next—"

His eyes were sympathetic. "You'll go over it in your mind a million times. Part of the healing, I guess—coming to terms with what happened. But one good thing came out of it. You can see how many people love you, and they realize just how much you mean to them. Aw, hey. Let me find a clean napkin." He dabbed at my eyes.

"Cliff?"

"Yeah?"

"I'm so glad Sam has you. But I'm glad I have you, too. You're my friend."

"We've been through a lot together, kid."

"I'm full now." I leaned back against my pillow. "Would you finish that cake?"

"Already on it," he said with his mouth full.

I laughed, then closed my eyes. "Why did they do it, Cliff? Even if they thought somehow they wanted to kill Camilla and me, well, that's not a very surefire way, is it? As we know, because we're both still alive."

"We'll find out," he said with a dark look. "We hope to have someone in custody today."

My eyes flew open. "What? You have a suspect?"

"No. Just a whole lot of determination."

"You know, your boss was at lunch with us that day. Rusty."

"Yeah? How come?"

"He was an old friend of Jane Wyland and Adam and James and all those guys. Back when they were young they hung out together. You and Doug might want to chat with Rusty, get his take on things. Maybe he has a suspicion."

Cliff's brows creased; for a moment he didn't answer me. Then he said, "Yeah, sure thing. I'm sure he's already on Doug's list if he was at Wheat Grass yesterday."

Another figure loomed in my doorway, and I said, "Your doppelgänger is here."

Cliff turned to greet his brother, and Sam West, looking clean and slightly less tormented and holding a small stuffed giraffe, walked into the room. Cliff stood and welcomed his brother with their habitual hug, then went to the door. "Lena," he said. "We'll find this person. Very soon."

"Okay. Camilla and I are going back to the letters. I've got nothing to do but read in here. I'll be like Inspector Grant in Josephine Tey's novel. Do you know the one I mean?"

Cliff looked at his watch with elaborate ostentation, and I laughed. "Stop it. It's a famous mystery. *The Daughter of Time*. This Scotland Yard inspector is confined to bed after he breaks his leg. He's bored, so he decides to solve a case of history—the crimes of Richard III. Whether or not he killed the princes in the tower. You know?"

Now Cliff looked interested, as did Sam. "Do you own this book?" Cliff asked.

"Yes. And I'm sure Camilla does, too. You come and borrow it."

"I will." He blew me a kiss. "See you later, slugger."

Sam moved toward me and handed me the giraffe. "Happy recovery," he said.

"Thanks. I'd offer you a bite of cake, but Cliff ate it."

Sam's smile was distracted. "How do you feel? Are you sure it's all right for you to eat?"

I sat up. "Sam. You don't need to worry about me anymore. I think it made you sick."

"Lena—"

"No. No more of this morbid stuff. We'll talk about it in three weeks when we're running around town and this is all behind us. Okay?"

He hesitated, toying with the edge of my blanket. "Sure, okay."

I looked at the giraffe, which was adorable. "This is lovely."

Sam said nothing. His skin still had a grayish look in the shadowy room.

I wanted to hold his hand, but I had an IV in one arm and I hadn't summoned the courage to do much with the other. I pursed my lips, and he kissed them. I said, "I know this must have been hard. After your family, and Victoria, and Cliff. And then me."

"I can't even express, Lena—the horror of Doug's phone call. I raced down to the church and they were just pulling you from the car. I heard you screaming when I opened my door. I'll hear it forever."

I sat up a bit straighter with the realization that despite my physical pain, Sam's trauma may have gone deeper. He had suffered too much loss, too much conflict. He was like a soldier forced to look once again at war. "Hey," I said, leaning my head against his arm. "I'm stronger than you think."

"Good."

"Guess what?"

"What?"

"I've been wishing I could spend more time with you, and I assume you're going to be visiting me a lot."

"You assume correctly."

"So I am deputizing you. I am going to work on this case in bed, and Camilla will work with me, and now so will you. It will do you a lot of good to feel like you're in control. To catch this person and make him answer for what he's done."

"For what he almost took from you. From me. From all of us."

"Yes. Will you help?"

"I will. Give me a task."

"First, grab that bag on the table there. Adam brought it, and it's full of food. You're going to eat some of it because I don't think you've eaten in a while. Then we'll go to step two."

Sam stood up and retrieved the bag. The moment he opened it the room became fragrant with the smell of good food. He found a leftover container with a tin lid and opened it to reveal some sort of delicious-looking pasta. "Do you want some of this?" he said.

"I just had a meal—the unhealthiest food ever. In a *hospital*. So I'm full for now. But I'll enjoy watching you eat, my Sam. Poor baby."

He took a bite, then several, and we both realized that he was starving. He held up a hand. "Okay, I admit it. I don't take care of myself while under stress."

I sighed. "Eat it all. You know we never even got to properly celebrate your birthday last month? You were too busy taking care of Cliff. You've spent far too much time sitting in hospital rooms and at the bedsides of convalescents. I had all these fun ideas, but they sort of went by the wayside."

He sent me an intense blue stare. "There will be all my other birthdays."

"Yes. I promise." I looked back at the giraffe. "For

some reason he looks like a Lester. I guess that's his name. Lester the giraffe."

Sam was eating again, but he smiled while he chewed and gave me a thumbs-up.

Camilla walked in then, holding her box of letters. She greeted Sam with her usual affection, and I said, "Sam's going to help us, Camilla." I sent her a be-seeching glance and willed her to read my mind, which she did.

"You will be a godsend, Sam. Lena and I were tak-ing our time with these, but it's clear now that we need to look through them more quickly, and with your help we can cover more ground."

"I'm glad to do it," Sam said. He finished the last bite of his pasta and got up to throw away the con-tainer; he washed his hands in the little bathroom and then returned to his seat. "Okay, ready."

Camilla opened the box and took out the note-books she and I had been using. "Sam, I'll give this to you because I don't know how well Lena can write notes with only one hand. Lena, if you find something you can call it out and we'll write it down."

"Good idea," I said.

Camilla handed small piles of letters to both Sam and me, and we got to work, Sam sitting on the wide window ledge and Camilla in a chair near my bed.

I looked at both of them, pleased to have them in my room, relieved that my surgery was over and we could concentrate on the task at hand. A beam of sun appeared on my bedcovers, and I studied it, feeling warm and heavy-lidded. Camilla said, "She's getting drowsy now," and I closed my eyes, allowing my head to relax into the pillow.

WHEN I WOKE they were still there, looking studious, scrawling notes in the silent room. I cleared my throat and they looked up and smiled at me. Sam jumped forward to offer me some water out of the big hospital cup, and Camilla patted my feet. "How long was I out?" I asked.

Camilla looked at her watch. "About two hours."

"Oh no! Did you find anything?"

Camilla shrugged. "This and that. Sam and I were just about to compare notes."

Sam sat back down in the window and the light made his brown hair look almost blond. "I did find something that might be significant," he said with a certain reluctance.

"What is it?" I asked.

He looked at Camilla. "You came here in late September to get married, did you not?"

"Yes, that's right."

He picked up a letter from his pile. "This one came to you in August. It suggests that James was actually supposed to visit you in England about a month or so before your journey, to help you make arrangements before you flew out."

Camilla frowned, thinking back. "Do you know— yes, I believe he was. Not a necessary trip, but we were both so lovesick that I think we manufactured reasons why he had to come out, even though I was coming to America soon."

Sam looked down at the letter. "But it says here that he didn't come."

"No, he had to cancel. It was something with his father, wasn't it? He was so ill at the time."

Sam shook his head. "He says that he didn't have the money for the journey. He had put aside enough for his ticket and his stay at a hotel, but he spent it."

Camilla's voice was toneless when she said, "Read it, Sam."

He lifted the letter and read the words of James Graham: "'I know how crushing this will feel; I am unbearably disappointed myself. But right now most of my ready cash is going to Dad's medical care, and I found myself with an unexpected expense—a large one—and I won't be able to make the trip. Please forgive me, Camilla. As it turns out I must fund the journey of someone else. It's a long story which I can share in more detail when you arrive, although I doubt I'll want to revisit this particular page in my history. I am so sorry, my love. More than you know.'"

Sam looked up at Camilla and me but waited for Camilla to speak. She said, "What is the date of that letter?"

Sam consulted the paper in his hand. "August twenty-fifth."

"And when did Carrie leave?" I asked.

Camilla smoothed her skirt. "It must have been around that time. She was gone when I arrived a month later. Had been gone for weeks."

"Might James have funded her trip to Chicago? Perhaps set her up in an apartment there?" Sam asked.

Camilla and I exchanged a glance, and she nodded. "I think it may well be the case."

Sam said, "Do you mind if I ask a couple of blunt questions?"

"We're here to find the truth," Camilla said placidly.

Sam looked at me, and I nodded. "I think we have to consider two things: first, why did James feel obligated to give his own money for Carrie's journey?"

"And second?" Camilla asked.

Sam looked at the floor. "Is it only for the missed visit that he is apologizing? Or is it for something more?"

Camilla surprised me by smiling. "I'm fairly certain I know the answer to that question, but this is good. This gets us closer to the truth. Let's go on the assumption that James funded Carrie's journey out of town. He used the money he would have otherwise spent on a visit to me, knowing that he would see me within the month. But I have questions of my own: Why was sending Carrie away so urgent? Why couldn't she have stayed in Blue Lake?"

I rustled in my bed. "The people at the restaurant were hinting that she was pregnant. Was there such a stigma on pregnancy in 1971 that a woman would want to leave town?"

Camilla nodded. "Oh, I think so, yes. And this town—lovely as it is—is rather narrow and provincial, even today. The poor girl would have wanted to go somewhere she could start anew. Perhaps tell people she was a widow. Avoid judgment, if in fact pregnancy was the cause of her flight, and if in fact she kept the baby."

I thought about this. "Camilla, you posed an excellent question in the restaurant. You told Rusty Baxter to find out if Carrie had indeed given birth to a child. If they knew that, they could do a DNA test and figure out the child's father."

Sam shook his head. "First of all, even if there is a child, there's no counting on his or her cooperation. Second, what would it prove even to find the child's father? How would that bring us closer to a murderer? At most, wouldn't it just cause some awkwardness for someone?"

I leaned back and thought about this. There was of course still the possibility that James Graham had fathered Carrie Wyland's alleged child, and that this was the deep, dark secret to which Jane Wyland had been alluding. Camilla believed that James would not have betrayed her in this way. So if another man in Blue Lake had fathered the child, why would that matter? Why would James feel obligated to get Carrie out of town? And why, at this late date, would the man care whether he was exposed as the father or not? The child, if it existed, was an adult now. I looked at Camilla. "It would still be good to know if there was a baby. We should deal with facts."

She nodded. "I agree. I'll see what I can find out. In fact, I think I'll pay a visit to Rusty Baxter. He seemed a bit reluctant to bring all this up again, didn't he?"

"They all did," I said. "I wonder why."

"We also need to talk to Adam," she said. "He must remember this. He was James's best friend." For a moment her face looked soft, childlike, with a slight downturning of the mouth. A vulnerable moment.

"I'll ask Adam about his availability. Perhaps he can visit us tomorrow. You'll be coming home, I think, and it would be a good distraction. You should rest for the first few days, and I know that goes against your nature."

I shrugged.

Camilla stood up with her box. "Sam, I'll claim those letters and your notes, if you please." He handed them to her. "Lena, you can keep the letters I gave you; I'll pick them up tomorrow. Meanwhile, I'll be going home. Star walked the dogs earlier today, but they'll need to go out in the yard, at the very least." She gave me a kiss and squeezed my hand, then walked toward the door of my room with the box of her husband's letters.

I sat up straight. "Camilla!" I almost shrieked it, and she turned in alarm.

"What is it?" She and Sam were both looking around, trying to find something that might have hurt me.

"You and I are both assuming that whoever hit my car was trying to prevent us from digging into Jane's allegations."

"Yes," Camilla said.

"So I was the only one hurt, but I wasn't the only target! You should not be driving around alone. I can't believe I let you do it before now."

She thought about this; she looked at Sam, who nodded at her and said, "She's right. For the foreseeable future, neither of you should travel alone. I'll go with you, Camilla."

"Nonsense. I can call Adam."

Sam shook his head. "I have to pick up some things anyway and make a couple of phone calls."

I pointed at the door. "Yes, both of you should go. I think I'm almost ready to sleep again, and if I don't doze off I can read the letters or watch that TV there. It's okay. I'm out of danger," I said.

"We need to call the police," Sam said. "When we're not here, a police officer should be."

Camilla agreed with this, and moments later they were on a call with Doug, who was apparently persuaded by their urgency. Sam hung up. "Chip Johnson is on his way. Camilla and I will stay here until he arrives."

I sighed. "Chip Johnson is annoying."

"We'll have him sit outside the room," Camilla said with a little smile.

CHIP WAS ACTUALLY nothing but professional. He arrived, checked in with me, and planted himself in a chair just outside my door. The nurses brought him coffee, and he refrained from flirting with them (for the most part). Now and then I heard the comforting squawk of his radio or the deep murmur of his voice, and this lulled me into a relaxed state. Just before I fell asleep something occurred to me. I stiffened and sat up with a crucial bit of knowledge—a name? a face?—and then it was gone.

What had I remembered with such suddenness, and why had it just as suddenly drifted away? I tried for a moment to bring it back, to concentrate it into being, but I was simply too tired.

I lay back on my pillows and attempted a gentle flexing of the fingers on my newly repaired arm. They worked.

Listless, I looked at the window, where the summer sun was back in full force and revealing every dust particle floating in the air. I watched as those tiny particles drifted, weightless and free, until the sun found my face and I closed my eyes against the brightness, then descended into a darker place.

❖ · 10 · ❖

*Have you ever felt as though something dark is
hovering over your life? Today has been strange
from the start, from the dead bird I found near
my car to the oppressive looming clouds that
seemed to intensify with each passing hour. It
feels like the setting of a Poe story, this creeping
darkness. I need you to be here, my love. The
light in my darkness, the brightness in my
storm.*

—From the correspondence of
James Graham and Camilla Easton, 1971

THE NEXT DAY a physician's assistant settled me in a
wheelchair and piloted me to a room on the second
floor, where a cheerful gray-haired receptionist ushered me into an office, and Dr. Salinger, with much
jovial conversation and a light touch, put a bright red
cast on my arm.

"For the Fourth," she said. "Tomorrow! You can
paint stars and stripes on it." Her short blonde hair was
slightly mussed, but somehow it looked fashionable.

"And you said it has to stay on for a month?"

"We'll check it at that point, yes. Then we'll determine whether or not you still need the cast."

"I want to thank you, Doctor. I know it was not a pretty sight. It's amazing, the work you do."

She patted my cast-free arm. "It's rewarding. I love to mend what is broken. Now, you can mostly do what you always do, but you need to keep the cast in the sling most of the time. That will stabilize it and advance healing. You'll adapt to being a one-armed woman in no time, and the time will fly. Really, all the worst is behind you."

"You're very persuasive. You should do TED Talks about positivity and healing and things."

"I've done one!" she said, her face bright and surprised. "But it was about the various types of fractures and new possibilities for treatment."

She was fussing with my sling now although our appointment was essentially over. I ventured to verbalize what I'd been thinking. "Doctor—what would you say about a person who intentionally crashes a car into people—intentionally runs them off the road? Do you think he has to be insane?"

For the first time her smile disappeared. "I can't guess at the person's mental state, but I can tell you from my experience of treating the injured that you don't have to be insane to commit acts of violence. There are all sorts of motives for that. But make no mistake about it—an act like that, assuming it wasn't accidental, results from extreme emotion. I would guess anger, fear, or hate. But that's for the police to figure out." She helped me back into the wheelchair, even though I was capable of walking. "Hospital policy," she said.

"Okay."

"Okay." She nodded at me, her face encouraging. "Meanwhile, Lena, you can go home within the hour. Have some lemonade, start getting out your sparklers and your face paint, and prepare for a nice Fourth of July. You can certainly go out, have fun, do whatever. Just be gentle on that arm, all right? I've got all my instructions written on your release forms."

"Thank you, Doctor."

She ran an assessing hand over the cast she had made, then nodded. "Good. Ready for action."

A FRIENDLY ATTENDANT named Carlos wheeled me back to my room to wait for Sam, who had not yet arrived. Chip Johnson sat in his chair in the hall, looking at his phone.

"Thanks for doing this, Chip," I said. "I know it's not the most exciting duty."

"It's been great," he said, smoothing his skinny mustache. "I got to sit on my butt. My favorite thing." He grinned at me, and I warmed toward him slightly.

Carlos wheeled me into my room and I stood up, thanking him. He waved and backed out with the chair, and I started to gather the few things that Camilla had brought me, putting them one-handed into a bag. I heard a woman's voice out in the hallway—a familiar voice. I turned to see Isabelle Devon, my old high school friend, looking tall and dark and lovely, and walking toward me with arms outstretched.

"Isabelle!" I shouted, shocked.

She hugged me gingerly. "My poor little Elle," she said, taking me back to the days of school when she, a junior, had decided to take Allison and me, mere freshmen, under her wing after we shared a class together. She used to call me "Little Lena," which she had then shortened to "L.L.," and that to "Elle." She mothered me during a time when I had lost my mother, and I had always looked up to her.

"What are you doing here? Did you come to town to apply for jobs?"

She took the things from my hand and began to pack my bag for me. I sat down in the chair that Sam had spent two days in. "I did visit the local animal hospital, on Allison's recommendation, and guess what? I'm hired. I already worked a shift while the doctor in residence ran some errands. He had two staff people leave—I guess they wanted to move out of Blue Lake—and he was in dire straits. So I already met a Blue Lake cat who is expecting kittens, and a Blue Lake rottweiler who tore a toenail, and a Blue Lake resident who sprained his wrist." She grinned at my surprised expression. "This is an eccentric little town. But I gave him some advice, then suggested the emergency room or his doctor's office. Then the boss came back and was very happy with me."

"Is that Dr. Pendragon?"

"Yes! What a great name."

"He's our vet! He takes care of Camilla's—my employer's—two German shepherds, and of my cat, Lestrade. He's excellent."

"He and I hit it off, which is why I took the job. I like it here! And how amazing that after all these years I'll be in the same town as you and Allison!"

I admired anew her tall form, her glossy black hair,

her elegant clothing of white linen pants and yellow blouse. I saw Chip Johnson peering around the door frame, clearly enamored with her. "You didn't answer my question, though. What are you doing *here*?"

"I stopped by to see Allison, of course. She's the one who badgered me to come to Blue Lake, so I had to come and see her." She studied my face. "Then she gave me the very unexpected news that my poor little Elle had been in a car accident. And that it may well not have been an accident."

"No," I said. "But I'll let my police friends worry about that. Like Chip there." I pointed at Chip Johnson, whose face quickly disappeared.

Isabelle looked all around the room and the little bathroom and tucked everything of mine into the bag. "There you go. You're all set."

"Great. I'm all ready for Sam. You don't have to stay now, but you must come over and meet everyone soon. My friend Belinda is having a party tomorrow for the Fourth, and I'm betting we can snag you an invite."

"That will be fun, if I'm not working. I know Arnie said he likes to be open at least a half day on holidays, in case of emergencies. Pets and fireworks don't mix."

"He's great, and so is this town. You'll love it here."

She sat down on the bed. "You said 'Sam.' Is that Sam West?"

"Yes. He—we're together."

"Wow! I read about him in the papers. I mean, everyone did. And about his wife." She tucked a lock of dark hair behind her right ear and glanced at me.

"They're divorced now."

"Oh, right. Anyway, it's pretty wild—you ending up here in the middle of that whole mystery. I can't wait to meet him."

I looked down at my cast, attempting a casual tone. "Are you seeing anyone right now?"

She groaned. "No! I'm done with men. But I did just fall in love with a Saint Bernard who was looking at me from a crate at the animal hospital. Arnie says he's up for adoption, so I'm strongly considering . . . I don't even have a place to stay yet, though. Allison is helping me work that out. She said there are beautiful apartments out by Green Glass Highway, so I'm headed there next. If not, of course I have an invitation to stay with her."

"She'll make you fat."

"I know. The best plan is to find an apartment, but I need one that allows pets. She also told me the place across the street from her is for sale—"

"Don't you dare!"

Isabelle held up her hands. "Just kidding. I know it's a house of horrors. But I do want to hear about it anyway. I missed out on all the drama by not living here, but to hear Allison talk it's been a nonstop adventure wagon for you two."

I shuddered at the thought of Nikon Lazos and his horrible sister, the people who had lived in that house. "Not an adventure at all. You're better off coming to town now, when those people can't come anywhere near you."

She jumped up and gave me another half hug. "I'm just so glad to see you, Little Lena. We're going to have fun!" She glanced up at the clock. "I have to run, though. Can I drop you off at home? Or no—you said Sam is coming. Well, I hope to meet him soon."

"You will."

She kissed my cheek and walked toward the door, leaving some lovely and expensive-smelling scent in her wake. "I'll be in touch, Elle!" she said.

When she went into the hall, I heard Chip Johnson scramble to his feet. "You have a nice day now," he said. I could almost hear him sucking in his stomach and smoothing down the perpetual cowlick on top of his head.

SAM DROVE ME home; he said Camilla was busy making some lunch for us, and she had asked Doug to stop by and fill us in. "Camilla talked to Rusty," he said. "She's waiting until you're home to tell us about that."

"Oh, I'm so glad to be going home. Oh, look! They got the paint off the Darrow statue. That's good to see."

"Yeah. It seems like a long time ago that we were talking about that at Allison's house. She's great, by the way. I always knew it, but seeing her in action at the hospital . . ."

"Yes. Thank God you were both there on that terrible day. Oh my God!"

I stared out the window, frozen with shock, and I heard Sam swear. "Lena, I'm sorry. I didn't realize—I had no idea they brought it here."

We were passing the service station at the end of Sabre Street, and I saw my own car parked there, crumpled beyond recognition, except for the bumper sticker that said "Booklover," in a little heart made of books. "Oh, my sweet little car. How—how did they get us out of there?"

"Lena, don't. Look away from it. I'm going to have that removed today. It's ridiculous of them to leave it sitting there. It should be in a police impound lot."

"Maybe that *is* the police impound lot."

I did as Sam suggested and turned away, focusing instead on his handsome face. He said, "Do you know who missed you? That menagerie at Camilla's house. They've been sitting in the window, all three of them, watching for you."

"I doubt it," I said, smiling. We turned onto Wentworth Street and then onto the rocky bluff road that led to Graham House. Something with honey-colored fur caught my attention on the side of the road, but then scuttled into the summer grasses. Sam turned into Camilla's driveway and, much to my surprise and pleasure, I saw two silhouettes in Camilla's living room window, with four alert ears perked up at the sound of the car. A burst of love fluttered in my chest. "Okay, two of them are there," I said. "I don't see Lestrade, though."

Sam parked the car and ran around to my side to open the door. "Let me help you. I'll run back down to get your purse and your discharge papers." I gave him my right hand and he pulled gently, helping me out of my seat and putting his arm around my waist as I climbed the stairs.

"Thank you. I'm fine, though. I'm getting the hang of it. It feels a little awkward, but I'm catching on."

Camilla opened the door and the dogs rushed forward. Camilla said, "Down," to them and they were appropriately polite, but they did some sniffing of me and my cast, and I scratched at their ears with one hand. I knelt to greet them and Lestrade appeared. He stalked toward us, moving in front of the dogs as though they weren't there, and he too examined my cast with interest.

"This is the reason I was gone, guys. But I'm back now. Hello, my little fuzzy friend," I said to my cat. He purred in response and stropped against my legs for a while.

"You see?" Sam said. "They missed you." He helped me back up; I felt lopsided and unbalanced.

Camilla said, "Lena, I have some lunch ready. Do you want to go upstairs, or wash up, or lie down?"

I shook my head. "I'm fine. Let's have our lunch meeting so I can hear what's happening."

"Good. I think Doug will be here any moment. There have been some—developments."

I looked at Sam. He had picked up Lestrade, who was purring madly now, and they were exchanging devoted looks. The unexpected love affair between my boyfriend and my cat had been sudden and surprising, but it was also very cute. "Good developments?" Sam asked of Lestrade's fuzzy face.

Camilla had turned and was already walking toward the kitchen. "Developments that might give us a way forward," she said.

WE SAT AT Camilla's table in the sunroom, cooled by air-conditioning but warmed by bright sunbeams. Camilla had made a big pitcher of lemonade and

Adam had brought a sandwich tray from Wheat Grass. I took a hearty gulp from my glass and watched Doug and Sam eat as though they'd both gone without for a while. There were five of us at the table: Doug, Sam, Adam, Camilla, and me. Doug finished a sandwich, glanced at his watch, and cleared his throat.

"I guess I'd better get started. We went to the homes of every person on Camilla's list, including our police chief," he said. "We asked to see their cars, all of which were intact. No sign of an impact to the front end of any of the vehicles."

"What about the people who live out of town?" I asked.

Doug nodded. "We sent Chip to Bluefield to look at the Fieldses' vehicles. That's Karina's married name—Fields. They have several cars, and they all passed the test. Ken actually enjoyed showing Chip around. A guy who knows his cars, Chip says."

I poked at my sandwich with one hand. "That's disappointing, sort of. I mean, I'm glad none of them did it, but—"

"No one is off the hook yet," Camilla said crisply.

Sam leaned toward Doug. "What about the child? Carrie's child?"

"Yes." Doug took out a folder and consulted a form. "As Jane's old friends suggested, Carrie Wyland moved to Chicago in August of 1971. We found her name in an old phone directory and then traced other documents to her address. From there we were able to get some more information, including the fact that she did give birth to a child, a boy named William, in April of 1972."

"So she got pregnant in July," I said. "In Blue Lake."

"It would seem so," said Doug, avoiding Camilla's gaze.

"Can we contact this William?" Camilla asked.

Doug took a sip of his lemonade, then met her clear eyes. "We are looking for him. His last known address was the one he shared with his mother, but neighbors we tracked down said that William moved out long ago, in the '90s. They weren't sure where he went. It looks like Carrie supported them both by working as a secretary to a local businessman. It's possible she ended up dating him, perhaps even marrying him. We're looking for a record of that, and we're trying to find the boy, as well. He's forty-seven years old, if he's alive."

"This is a good start," Camilla said, nodding. "I spoke to Rusty Baxter, who told me much of what Doug just told us. And the fact that he had liked Carrie Wyland—a tidbit which we already knew. He said she was the one girl he had never flirted with because he thought there was something sweet and vulnerable about her. He claims he was a bit brokenhearted when she left town."

It was quiet for a moment; a cardinal pipped on Camilla's bird feeder as we contemplated the lost life of a woman who, as a girl, had for a brief time lived in this house. I wondered if someone could tap into the spirit, the energy, not of a soul who had died, but of one that remained in the past.

Adam held up a leather-bound book. "I've brought photos. Who knows if they'll be any good to us, but they might spark some questions in you, or some memories in me."

"Wonderful, Adam," Camilla said, touching his hand. "We'll do that right after Doug leaves, if you don't mind staying."

"Of course not." Adam reddened slightly; he always looked pleased when he had Camilla's approval. To Camilla's credit, I don't think she realized how much power she had over Adam's emotions.

Sam was still looking at Doug. "Hang on. What about *Lena*? Someone out there almost killed her and Camilla, and they're walking free. Can't you check how many of these people have two cars listed to them? Is there something else you can hunt down besides cars?"

Doug looked pleased. "You should be a cop, Sam. Yes, we're still looking into the titles in the name of every individual involved. That takes longer than you'd expect. We're running into some red tape, but we're persistent. And in regard to Lena and Camilla, I'll need to make a schedule of protection. We probably don't need anyone while you or Adam can be here, but obviously I'll want someone watching overnight and occasionally in the day."

Sam sat up straight. "I am offering myself as twenty-four-hour protection until this is resolved. But we go back and forth between two homes . . ." He looked uncertainly at Camilla.

Adam raised a finger. "I can move into Graham House for the foreseeable future. If you don't mind, Camilla."

Camilla covered Adam's hand with her own and

sent a mischievous glance to me. "Our knights," she said. "I suppose this should offend our feminist sensibilities, but since I don't feel capable of wrangling with an intruder and Lena has only one arm, I think we would both be glad of any protection offered. To be honest with you, I still haven't emotionally recovered. It was such an overwhelming impact. To think that someone flew up behind us in that—death machine—and intentionally ran us off the road—it's just unbelievable."

"I saw him," I said suddenly.

"What?" Doug and Sam yelled together.

"I mean, I think I did. It keeps coming back and going away. I think I saw the driver, but I don't know who it was."

Doug looked puzzled. "What do you mean?"

"I had a vague memory, in the hospital, but I kept falling asleep. The nurse in recovery said that I called out a name, but it wasn't Sam or Camilla. She said it was a strange name, but she couldn't recall what it was."

Doug's computer was in his hand. "What's this nurse's name?"

"Uh—Amy, or—no, Annie! Her name was Annie."

"I'll talk to her," he said.

"Okay. Then Sam said I talked in my sleep and said something about an evil spirit."

Sam nodded. "But not a name."

"No, but I have this vague memory, from when I was lying next to the church. I could see the stained glass windows glimmering in the weird light, and I was thinking of saints and angels, and another face was there, and I thought, *Demon*."

"What do you mean, a face was there? As in, with the crowd of people at the wreck?" Camilla asked urgently.

I shook my head. "No, I don't think so. I just mean, crowding into my thoughts. Trying to rise to the top of my consciousness. It's been toying with my brain ever since. When Doug asked me if I'd seen the driver, for a second it was there, but then it was gone. It's very frustrating." Inexplicably, I was on the verge of tears.

Doug waved a hand in front of me, as if to erase my sadness. "No big deal, kid. It will come back, and when it does we will be on that guy so fast he won't know what hit him."

Sam leaned closer to my chair. "It's okay, Lena. You've been through a trauma. You can't be expected to have everything intact yet, including your memory. When you relax, it will come."

Everyone nodded at this, and I laughed a watery laugh. "Okay, thanks. I just have one worry."

"What is it, dear?" asked Camilla. Adam pushed a plate of cookies toward me.

"Let's say I did see him. That we locked eyes in that millisecond before the crash. If so, then he knows I saw him, right? Because *we looked at each other.*"

Because we five had been through a great deal together, and because the people around me respected me, they didn't pretend that this wasn't a concern. Doug pursed his lips and tapped his fingers on the table. "Which is why we'll make sure that you always have security. Sam? Adam? When's the last time either of you shot a gun?"

* * *

DOUG LEFT WITH a list of things to pursue, along with the docket of tasks he and Cliff had already assigned themselves. Camilla had thanked him warmly for coming to see us personally—a privilege Doug had afforded us since I had come to Blue Lake.

Camilla, Adam, Sam, and I had remained at the table so that Adam could share some photographs. We sat together and he held up a loose pile of slightly yellowed pictures. "These were just lying around in boxes and books and things. Pictures people gave me or I took myself but never bothered to catalog. I just grabbed the ones that were from around that time."

The first one he handed to me was a picture of Adam and James standing in front of a brick wall and a well-tended flower bed. "That's us in school. Seniors at Blue Lake High."

"Oh my gosh, you are both so handsome!" I said. Adam was tall and dark with rather wide-set eyes and pleasing, symmetrical features. James was about an inch shorter, with lighter hair but similar handsomeness.

"You could have been brothers," Sam said, perhaps thinking of himself and Cliff.

"We were, in one sense," Adam said. "We were—devoted to each other. I don't suppose young men think in those terms today, but we had a lasting friendship because of it. Because of our loyalty."

"When did you first meet?" I asked, still studying their faces.

"In grade school. Third or fourth year, we were seated together at the same table. Never really separated after that." Adam's smile was bright, but there was a touch of sadness in his eyes.

Camilla held up another photo. "This one has all of the boys. Adam, here you are with James, and who is this? Rusty?"

"Yes. And that's Travis, and Horace in the background."

I leaned in to look. The young men were seated on a fence in front of a field I recognized. "That's Blue Lake! Right by the old Schuler's barn," I said.

"Yes," Adam agreed. "No billboard back then, and those trees still obscured Green Glass Highway. Funny how you can look at then and now and remember both worlds."

"Where's that other man? The one who said he was studying when you all got together?"

"Paul Graves? He didn't really hang out with us. Except in the pub, I guess. He was there because of his father, who obviously wasn't a part of our group. He was just a local businessman."

"What about Karina or Jane or Carrie? Where are they?" Sam asked.

Adam shrugged. "You know how it is when you're teens. You mostly hang with the guys, but you *talk* about the girls."

We smiled, and Adam passed some more pictures around; we looked closely at them, then handed them to the next person at the table. For a while we did this in silence. Adam was on my left, Sam on my right.

Often when I handed Sam a picture, his hand would linger for a moment on mine. Since my accident he seemed to take every opportunity to remind himself that I was physically intact.

Finally, Camilla held one up in triumph. "I have Carrie!" she said.

We all jumped up and crowded around her, Sam and Adam taking care not to jostle my cast. I peered down at the photo in Camilla's hand. In it a blonde woman, perhaps about twenty years old, smiled at the camera. She wore a white T-shirt with a yellow daisy appliqué, and she was sitting at a table in front of a cake. A birthday party? I looked more closely at her face. It was pretty, with wide eyes and a slightly pointed nose, and full red lips. Her hair, which looked thick, was tied into a careless tail that had spilled several strands that hung delicately around her face. Overall it created a casual but attractive image.

"She's lovely," I said. I peered more closely to read the date stamp on one white margin of the picture. "The date says August 1971," I said.

"Right before she left," Camilla said. "Perhaps that is a going-away cake. Do you recall, Adam?"

Adam shook his head. "I don't even recall this gathering. Or why I have the photo. It might just be my failing memory, but—I don't remember Carrie very well. She wasn't in our class at school, and if she tagged along with Jane now and then, I didn't really interact with her. James and I were generally engrossed in some conversation together or with Horace or Rusty or Travis or one of the fellows from school."

I studied Carrie again. Was I imagining the fact that her smile looked sad? "She was already pregnant here," I said. "And she knew it, but no one else did."

This silenced everyone. Then Sam said, "At least one other person probably knew."

I watched Camilla as she processed that idea. "Unless she left town to prevent someone from knowing. Let's consider these possibilities: Carrie knew she was pregnant, and so did the man who made her pregnant. If that was the case, then perhaps she was leaving because (a) he didn't want her or the baby, and she was mortified, or (b) he did want her and the baby, but she didn't want him.

"But let's suppose Carrie was leaving and the father of the child never knew she was pregnant. Then we might consider that (a) she left because she didn't want him to know—if so, why?—or (b) she left because she was afraid he would find out. Those are a few possibilities. What am I missing?"

Sam raised his hand. "That she left because someone told her to."

"Why?" Adam asked. "To protect his reputation?"

Camilla pursed her lips in a thoughtful expression. "It could be—but in that case, why wouldn't that person pay her way out of town? He might be desperate enough to cover those expenses and set her up in an apartment. Why would James feel obligated to do it? I think everyone at this table is willing to give my dear James the benefit of the doubt. If he paid for that girl to leave town, it was because he was helping her."

We thought about that. "But if that's the case, it seems more likely that the father didn't know," I said.

"Because otherwise wouldn't he question James's involvement? Resent it, perhaps?"

Camilla lifted her notebook. "Let's not forget these things we learned from James's letters." She read them to us, holding up a finger for each new item:

"He was agitated in the months before I arrived. He told me that he couldn't come to see me because something else had come up.

"He wrote about family and the realities of blood. He could have been speaking of his family, or mine, or—someone else's.

"He spoke about losing trust in the people you grow up with. Couldn't that have referred to the old gang? The boys in the picture there, or the girls? And if so, how did he lose faith in them?

"He said—" She paused and stared at the paper. "He said he had seen the darkness of the human heart."

She looked back up at us, her eyes wide. "And then he asked me to pray for him."

Sam shook his head, processing these ideas, and then pointed at Adam. "You were here with him at that time. You must remember what was upsetting him."

Adam leaned in, pushing aside the pile of pictures still in front of him. "I do recall the time. James had been quite busy at work, and then had his father to care for at night. I didn't see a lot of him then—some occasional outings on weekends."

"Do you remember him being distressed?"

"Yes." Adam's handsome face looked sad. "But I fear I missed something very important because I thought he was just sad about his father. As I recall, I assumed his father was dying, and when James was reticent I realized it would be rude of me to press him for information he might not want to give."

"Of course. You and James were both so good and kind, even as young men," Camilla said.

Sam looked unconvinced. "Is there anything you can look back to now—a diary, or a letter, like Camilla's pile there—to give you some insight?"

Adam bit his lip. "We lived in the same town, so we didn't really correspond. But I'll keep digging."

Camilla said, "Let's assume that James's comment about 'the darkness of the human heart' applies to whatever happened with Carrie. That would push us toward Sam's theory that she needed to be protected from something. Or someone, perhaps. Whatever it was disillusioned James and prompted him to spend all of his ready money on that young woman."

I had returned to my chair, but I sat up straight with a new thought. "But Camilla, if there was some secret involving Carrie, she never told her family!"

"Why do you say that?" Camilla asked.

"Because Carrie died a couple of months ago, according to Marge, and after that Jane was perturbed, distressed, until she came marching to your house to address some long-ago grievance, some secret that James Graham had kept. Perhaps she was indeed assuming that James got Carrie pregnant and then forced her out of town. But if that's not correct, as we all believe, then that means Carrie never told her sister what really happened, but instead allowed her to draw her own conclusions."

We all sat in silence for a moment.

Then Adam said, "Why would a girl like Carrie, who loved and admired Jane, not *immediately* confide in her own sister?"

"Because she was ashamed?" Sam asked.

"Or because she was afraid," Camilla said.

There are some things, Camilla, that I think I'll never tell you.

—From the correspondence of
James Graham and Camilla Easton, 1971

CAMILLA FINALLY BROKE up our meeting, saying that I needed rest. She gave everyone some letters to study, with the strict order that these precious missives must all come back to her. "Adam, if it's all right, I'll hang on to your photo album," she said. "Lena and I might have some questions about the pictures. I think we've looked at all these loose ones."

Adam murmured his agreement, then said, "Sam, if you'll stay here for the time being? I'm going to go home and pack a bag. I'll be back in an hour or so." Sam nodded. Camilla offered to put the loose photographs in a folder, and Sam and Adam stood by the window, discussing the logistics of their "guard duty."

I wandered out of the room and gravitated to Camilla's office. I sat down in my purple chair, which I connected with the creative wavelength that traveled between Camilla and me when we collaborated on books. I wanted to be writing now, to be in Delphi on a dark night when our main character, Lucy Banner, stepped carefully over the stony path, hoping not to make a sound that would alert the men in the tavern to her presence. We had left her in danger and alone; I wanted to guide Lucy through that rocky terrain and through our complicated plot so that she could emerge victorious with her new lover at her side.

With a sigh, I leaned back in the chair, my red cast poking out of its sling and looking strange against the plump chair arm. Lestrade wandered in, jumped on the opposite side, and began to make dough with his paws on the purple upholstery. I petted his fuzzy face and he purred, his eyes slitted in a pleased expression. "A lot has happened in this room, buddy. Did you know there's a secret chamber behind that wall over there? And did you know I once came face-to-face with a murderer in here? Or that I helped to write two novels with my idol, at this very desk?"

Lestrade tucked his legs underneath his body until he resembled a fluffy boat. He did not look impressed by any of my information. "You're hard to please, Lestrade. But I do love you."

His eyes were fully closed now, but he was still purring.

I sighed again and leaned my head against the chair. Lestrade had made closing his eyes look pleasurable, so I tried it, too . . .

"Lena?" Sam stood before me, tall, handsome, serious. "I'm sorry to wake you, but Camilla wants to know if you'd rather rest upstairs, or at my place?"

"I could write," I said.

He shook his head. "She said you would say that, but she claims she is unavailable to work for the next day or two."

I curled my lip. "That's just her being protective. How hard is it to write? I would just sit in this chair."

"You are tired, though. You fell asleep in here."

"Whatever," I said, unsure of my mood.

Sam smiled, and I felt better instantly because I hadn't seen a genuine smile from him since before the accident. "Fine," I said. "If Camilla's taking a break, then you and I can work on this mystery and catch this murderous person before he strikes again."

"Sure. We can read more letters, if you like, or look at Adam's book."

"Maybe we should go back and talk to Adam's old group, one by one. Away from the influence of their friends."

Sam nodded, running his hand through his slightly mussy hair. "We could, but we might be stepping on the toes of the police, since they're probably doing just that."

"Huh." I stroked Lestrade's ears. Sam knelt in front of me and began to pet him, too. Lestrade's purr grew louder. Heathcliff and Rochester, always pleased to see a human at their level, came padding in to sniff at Sam and to put their wet noses on his face. He laughed and patted their big heads.

"All the animals in this house are spoiled— Camilla's right. I wonder if Star Kelly is going to walk them today. Oh!"

"What?" Sam looked up, surprised at my tone.

"Star and her father were there. At the lunch, right

before our crash. They heard everything Camilla said."

"Okay—?"

"I mean—that probably means nothing, but they should be on Doug's list, I guess. How well do you know Luke Kelly?"

Sam shrugged. "Not well. I consulted him once, when Victoria was missing, to see what my options were."

"Regarding what?"

"The law. The public. I was persona non grata with them both. I got death threats; you know the drill. Nowadays there are people who go straight to the rhetoric of violence—no attempt at thought, or conversation, or resolution. Just *I'll kill you because I don't understand you.*"

"It's horrible." I stared at my cast. Was that what had motivated the person who had rammed into Camilla and me? But why? Surely, they knew that the police, and not just the town mystery writers, would be investigating Jane Wyland's death?

I said as much to Sam, and he shook his head. "I have no better idea than you, but I'll tell you one thing I learned from more than a year of isolation: you take every threat seriously, and trust no one until they've earned your trust. Doug asked if I have a gun, and I told him that I do. I never really wanted one in my house, but—you get enough threats, and you figure you might want to be able to defend yourself."

I shivered.

"Are you cold?" Sam asked, solicitous, leaning

forward to reach for one of Camilla's flannel throws on a side table.

"No. Camilla's air-conditioning isn't *that* effective. I just had a shiver, like the kind they say you get—what is it? When someone walks over your grave?"

"I don't know. Is that an expression?"

I yawned. "I think so. It's gruesome, though."

"How about if I help you upstairs and you take a nap?"

I shrugged. "Only if you and Lestrade lie there with me."

Sam leaned in, smiling, and kissed me softly. "I would love to do that. Let me just make two quick phone calls, and then I'll carry your cat upstairs for you."

He stood up, pulled his phone from his pocket, and stepped out of the room.

I smoothed Lestrade's unruly eyebrows. "Soon things will be back to normal, buddy." He opened his eyes to give me a bored glance, and I realized that, in his leisurely cat world, nothing had really changed.

WHEN I WOKE I was on my bed alone, although Lestrade was nearby, watching birds from my bedroom windowsill and making low chuckling noises in his throat. I lay and looked at the ceiling, my left arm feeling like a block of cement against me. I recalled a character in Camilla's novel *The Villainous Smile.* Her protagonist, Prudy Penrette, had been strolling with companions in the woods on her cousin's palatial estate when she was shot in the leg by a wayward hunter's bullet. While convalescing in a bedroom in her cousin's giant, drafty house, she started to wonder whether the injury had in fact been accidental.

I'd felt such horror as a reader, realizing, along with Prudy, that her cousin himself had the best motive for wanting her dead, that he was in debt and would inherit her trust fund if she died. Slowly it dawned on her that she was helpless as a patient at his hundred-acre residence, with no access to the outside world and her cousin himself checking on her several times a day. She grew to dread the sound of his tread on the stairs, the shadow of his elongated form on the wall as he approached her bed, smiling and asking after her health.

Smiling. Camilla had taken the title, *The Villainous Smile*, from a line in *Hamlet*. The young prince complains "that one may smile, and smile, and be a villain," as he contemplates the crimes of his nefarious uncle. And here I was, able to move but partially disabled by my cast, wondering which smiling person in Blue Lake hid the dark heart of a murderer. I no longer wanted to be alone, not even in the room that I loved, and which had been my haven for almost a year.

"Hello?" I called tentatively.

Moments later Camilla's face appeared in my doorway. She must have been in her room. "Oh, you're awake. Did you have a nice rest?"

I sat up, and she came to sit on the edge of my bed. "I guess so. I was kind of scared just now, so I wanted company."

"Scared?" She smoothed my blanket in an automatic gesture.

"Remember Prudy Penrette?"

"The Villainous Smile," she said. "I scared *myself* writing that one."

"Yes. I was reminded of her, lying on this bed, in this town that I had assumed would be my new start, my haven. Just like her. And at first her cousin seemed so solicitous and friendly—it was amazing, the way you let the horror slowly creep into that plot."

She patted my leg. Camilla had been patting various parts of me since the accident; like Sam, she seemed to want to find ways to comfort me, or perhaps to atone for what had happened, despite her innocence in the matter. "Probably not the best story to think about right now."

"No. I was thinking about *our* story, too, our Lucy, but then I got tired."

I must have looked wistful, because she said, "We'll get back to it very soon. Just a day or two for you to feel like yourself again. Tomorrow is the Fourth, and you'll want to go to Belinda's party. After that—back to work!" She pointed at me with a feigned stern expression that made me laugh.

"Oh! Camilla, I meant to show you something. Look over there on my desk."

She got up and walked to the wood desk that dominated the south wall of my bedroom. The books from Belinda were stacked neatly there.

"Old library hardbacks! Where in the world did you find these?"

I struggled to the edge of the bed, feeling a bit like

a bug on its back. "Belinda gave them to me. Her library has all new editions, so she thought I might like these old ones. They're in fairly good shape, and I do love those original covers. The artist was a genius. I even know her name, because I read every word, even the copyright pages and the tiny notations that no one generally sees. Persephone Drake."

"Oh yes! I met Persephone a few times in New York. A very talented young woman. Well, young at the time. That was in the '80s. She still does the occasional cover for me." Camilla picked up one of the books and glanced at the inside flap, then the back cover. "My, it doesn't seem that long ago." She turned to grin at me. "But copyrights don't lie."

I smiled back but grew distracted by the sound of voices on the main floor. "Is Sam talking to someone? Or is that the television?"

Camilla walked back to me. "Cliff is here. He had some questions for me, and then he and Sam got to talking."

"Sam is so restless. He was supposed to be lying in here with me. He didn't get much sleep while I was in the hospital. You probably didn't, either." I glanced in the mirror over my dresser and briefly caught her eye, but then she moved briskly away.

"I'm all caught up on rest. I don't know about Sam. I agree with you; he is a bit of a restless soul. You'll have to adapt to that, Lena."

"Or put him in a cage," I said. My voice sounded wistful, and Camilla looked surprised. Then she patted my arm.

"Shall we join them downstairs?"

"Yes—not to sound like a teenager, but do I look all right?"

"You look lovely. A little bit of bed hair. Let me find a comb." She located one on my dresser and did a quick styling of my hair.

"I feel kind of grungy," I said. "I'd love to take a proper shower."

"Tomorrow morning you can do just that. Sam Googled information about how to keep a cast dry. He has all sorts of ideas involving plastic bags and duct tape."

"Sounds great. Okay, I'm ready."

Camilla and I moved carefully down the stairs, our eyes on the dogs who waited below. I could still hear Sam and Cliff talking, but I hadn't yet made out the words. Sam's voice was raised slightly. I thought I heard him say, "I'll do it, Cliff, if I have to," and then we were at the foot of the stairs and turning the corner, and both men, surprised by our entrance into the hallway where they stood, affected a casual air.

"Hey!" Sam said, coming forward to kiss my cheek. "You look terrific."

"Thanks. Hi, Cliff," I said. He was wearing his Blue Lake police attire of khaki pants and blue polo with the PD insignia. "Are you just getting off work?"

"No. Going on duty in about an hour, but I wanted to come by and talk to Sam about this and that. And I had a couple of things to ask Camilla."

"No questions to ask the other victim?" I asked lightly. Clearly, I was being left out of the loop about something.

"Not just now," he said. "But I do need to get going.

I'm heading to Sam's to pick up something he has for me."

"Oh, let me go, too!" The words burst out of me and I realized just how claustrophobic I felt. Cliff and Sam looked at me with blank expressions.

"Go where?" Sam asked.

"To your house. Just a short walk. I feel like I need fresh air. It's been days since I could just go outside and breathe."

My three caretakers exchanged a concerned glance, and I groaned. "Oh, come on! I'd be walking between an armed police officer and a very protective boyfriend. And going approximately, what—fifty yards?—to Sam's driveway."

Cliff studied my face for a minute, then nodded. "Of course, you want fresh air. It's pretty nice out right now, too. Sure, come along, kiddo. Sam and I will flank you like mighty pillars." He leaned toward me, projecting his "bigness" by puffing out his chest and thrusting his arms out from his sides.

I laughed, but I noted that Camilla looked unhappy. "Bring her right back, Sam."

"I will." Sam put an arm around Camilla's shoulders and said, "I promise."

"Oh, wait," I said. "Who will guard Camilla?"

Camilla looked surprised. "Adam has returned, dear. You were asleep for a couple of hours. He's in the sunroom, looking through those photo albums."

"Oh. All right, then. Sam and I will help him when we come back."

"He'll be grateful, I'm sure."

Soon enough we were in the driveway and I was

taking deep breaths of Blue Lake air. The men marched on either side of me like affable jailers. Cliff seemed more relaxed than Sam did, but I noticed that Cliff's eyes, even while he bantered with me, were always scanning the landscape.

"Did Sam tell you what I said about Luke Kelly?" I said, poking Cliff's arm.

"Yup. He's on the list, as of now."

"What more have you and Doug learned?"

"Not much. Still interviewing people." He peered down at me. "We've got this, Lena."

"I know." But, in the past, they had been more willing to talk to me. Now, because I had been broken, I was being left out. I understood the protective impulse, but I didn't plan to put up with it for long. We reached the end of the long driveway and turned onto the rocky road that led to Sam's house. "I certainly have much more appreciation of what poor Jake went through," I said.

"Jake? Oh, that reporter friend of Sam's?" Cliff said.

"Yes. He broke his leg, very badly, back in winter. I saw it happen; it was . . ."

"Lena! Are you okay?"

They were both bracing me; I had nearly collapsed right there on the ground. The memory of Jake's horribly twisted leg, and his groans of pain, had suddenly overwhelmed me. "I think I almost fainted," I said, going for a joking tone. "I guess this isn't the time to focus on gory images."

The men exchanged a glance over my head. "The doctor said this might happen," Sam said, trying to be gentle but also sounding a bit accusing. "This isn't just a reaction to Jake's injury, it's a reaction to your own."

"Great. I'm insane now, is what you're saying."

Cliff laughed out loud. "You're not insane. And I think you're right—you needed this fresh air. Do you think you can make it to Sam's without breaking, little teacup?"

I punched him with my good hand and felt much better. Cliff rumbled out a laugh and even Sam was smiling broadly when we all paused, arrested by a strange sound.

"What is that?" I said. "Is that—it sounds like a cat." It was, in fact, a tiny mewing, loud but somehow frail. I looked along the edge of the pebbled road, where summer grasses and wildflowers edged the path. I remembered that, when Sam had driven me home, I had seen something furry that wasn't quite the color of a squirrel or a chipmunk . . . Finally I spotted a tiny yellow ball, and I lunged in. It was a kitten, no more than seven or eight weeks old, mewing furiously at us. "Oh my goodness!" I said, scooping him up. "Sam, hold him! I can't cuddle him with one hand."

Sam took the tiny cat, who was already purring madly. It nestled immediately against Sam's chest and closed its eyes, which made Sam laugh. "What a cute little guy! Now, where could he have come from? He's too little to have traveled far on his own."

Cliff pointed down the bluff. "People dump them. Someone could have driven down Wentworth, stopped at the bluff road, and just tossed him in the shrubbery. He looks pretty hungry."

We walked the final steps to Sam's door. Sam

handed Cliff his key so that he wouldn't have to dislodge the little cat. "Poor guy. I guess I needed a pet at this place, right, Lena?"

"Oh yes! I think that would be wonderful. What would you name him?"

Sam lifted the kitten to look into its tiny face. The ball of fluff seemed indignant at losing his spot against Sam's chest, and he let out a fierce (but cute) meow. Sam laughed. "Well, I see that he is a boy. I'm thinking this is Geronimo."

"Perfect," I said.

Sam seemed to be warming to the idea of a pet. "I even have some kitty litter left over from last winter. I used it to create traction for my car in the snow."

"And you have a box here from the mailman. You can cut it down and create a makeshift litter box until you're able to go out and get one."

We walked into his main hall and turned into his big and beautiful kitchen. Sam set Geronimo on the tiled center island and the kitten, now the focus of attention, chose to become casual. He lifted a paw and began to lick it. He was truly lovely, with marmalade-colored fur and pale cream–colored stripes. His face was tiny and sweet, but I could see that Geronimo would grow into his noble looks. "I have one concern," I said to the men who looked more like boys as they played with the cat.

"What's that?" Sam asked, poking Geronimo in his belly.

"If someone dumped him, wouldn't it be more likely that they were dumping a litter? Geronimo was right by that big, hollow log. What if—?"

Cliff had already jogged down the hall; I heard him slam out of the door. Sam clearly wanted to join him. "Go," I said, laughing. "Find them, if they're out there. I'll watch the baby."

Sam kissed me and followed his brother. I took my phone from my pocket and dialed Isabelle, who had programmed herself into it at the hospital.

"Elle? Is that you?" said her bright voice.

"It is. Hey, are you working right now?"

"Nope. Just looked at an apartment. I think it's a keeper!"

"That's great! Would you consider making a quick house call? Sam found a stray and I want to make sure it's okay. And if you happen to have any kitten chow in your vet-mobile, can you bring some along?"

She laughed. "I don't, but I can stop at that little store on Wentworth and get some. Give me directions, I can be there in ten or fifteen minutes, depending on where you are."

I thanked her and told her how to get to Sam's place. Geronimo had started to investigate the edges of the island and I feared he would jump, so I scooped him up and set him on the floor. "Thanks, Belle. See you soon."

I found a little bowl in Sam's cabinet and filled it with water, which I put in front of Geronimo. He took some dainty sips, his pink tongue darting. I heard shouting outside, then laughter, then more shouting. I wasn't sure what this meant. I studied Geronimo's little face, now drooping with a water beard. "Do you have a family?" I asked him.

His green eyes told me nothing, but moments later

Sam and Cliff did. They marched in, laughing and euphoric, holding three more kittens: two gray and one black with a white patch over one eye and a scarf of white fur around his neck, along with four white paws. "We're pretty sure we got them all," Sam said. "These guys were sticking close together. We think Geronimo was their scout."

They set the other kittens on the floor by Geronimo, and the four had a reunion in the form of sniffing and swatting. "I'd better make that litter box," Sam said, jogging away. He called over his shoulder, "I do *not* want four cats, Cliff. You're taking two."

Cliff laughed. "Fine with me. I like cats. Since Sam probably wants the one he named, I get first dibs on these other ones." He did a quick examination. "All male except the black one. They're pretty handsome little things."

"They're adorable! Who would dump these sweethearts in the woods?"

We played with them until Sam returned. Cliff said, "I'm going to take these guys." He held up the two gray cats, who dangled with placid expressions. "Meet Jeeves and Wooster."

Sam and I laughed. "Great names," I said. "I didn't realize you were so literary, Cliff."

"I'm a man of many distinctions," he said as we petted the soft fur of our new friends. Sam finally scooped them up and showed them all the litter box. "You'll have to keep them a few days," Cliff said. "I won't have my place set up for a while. I can hit the pet store tomorrow morning—let me know what you need."

"Meanwhile, I have to feed them," Sam said.

There was a rapping at his front door. "Problem solved," I said. "I asked a vet friend to come and take a peek at them."

"A vet friend?" Sam asked blankly. "Do you mean old Arnie Pendragon?"

"Hang on," I said. I jogged to the door and admitted Isabelle, who still looked fresh and lovely in her white linen pants. She held a bag of kitten food in the crook of her arm. "Hi, Belle. Come in. I have lots of introductions to make."

We moved into the kitchen, where Sam and Cliff both looked quite surprised to see my tall, pretty friend. "Guys? This is Isabelle. Remember I mentioned her to you, the day you put in the air conditioners?" That seemed like a long time ago, somehow. "She just got hired at the Blue Lake Animal Center. She has very kindly agreed to take a look at these kittens and make sure they're okay. And she brought food."

Sam moved forward first and shook her hand. "So nice to meet you! And thanks so much for bringing food. I'll find a bowl." He went to his shelves and began rummaging around.

"Nice to meet you, too, Sam," said Isabelle, setting the food bag on the island.

I pointed at Sam's brother. "This is Cliff Blake."

Isabelle shook his hand. "Hey, Cliff."

"Welcome to Blue Lake. Congratulations on your new job," Cliff said, with his charming smile. I remembered him smiling at me in a similar way when I met him for the first time in Camilla's driveway.

"Thank you!" Because she was Isabelle, she was already picking up kittens and looking totally at ease in Sam's kitchen. "Well, these guys couldn't be more adorable." She set Geronimo on the island and expertly examined his ears and eyes. "No mites," she said. "These are lovely pink ears."

Sam returned with a couple of small bowls. He opened the bag of kitten food, poured it into the bowls, and set them on the ground. The three kittens on the floor were immediately drawn to the scent and tripped over each other in their eagerness to eat. Geronimo started to squirm, and Isabelle laughed. "Okay, join the party," she said, putting him on the floor, where he wiggled until he got a spot at one of the bowls with his sister.

Isabelle grinned. "This town has the most amazing animals. I'll get to those other three in a minute. The orange guy looks great. Nice teeth, clean ears. He doesn't have fleas, which tells me he hasn't been outside for too long. You said he's a stray?"

"We think they might have been dumped at the edge of the road there," Cliff said, pointing toward Wentworth Street.

"Well, weren't they lucky? Stroll up a rocky path and find a place in the castle," she said. "This is a gorgeous house."

"Thanks," Sam said. "How do you and Lena know each other again?"

"High school buddies," Isabelle said. "Newly reunited in the unlikely location of Blue Lake, Indiana."

Cliff laughed. "It has that feeling, doesn't it? I felt like I was walking into Brigadoon."

She studied him. "You're not a townie?"

"No—from Saint Louis, originally."

"I went to college at SLU!"

Cliff leaned toward her. "I lived not far from campus."

Sam, his eyes elsewhere, laughed and pointed at the floor. "Look at these cats."

Two of them had climbed inside the nearly empty bowls and were on their way to falling asleep. Isabelle grinned. "Don't move them. I'll examine them on the floor." She got down on her knees. "Oh, you are so cute!" she said. I stole a glance at Cliff, who hadn't looked at anyone but Isabelle since she had walked in the room.

Isabelle stood up. "Bring them to the center in a couple days, Sam, and we'll do the full exam. But I don't see anything to worry about right now. If you notice anything strange about their poop, like an unusually bad smell, then we can check for worms, but these guys seem healthy to me. Guys and one gal, I mean." She picked up the little black kitten with one white eye, a white bib, and four dainty white paws. "You are sweet," she said, kissing the little kitty face.

"I'm taking the two gray ones," Cliff said.

"That's great. I'm so happy you guys are adopting them. Good for you!" Isabelle clapped a congratulatory hand on Cliff's arm, then studied the logo on his shirt. "Are you a cop?" she said.

"Yes, ma'am."

"I was toying with calling you guys," she said. "I got so frustrated on the way over here. Some drivers just shouldn't be on the road."

"How's that?" Cliff asked. His phone buzzed in his pocket, and he took it out to glance at it.

The black kitten had climbed up to the vicinity of Isabelle's bosom and curled into a fluffy ball, purring madly. Isabelle supported her with one gentle hand. "There was this guy in front of me, driving too slowly, with a car that obviously wasn't roadworthy. It was totally out of alignment; he could barely pilot it down the road." She was laughing as she said it, so she didn't immediately notice the tension in the room.

Sam moved closer to her. "Where was the damage? On the front?"

She looked up from her study of the kitten. "What? Oh—I mean, it must have been. Yes, it was, because when I passed I turned to glare, but got distracted by the smooshed front end. God knows why they were driving that thing at all. Have it towed, I say."

Cliff grew official; he seemed to grow taller as he questioned Isabelle. "Did you catch a license number? Or part of one?"

She shrugged. "That's why I was tempted to call. They had no plate at all! Isn't that illegal?"

"What color was the car?"

"Blue. A pale blue."

"Make? Model?" he asked.

She hesitated, looking at me. "I—don't notice stuff like that."

"Neither do I," I said.

Cliff was dialing his phone with one hand and digging for his keys with the other. "Where were you? Was this on Green Glass Highway? How long ago?"

Isabelle finally realized that the driver might have been more than just an annoying motorist. "Oh—my God. It was maybe ten minutes ago. Yes, Green Glass

Highway, right near that billboard about the guy who sells fireworks. Mad Mike. Yes, that's where I passed him."

Cliff was moving toward the door. He turned back and beamed an intense gaze at Isabelle. "Did you get a look at the driver?"

She shrugged and sent me an apologetic glance. "No—just—I noticed gray hair. That's all."

Cliff nodded and said, "I'll be in touch," as he ran down the hall. I heard him calling the station. "Karla, put out an all-points bulletin . . ." And then he was gone.

Geronimo was trying to climb Sam's leg. Sam pulled the tiny claws from his pants and lifted the kitten, scratching its ears with a distracted expression. He said, "God, I hope Cliff gets him."

Isabelle was distressed. "I didn't realize. Lena, I'm so sorry. It never once dawned on me that it could be related to your accident. I've been here one day and I've already encountered several eccentric drivers, so—"

"Of course, you couldn't know," I said. "It was great that you even thought to mention it to Cliff."

She nodded, thinking, and then she pointed at the black kitten, now dozing on her chest. "Have you named this one?"

Sam smiled. "Not yet. Waiting for inspiration. Hey, how is it that a little orange guy like this can have a sister with black fur?"

"They most likely had different fathers," Isabelle said.

Sam stared at her. "What?"

"When a cat is in heat she can have multiple

partners, and a litter of kittens can be composed of more than one sire. People don't always know that."

"I didn't," Sam said. He looked at Geronimo. "So he and she are half siblings. Like Cliff and me."

"Oh, that's right! You have a half brother! I read about your reunion in the paper. I guess I should have seen the resemblance," Isabelle said.

For some reason I was thinking of the old hardback copies of Camilla's books that sat on the desk in my room. "Do you know what? Camilla wrote a novel, back in the '70s, in which the heroine had amnesia. She was wandering in the woods, just like these guys, and she was found by a local recluse, who took her in and tried to help her piece her story together."

"That's wonderful!" Isabelle said. "Life imitates art."

Sam's expression was wry. "I guess in this parallel I am the local recluse."

"You should name her after that heroine, Sam."

He smiled at me. "What name is that?"

"Arabella Martin."

Isabelle peered at the little cat. "Oh, what a lovely name! But such a big name for a tiny girl."

"She'll grow into it," said Sam. "I like it."

We chatted with Isabelle for a bit longer, but Sam kept glancing at his watch, and I at the clock on his kitchen wall, and the tension generated by the unknown grew palpable. Thoughts were tumbling around in my mind as I struggled to make polite conversation. Would they find the man with the crumpled car? Would we actually learn who had tried to run Camilla and me off the road? And would we, at last, learn the secret behind Jane Wyland's death and Carrie's departure?

They were tantalizing thoughts, and by the time Isabelle said good-bye and left Sam's house, my stomach was in painful knots.

· 12 ·

*Do you have an old friend, Camilla, who be-
comes your rock when times are hard? Who
would defend you against a crowd, protect you
in a storm, probably die for you if it came down
to your life and his? I have such a friend, such
a blessing, in Adam Rayburn.*

—From the correspondence of James Graham
and Camilla Easton, 1971

WE RETURNED TO Camilla's and told her about the
blue car and, when we had calmed down a bit, about
Sam and Cliff's new kittens, all four of whom Sam
had locked into his office with food in one corner and
a litter box in the other. When we left, they had all
been asleep in a sun spot under the window, piled on
top of each other with careless sibling affection.

"How sweet," she said. "I want to come and visit
them soon, when all this is over." She looked at her
watch, just as Adam and I had done. Perhaps there is
no one human gesture that can convey at once the
sense of impatience, urgency, helplessness, and tension as can a mere glance at a watch or a clock. Time,
the enemy and the informant.

Sam saw this, too, and said, "Cliff knows what he's

looking for. A car like that is easy to spot, and there are security cameras here and there. Someone will have seen it. Every cop car will be looking for it."

"Yes," Camilla said, her expression absent. "Meanwhile, dear Adam has been laboring over these books, trying to sort people and events. Perhaps we should offer him some help."

"Of course," I said. "It will be good to do something constructive."

We went to the sunroom, where Adam sat with a replenished pitcher of lemonade and a pair of cheaters on his nose. He looked like an elegant professor. He glanced up when we walked in and smiled his charming smile. "Oh, reinforcements! Thank goodness. At this point, one picture is blending into another."

"Thank you for bringing these, Adam. Was it a challenge to find them?" I asked.

He shrugged. "I did a lot of downsizing before I moved to my current apartment, so I am pretty streamlined. All the photo albums went in one cabinet."

"What would you like us to do?" Sam asked.

Adam rubbed his gray head. "Well, let's see. That stack over there are books I've looked through and not found anything striking. This stack here contains books with some photos you all might want to see—I marked them with bookmarks. And these last four are the ones I haven't yet gone through. I have a fair number of albums because I fancied myself something of a photographer back then. I think I had the glamorous notion that I was the chronicler of our youth."

"You're still an excellent photographer!" Camilla said.

Adam smiled. "Thank you. I certainly have some lovely subjects to photograph in Graham House. Sam, would you like to take one of these? And Lena and Camilla, why don't you look at the pictures I've marked, see what you make of them?"

"That sounds fine," Camilla said. Sam nodded and took one of the photo albums that sat in front of Adam. I selected one of the books that Adam had pre-marked and set it on the table in front of me. Camilla waited until Adam made eye contact with her. "You'll never guess what Lena and Sam found in the underbrush."

She began to tell him about Geronimo and the others while we all turned pages and studied images. Adam laughed gently and asked Sam some questions, but I lost track of their conversation as I became absorbed by the faces in front of me. They were recognizable faces, almost, but they were different from the people I knew today or had met in the restaurant. Marge Bick, or Marjorie Allan as she was known then, was impossibly thin and somehow taller-looking. Karina Thibodeau looked like the pretty granddaughter of the woman I'd met at Wheat Grass, and the men were even less recognizable, barely more than teenagers, with sticklike legs and sheaves of dark hair.

I saw a picture of what looked like Horace Bick's birthday; he sat at the head of a table in someone's house, wearing a child's birthday hat and laughing heartily while his friends sang to him. Marjorie hovered behind him, her look doting and slightly possessive.

In another picture at the same gathering, Karina chatted with Rusty Baxter, his hair flaming under the light of a chandelier. Karina was speaking animatedly but Rusty, whose expression was serious, was looking over her shoulder at someone else. I held the photo closer to my nose to study the people against one wall. It was a slightly blurry shot and the photographer had been focusing on the two people in the foreground, but I could just make out the other people against the wall: Travis Pace, James Graham, and Carrie Wyland. They all looked rather grim, and they were all staring at Rusty and Karina.

I pulled the picture out of the plastic. Adam was on my left, so I had to lean over, twisting my right hand, to touch his shoulder. "Was there something between Rusty and Karina at some point?"

"Hmm? Uh—not that I know of. Karina did like him, I think."

"Might Travis have been jealous? Did he have a thing for Karina? Or was he a good friend of Rusty's? He seems upset about something in this photo, doesn't he?"

Adam studied the picture. "They all do, now that you mention it. Not one happy person in that picture except for Key. That's what we called Karina."

I looked again at Carrie, who seemed to be standing rather close to James. Were their hands touching?

With a sudden wave of guilt, I sat up and stole a glance at Camilla. Could she read it on my face? It had just been a fleeting suspicion, a moment's doubt—and surely it was nothing. I put the picture back in the plastic and, from this more normal distance and in the glare of the sun on the page protector, the picture seemed like what it was—a scene from a birthday party.

Camilla looked up, her eyes bright and alert. I knew she could read my mind, so I hastily averted my gaze and turned the page to the next one Adam had marked. This page had an attractive color picture of the Wyland sisters, Jane and Carrie, and it made me gasp.

"What is it?" Sam and Camilla said in unison.

"It's Carrie and Jane. They look—so loving. So connected. Look how protective Jane seemed, even then." I held up the picture so that everyone could see what I had seen. Carrie, sitting on a brick wall with the bright waves of Blue Lake behind her, and Jane, standing next to her with an arm slung around her sister. Carrie was looking at the camera, squinting in the sun and smiling shyly at the photographer, but Jane was looking at Carrie, her mouth curled into a fond and indulgent expression.

"Yes, clearly a sister who doted on her younger sibling. Almost as though she were her child. Yet there were only a few years between them, right Adam?" Camilla asked.

Adam had been studying the picture, too, with a rather odd expression. "Hmm? Oh yes, yes, a couple of years."

Now Camilla's clever gaze was on him. She always seemed to know where the secrets were. "Adam? Is everything all right?"

"Yes—I had a memory. It's vague and fuzzy right now. Let me wait until it bobs to the surface."

This I could certainly understand. My own elusive memory of the murderous driver, if indeed I had such a memory, had not returned.

We all went back to studying our pictures. Sam turned a page in his album and pulled something from the plastic sheath. "Adam? This is a letter or a note. It has your name on it."

"Oh? I didn't realize I had put anything like that in there. Let's see."

Sam handed it to him, and Adam pulled the missive from its envelope. He read a few lines and his face turned red and rather miserable. I had seen him look this way once before, more than nine months ago, when he'd been forced to admit his love for Camilla in front of me and a restaurant full of people.

Camilla's voice was gentle. "Adam? Are you all right?"

"Yes." He folded the letter and tucked it into his shirt pocket. "That shouldn't have been in the photo album. I'll file it with my papers later on."

We went back to our work, but stolen glances at Camilla and Sam told me they were just as curious as I was about the letter, and even more so about Adam's reaction to it.

I turned another page and found myself looking at some pictures from the Lumberjack or the Mill Wheel. There was Paul Graves with a man I assumed was his father (and he was in fact wearing an apron that said "Timber!" on it). Young Graves was smiling vaguely and seemed to be avoiding eye contact with his father, who was saying something to him. I wondered who had snapped the photo of what seemed to be a private conversation. In another picture was James Graham, handsome and grinning at a young Adam Rayburn. They stood beside a bar full of glistening bottles. James was wearing a button-down shirt and a pair of jeans, and across his chest was a sash that read "Fool for Love." Young Adam was pointing at the sash and grinning. The picture, perhaps even more so than the one of the Wyland sisters, conveyed the strong bond between the two people who stood so easily together, happy in each other's company.

Wordlessly I held it up to Adam, who chuckled. "Ah yes. James was so busy then, and he and Camilla were both being so practical about the wedding, that he claimed he wanted no bachelor party at all. I had to surprise him one night at the Mill Wheel. I had one of the girls make that sash, and we had a cake and drinks and such. It wasn't a very big endeavor, but I think James liked it. As I recall, Camilla arrived the next day." His eyes grazed Camilla and then looked away again.

Now I was extremely curious. Normally Adam couldn't get enough of gazing at her, or of drinking in her attention. Today, sorting through the records of his past, he seemed to have struck a vein that caused discomfort. For the second time I had a moment of doubt. Was my image of Adam an illusion? My image of James? Surely Camilla was the person I believed her to be? I cast a quick glance at her, studying her face as she peered at a picture in her hand. She looked elegant, as always, but a bit tired today. She would be turning seventy in October, and I was in the process of planning an extravaganza of a birthday party (in conjunction with Adam). Despite this milestone birthday, I had never thought Camilla looked her age. Her face had few visible wrinkles, and her energy generally matched mine. Since Jane's visit, though, she hadn't looked herself, and the summer light harshly delineated the lines around her eyes and mouth.

She looked up at me and narrowed her eyes slightly. She was reading me.

I focused on my work, turning pages and studying faces. I felt Sam stiffening before I heard him gasp. "Camilla," he said.

"What is it?" She was on her feet and moving toward his chair before Adam and I had finished exchanging a surprised glance. Then we stood as well and moved behind Sam.

He held up a photo that Adam had taken, once more of a group, seemingly at a gathering. Adam leaned in, squinting. "That was the same day. Horace Bick's birthday. We went out to the pub after the party at someone's house—Marge's, maybe."

"It looks like everyone is having fun," I said, noting that Marge and Horace were dancing with hilarious expressions, and Travis Pace was deep in conversation with James and Paul Graves.

"Look behind them," Sam said. "In the booth."

I peered in and said, "Is that Rusty? And Jane?"

"No," Camilla said. "It's Carrie. And she's crying."

13

*Remember that line in Shakespeare, Camilla?
"That one may smile, and smile, and be a
villain."*

—From the correspondence of
James Graham and Camilla Easton, 1971

DOUG WAS BACK at Graham House, studying the photos that we had found so significant. "There's something here," he said. "The question is how to decipher these images." He looked at Adam, who had seemed unlike himself for the last half hour or so. "There's nothing you can remember about this day? This event?"

Adam shook his head. "I know it was a party for Horace. I don't really recall the dramas of those days—who liked whom or who upset whom. Would anyone remember, after forty-odd years?"

Doug's face looked wise, and a bit worried. "I think *someone* does."

I pointed at the picture in his hand, the one in which Rusty sat across from a crying Carrie Wyland. "What about Rusty? He told Camilla that he had special feelings for Carrie. That she was different from the other girls. It would have made a big impression on him if she sat in a private booth with him and told him something that made her cry."

"You're right." Doug tucked the picture carefully into a file folder Camilla had offered him and removed his keys from his pocket. "Time for me to have a chat with the chief." He started to head for the door, then turned back. "Do you feel well enough to come to Belinda's party tomorrow? She really wants you there, all of you. But especially you, Lena."

"I know. I'll be there."

Sam came in, holding a bottled water. He and Camilla had been talking in low tones in the kitchen. It had started to bother me how many conversations were conducted out of my hearing range, how many people seemed to be avoiding my gaze.

"We'll both be there," Sam said.

Doug turned to Adam. "How about you and Camilla?"

Adam looked up, his expression far away. "Hmm? Yes. Of course, we'll attend. Looking forward to the party and the fireworks."

"Blue Lake does us proud with the fireworks," Doug said. "You've never seen them, have you, Lena? You'll be amazed."

"I'm ready to be amazed," I said, forcing a smile.

Why, in one horrifying moment, had I felt as though I hated them all, every person in that room? The feeling disappeared almost immediately, and then I was left with a horrible, hollow remorse.

Doug waved at all of us and walked to the front

door, the tools in his police belt jostling and jangling. I turned away from him in time to see Sam and Camilla exchanging an inscrutable glance. Then Camilla saw my face and said brightly, "I don't think I can wait any longer—I need to meet these new kittens."

JULY 4TH BROUGHT more hot weather and a slightly overcast sky. Camilla insisted that I rest for most of the day. I did my best to take a makeshift bath, then spent much of the time brooding in my room, petting Lestrade and answering the calls and e-mails of concerned friends and relatives who had just heard about my accident. I was relieved when Sam arrived, late in the afternoon, to drive me over to Belinda's. Camilla and Adam followed in their own car since they expected to leave the party earlier than "you young people," as Adam put it.

Belinda's house actually belonged to her parents, but they had retired in San Diego and they now rented it to her for a reasonable rate. It was a lovely home, not on the lake but with a distant lake view and a multitude of windows, making it feel both airy and bright. She had decorated with a whimsical but elegant style, and we were led on a tour of the place, starting in her plush bedroom, where the queen-sized bed was covered with a white coverlet and pink and red pillows and surrounded (of course) with white wood bookshelves; this room felt like the most comfortable library ever.

"I would spend all my time up here," I said.

Belinda laughed. "Okay, then there's a bathroom down there, along with a guest room, in case you ever want to get away from it all." She sent me a quick, smiling look that I couldn't quite interpret. Then she led us all—Camilla, Adam, Doug, Sam, Allison, John, and me—back down her wood staircase to the main floor, where an open-plan kitchen widened into a dining and living room area. The hardwood floors gleamed under one central Turkish-looking rug of blue and turquoise. I said, "It's beautiful, Belinda. I can't believe I've never seen your house before."

She shrugged. "It's because we always go out for lunch and dinner. Or meet at Allison's, because she's the perpetual hostess."

Allison raised her hand. "True! I love hostessing, but this is a great house, Belinda. I guess we'll have to take turns. The Blue Lake Social Club."

"It's a very select club, though," Belinda said. Like me, she was an introvert and chose her friends carefully.

"Speaking of which," I said. "No one has signed my cast. I'm feeling forlorn."

Doug ran to Belinda's kitchen, where he opened a drawer with the ease of a man familiar with the space. "Here—a black Sharpie. Just what we need for this job!"

The whole group surrounded me, passing the marker around and cracking wise about my red cast. "It's patriotic," I said.

When they had all finished writing, we moved out onto Belinda's deck, which bordered on Moonstone Park, one of three public parks in Blue Lake. "We would be able to watch the fireworks from this patio if it weren't for these trees," Belinda said, waving her hand at the stately elms which shaded her property.

"The wooded lot is great for privacy, but bad for viewing the Fourth festivities, so we'll have to mix with all of humanity in the park there. Still, it's not far to walk."

I studied my cast in the afternoon light. Doug had written, "Don't ever do this again," and then added "Love, Doug." Good advice, I thought wryly. Camilla's note said "Heal quickly, dear Lena," while Adam had gone for an impersonal "Happy Fourth!" Sam had scrawled just his name and a heart. Allison wrote, "I will always take care of you," with a bunch of x's and o's. Belinda wrote, "Get well, my friend," along with her name.

"Anything good?" Allison asked, sitting down beside me in one of Belinda's patio chairs.

"They're all good. Good friends."

"You're a fine friend, too. I am glad to see your color looking better. Are you in pain?"

"No. But I still have pain pills left."

"Any side effects?"

"No, not that I—well, I'm kind of emotional."

Allison nodded. "Yeah, that can happen. You can feel a bit off-kilter."

"I do. And—I don't know. It's stupid."

She leaned in and touched my knee. "What's wrong, sweetie?"

"I feel like people are talking behind my back. I'm not a child. I don't need to be managed. And I—I'm tired of them whispering."

Allison didn't laugh. "It's a common complaint of patients. They don't like feeling helpless or being treated as though they are."

"Yeah, there's that. But it's more than that. It's this constant—talking about me behind my back. Like people are conspiring or something."

Allison's dainty eyebrows rose. "*These* people?" She waved a hand at all of our friends.

A surge of resentment made me say, "Yes, all of them." And then, a new wave of emotion: remorse. "Oh God, what's *wrong* with me?"

My friend studied me for a moment. "Nothing's wrong with you, Lena. There might be something wrong with your medicine, though. Do you have it with you?"

"In my bag. Right there by the door."

She got up to retrieve my purse, then sat back down. She dug out my pill bottle and studied the label. Then she pursed her lips.

"What?"

"Um—I wonder if you might want to talk to Dr. Salinger about this. Most patients can take this without a problem, but some get side effects."

"Like what?"

Her pretty blue eyes met mine. "Paranoia."

"Oh."

"Have you been feeling paranoid?"

I tried to recall my various moods and thoughts over the last two days. "I don't know. Define 'paranoia.'"

Allison's tone became brisk and clinical. "It's a range, of course. From just misreading cues to feelings of mistrust to extreme fear that someone is out to get you."

"Well, I don't think I am experiencing those things."

I was watching Sam, who was in a conversation with Doug at the edge of the patio. They spoke in low tones, their eyes scanning the patio every now and then.

"Didn't you just say people were talking behind your back?"

"They actually *were* talking behind my back."

"Or were they just talking?"

I had no response to this.

"Lena, I do think you should speak to the doctor. And tell her that you thought someone was in your hospital room."

"There *was* someone in my hospital room! Or I dreamed it. I don't know. It seemed real."

"Think for a minute. Have you been feeling mistrustful?"

I remembered those dark moments I'd experienced when we had all been looking at pictures. Adam had seemed almost sinister, as had James in one of the photographs. I had considered the idea that James was lying, that Camilla believed in someone who wasn't what he seemed. But then even Camilla had seemed rather menacing for a moment there . . . "Oh boy. Yes, I think she needs to change my medication."

"When's the last time you took a pain pill? The effect can grow over time."

"I just took one half an hour ago," I said.

She patted my hand. "If you can do without them after that, abstain. And then make a point of calling the doctor's office tomorrow. Meanwhile—don't trust your most negative thoughts."

"Okay." My mood was plummeting again with the knowledge that my brain was controlling me—or, perhaps more specifically, my medicine was controlling my brain.

Allison was looking at the group on the deck. "Oh, hang on, John's beckoning to me. I'll be back. You relax there." She kissed my cheek and skipped across the wood planking.

I turned my attention back to the spot where Doug and Sam had been talking, but they were gone. I scanned the area until I spotted Sam's blue shirt and plaid shorts, but this time he was talking to Belinda, who spoke up into his face with an animated expression, occasionally pushing her glasses up on her nose. Sam seemed to be protesting something she said; his brow furrowed, and he lifted his hands in a defensive gesture. Belinda spoke again, and Sam's shoulders sagged slightly.

I crossed the patio until I stood next to them and heard Sam saying, "That's not how it is."

"Hi," I said.

They both turned and smiled those fake smiles that I had been seeing since my operation—the smiles of people with something to hide. "What's up?" I asked.

Sam pointed at the park. "I just wanted to find out what time the festivities begin. I didn't watch last year, and I'm excited to see them."

"And when do they begin?" I asked coolly, not believing him.

Belinda shrugged. "They didn't give a certain time on the Blue Lake website. It just says that fireworks begin at dusk."

"Huh," I said. "Well, we've got an hour or so then, right?"

"Yes." Belinda brightened. "Lena, have you been to the buffet table?"

"I found a drink, and one of those little taco things. It was very good."

She took my arm. "Come back. I want to show you some of my special treats. I'm trying to give Allison a run for her money."

"Okay," I said. "I'll do that." I was going to walk away and leave Sam there out of an inexplicably perverse feeling, but he slung an arm around me and said, "Me too." He kissed my hair, and I melted under his soft touch. What was *wrong* with me?

We went back into Belinda's house and saw Isabelle at the door, tall and pretty in a blue cotton dress. "Knock, knock. Sorry I'm late! I covered the first shift. No animals harmed by fireworks at this point, thank goodness. Hopefully Arnie won't encounter any, either." She said all of this rapidly, breezily, on the threshold, after which Belinda ushered her in and I introduced them.

"Thank you for including me," Isabelle said to Belinda, handing her a wrapped package and a rose. Isabelle had always been an elegant gift-giver.

"Of course. I've heard a lot about you," Belinda said, sniffing the flower and closing her eyes.

I leaned toward Sam. "Is Cliff coming to this?"

"He said he'd stop by later, matchmaker." Sam grinned at me.

"By the looks of things at your house yesterday, I don't have to do any work in that regard."

"Yeah. That's good. She seems nice." Allison and John had joined Belinda, and Isabelle had become immediately immersed in a conversation with them all.

"She is. How are my sweet kittens today? Brave Geronimo and Sweet Arabella? And Cliff's gray duo?"

He held my face in his hands and studied it for a moment, then let go. "They are all fine. I had thought that their smallness would keep them off of the furniture, but it has not kept them out of anything. They also refused to stay in my office, so they currently have run of the whole house. I took first watch of Graham House last night and then Cliff relieved me. I went home and crashed, and when I woke up Geronimo was curled up on my neck and either Jeeves or Wooster was in my hair. I found the other two in my fruit bowl."

I sniffed, smiling. "Fate brought them to their new home."

"I'll be glad when Cliff takes his two. He's busy kitty-proofing his apartment. It's hilarious how seriously he's taking the whole thing. He's actually building them a cat tree with some scrap wood."

"That's great! Have him build you one, too. It will keep them from clawing your furniture if they have some nice wood to dig their nails in."

He glanced out the patio door. "It looks like the park is filling up. I wonder if we should drag some lawn chairs over there and stake out a claim? I don't want people jostling your cast. Let me get the guys to do that with me." He jogged toward Doug, then John, and the three of them disappeared out the door.

Camilla stood in front of me then, holding out a

cupcake. "You look as if you could use some sugar," she said.

By nightfall Cliff had joined our group and we had wandered over to the park grounds. I held Sam's hand with my good one, and his grip seemed to grow tighter as we plunged into the throng. The people of Blue Lake chattered cheerfully, calling out to each other and waving as they saw friends across the grass. Children occasionally screamed with high-pitched voices, and I jumped at the jarring noise.

Sam peered at me in the dark. "This might be too much for you. Do you want to go home?"

I did, actually. I wanted to hold Lestrade, or Sam's kittens, in an empty, quiet house, but I felt just recalcitrant enough to deny it. "No, I'm fine. Stop worrying over me, Sam."

"Okay," he said. I couldn't see his expression, but his tone made me feel guilty.

A figure loomed up in the dusk. "Hello, Lena." It was Marge Bick, and behind her were Karina "Key" Thibodeau and Horace Bick. "We heard about your accident! I'm so sorry, dear."

They stood side by side now, three silhouettes against a dark gray sky, and they seemed to float and billow with the slight breeze. "It wasn't an accident," I said. "It was intentional. Someone slammed me from behind." I wanted to see a reaction, but of course I could barely see their faces. Karina grabbed Marge's arm, seemingly for support.

"Do the police know this?"

"Yes, of course. They're looking for our assailant as we speak."

Karina said something softly, under her breath, and Marge shook her head. "Anyway, I'm glad to see you and Camilla are all right."

"Thanks, Marge," I said.

"Be careful," she told me with an odd expression. Horace, never a man of many words, put his hand on my shoulder, perhaps as a vague benediction. Then the three of them moved away. "I need to find Rusty," I heard her say.

"That was weird," Sam said.

"Yes." Why had Marge warned me to be careful? Did she know something? Was an assassin lurking in the dark? How had Doug thought it was all right for us to be here in the open, when a random bullet could be masked by the sound of the fireworks?

In retrospect, Karina's eyes had seemed almost hostile, glowing weirdly in the darkness. She had been the one, back when Camilla and I spoke with Jane's old friends at Wheat Grass, who had put forth the theory about James Graham. Who had insisted, when no one else would say it, that James Graham had been suspected of making Carrie pregnant. But had people really suspected that? Or had Karina just wanted it to seem that way? Might Karina have been jealous of Carrie? She had loved Rusty Baxter—isn't that what Marge had said? And Rusty seemed to have been close to Carrie . . . Thibodeau was a very distinctive name. I recalled what Nurse Amy had said in the recovery room: I had called out an "unusual" name.

Was Karina watching me now, in the dark, waiting

for a chance to silence me? Was it her face I had seen in the rearview mirror?

A sudden explosion in the sky made me scream out loud, but my voice was drowned out by the roar of the crowd at the sight of the first pyrotechnic display—a blue, green, and gold layered flower, sparking and fizzing above us and occasionally popping loudly as new layers burst forth. I flinched against Sam and he held me more tightly. "This was a bad idea," he said in my ear. I nodded.

He looked around for our nearest friends. "I'll just tell—" and a new explosion drowned him out. In the changing, strobe-like light I caught brief glimpses of people I knew: Kerry, the proprietor of the coffee shop; Lane Waldrop, her husband, Clay, and their two children; Paul Graves and a woman I had never seen before. I even thought I caught a glimpse of Dr. Salinger in the red light of a particularly noisy firework.

I shifted my gaze to our own group and saw that Camilla was watching Adam, who was talking to two men: Travis Pace and Rusty Baxter. The three of them huddled close together, straining to be heard over the noise. I watched their silhouettes in the deepening blackness, but suddenly they were all illuminated, and Travis and Rusty turned to look directly at me, like monsters in a horror movie who had been trained to home in on their prey. I jumped in my seat and Sam's arm tightened around me. "What does Adam have to say to *them*?" I said.

A moment later Paul Graves strode out of the darkness to talk with the other three. Once again, three faces turned to me. Why did they all look hostile, with expressions that bordered on hate? "Sam," I said. "I don't like them." Karina and Marge hovered not far away from the group, and suddenly they were all there, the people from the restaurant table, and the next burst of light illuminated their pale faces, then turned them into mere shadows again. A thought, a memory, a silhouette came back to me, and was gone.

"Let's go," Sam murmured. We stood up, and the group of men, sans Adam, came to stand before us. A shiver ran through me, despite the warm air.

"Hello, Lena," Paul Graves said. "I'm so sorry to hear of your accident."

"It was a collision," said Camilla's firm voice. She appeared at my side and lifted her chin at the three men. "And it clearly was not accidental."

Rusty held the last bit of a corn dog in his hand; a vendor on the sidewalk was getting rich tonight from the Fourth crowd. He pointed the stick vaguely at us and said, "Let's calm down now."

"I am calm, Rusty," Camilla said. Even in the dark, her eyes were bright and intense.

Travis Pace, holding a light jacket despite the heat, sounded petulant when he said, "It wasn't necessary to search our houses. We're all old friends, for God's sake."

Camilla turned her laser eyes on him. "I would think you'd want them to find the perpetrator, Travis. Lena was nearly killed. I could have been killed, as well. Someone wanted it that way, and someone is bitterly disappointed."

"Oh, don't be ridiculous," Travis said. Paul Graves nodded his approval.

Camilla's hands were on her hips. "How is it ridiculous, exactly? Jane Wyland is dead—shot to death. Lena's arm was brutally broken. What exactly are you angry about?"

Travis took one step back, literally and figuratively. "I'm not saying they shouldn't investigate. I'm saying that you shouldn't let your suspicions make you turn on old friends."

"You were *James's* friend," she said. She was about to say more, but instead she turned and walked away.

There were no forthcoming apologies from the men who faced us underneath a canopy of fireworks. Their emotions seemed somewhere between confused and furious, but I wasn't sure why they would be angry. Did they feel defensive? Shouldn't only one of them feel that way? Or had it been a conspiracy?

Another sulfurous boom in the sky made me jump. Sam said, "We were just leaving, if you don't mind."

He put a hand around my waist and guided me past the glowering men and toward Belinda's patio. Another shadow appeared beside us. Rusty Baxter was there, looking earnest. "Listen—oooh, that was a good one! Look at that, Lena! My daughter used to call those 'princess dresses.' All that pretty gold and white."

"How can we help you, Chief?" Sam said.

Rusty started to speak, but Doug and Belinda came running toward us. Doug patted Sam's arm. "Allison's got the key and will lock up the house. We have to go— Belinda just heard that our vandal has hit the library."

"Oh no!" I said, looking at Belinda's distressed face.

She sighed. "Yeah, I'm afraid so. I have to go see the damage. Frank, our janitor, said it seems like it's just the legal section."

A weird alignment of thoughts happened in my brain under the persistent explosions in the sky. Doug and Belinda started to walk away, toward the house and Doug's car, but I ran after them. "Doug! Belinda! Wait."

They turned, surprised, on the verge of her patio. "What's up?" Doug said, looking at his watch. *Ah, the watch again*, my brain said. The tension and uncertainty of time.

"The legal section," I said.

"What?"

"This vandal—what was it that he hit on the day you guys were putting in our air conditioner?"

"What? Just a bus bench. We've got to get going."

"Wait. Do you mean one of those benches with the ads for Luke Kelly's law office?"

"Yes." He moved closer. "Why?"

"Because, look at the pattern. The statue in the park is of Clarence Darrow. A *lawyer*. The library is hit, but only in the legal section. And Luke Kelly is a lawyer. A very specific lawyer."

"And you're saying what?"

"I'm thinking someone might have a pretty big grudge against lawyers right now."

He leaned in so close that I could see his gold-brown eyes, and those eyes seemed to read some knowledge in mine. "I've got you. Let's go, Belinda." He turned back once. "Thanks, Lena!"

Sam appeared next to me, looking dazed. "I thought he was about to kiss you."

"No—we were exchanging brain waves. He doesn't want to kiss me, Sam."

"I do."

I squeezed his hand, but Rusty Baxter, who hadn't gone very far away, was beside us again. "Lena, I'm sorry to bother you, but I want to make something clear."

This whole day had seemed off-kilter, and I had experienced enough. "Rusty, I'm not in the mood." Then, prompted by I don't know what, I whirled around and faced him. "You know what? I think you're all hiding things. You all know more than you're saying, and Camilla and I are going to find out whether you tell us or not. I saw that picture of Carrie crying in the restaurant. I saw your face. You said you liked her, and you wouldn't forget a thing like that." I pointed my finger in his face. "So you're lying, Chief. They all are."

Sam leaned in front of me. "Lena's pretty exhausted, and on medication."

Rusty Baxter nodded. "She's also right. I didn't forget what Carrie told me, but I told all this to Doug when he came to my office. She was upset because she had visited my dad that day at the station. My dad was chief then, did you know?"

Sam and I nodded, waiting for whatever unburdening Rusty wanted to do. "I was there when she came into the station with James Graham. She asked to see my father. When she came out she was crying. She and James left together. That was all. I cornered her at the party and asked what she had been crying about. I wanted to be a brave knight to protect her—from

James, if need be, or whatever was bothering her. I think I was in love with her."

A series of explosions sounded in the sky, and the audience roared. "What did she tell you?" Sam asked.

He shook his head. "Nothing. I just made her cry again." For a moment I thought I could see the eyes of the young man that he had been shining through the eyes that looked at me now. "Believe me, if there were some way I could go back in time and find out what Carrie told my father—and *why* she told it to him—I'd be glad to do it. But there's no way to go into the past."

"Maybe Carrie kept a diary," I said dully.

"What?" Rusty looked startled.

"I said—"

"I heard you. And I'm wrong. There *is* a way to go back!" He looked something between urgent and euphoric. "Come to the station with me right now—we'll settle this thing!"

"What?" I said.

"You were leaving anyway, right? Let's go to the station. My dad used to keep a diary. Nothing official, just his way of winding down after work each day. It's an old leather tome, and I actually keep it in my office as a memento. A prop, really. I haven't opened it in years."

"Why didn't you look up Carrie's information long ago?" Sam asked, his tone skeptical.

Rusty looked sad. "Because life moved on. I got married." He looked at me. "And I forgot."

"Let's go," I said.

We rushed through the darkness toward the street where Rusty Baxter had parked his car. Rusty said,

"One of you lovebirds get in front so I don't feel like a limo driver."

Sam obliged him and climbed into the passenger seat after helping me into the back.

It wasn't until the car had pulled away from the curb and the night around us grew quieter, the fireworks and crowd chatter receding, that I looked at the back of their heads and considered that it might be a trap.

14

I cannot bear to see a woman cry. If I saw you cry, I think it would kill me.
—From the correspondence of James Graham
and Camilla Easton, 1971

THE CAR WAS dark and smelled vaguely of cigarettes. Behind us the sound of exploding fireworks put me in mind of war, conflict. The sky brightened with an orange light, then grew dark again. The car's motor was barely audible beneath the relentless pop pop pop—not just from the park but from all around as people set off homemade fireworks in their yards and driveways, the noise as jarring as gunfire. We were surrounded.

Rusty's hands sat large and pale on the steering wheel, and his speedometer rose past the legal limit the moment we hit the highway. "Rusty, you're speeding," I said, my voice sounding brittle to my own ears.

"No problem, I know the chief," he said. Perhaps it was a joke, but he didn't smile when he said it, nor did I. His eyes met mine in the rearview mirror; his normally jovial expression had a hard edge to it.

We hurtled down the dark road, and I wondered at our foolishness. Why had we climbed into a car with Rusty, a man who was a *suspect* in Jane Wyland's murder? A man who had been in love with Carrie Wyland? A man who, even now, carried a gun?

I tapped the back of Sam's seat with my foot.

He turned toward me. "Are you all right, Lena?"

I sent him an urgent glance, but then Rusty's eyes were watching me again in the rearview mirror. My eyes dropped to the speedometer, which had crept up to seventy miles an hour. "Why are we going so fast?" I asked.

Sam turned to look at the gauge and raised his eyebrows. "Rusty, the limit is fifty on this road. How about if you slow down? You're making Lena nervous."

"I'm feeling determined," he said. "I think we're onto something. I think we three are about to discover something important."

"Slow down," Sam said.

Rusty shrugged and decreased his speed. "I can't believe I never thought to look at that old book, not once. I never made the connection between his little hobby and the actual history he was preserving about this town, about the people in it."

His words slurred slightly, and I wondered if he had been drinking.

I tried to sound firm, authoritative. "We should call Doug, too. Someone else, to meet us at the station." The last thing I wanted was to be alone in a building with this man.

It was fully dark now, and we could see occasional signs of fireworks from neighboring towns—distant bursts of color on the horizon, illuminating the gently lapping waves of Blue Lake. Rusty rolled his window partway down and a gust of cool air hit my face. I hadn't even grabbed my purse on the way out. Now I longed for it; I wanted to dig in it and find my keys, to curl my fingers around them and let the sharp ends jut between in a makeshift weapon. I had only one good arm, but it was strong . . .

Rusty's police radio squawked in the front seat and he flicked it off with a quick motion. Was he allowed to do that? I met his eyes again in the mirror, and they narrowed at me, suspicious or angry or assessing.

"Rusty, watch out!" Sam yelled, and Rusty hit the brakes as two deer darted across the road and disappeared into the forested land on our right.

The moment hung suspended and I heard, once again, Camilla's screams, felt the impact, and saw a face in my own rearview mirror, eyes narrowed at me in a similar manner . . .

It was there, but then gone, maddeningly elusive. I dug my nails into my hands.

"Everyone okay?" Rusty asked.

Sam turned to look at me, wearing his concerned face. Hadn't that been his expression since the day we met? Always concerned, always watchful. What was he watching for? It was like . . . surveillance. "Lena? Are you all right?"

"Fine. Shouldn't we have turned right there?" Panic fired through my system as Rusty bypassed the police parking lot.

Rusty shrugged. "Going in the back way."

I had not realized there was a back entrance, but

there was, and we drove to a well-lit door that said "Police Personnel Only."

Rusty parked the car and turned off the engine; the shadowy lot was empty, and we sat for a moment in the dark while he dug in his pocket for something. I feared it was a gun.

"Sam!" I said.

He looked back at me, surprised, and Rusty held up a key. "Here we go," he said.

I was trembling, almost as much as I had been in the hospital when my arm had been hanging, broken and bleeding, at my side.

Sam and Rusty got out; Rusty moved toward the back entrance, and Sam opened my door. He leaned in and said, "Oh my God! What happened? Did that scare you, with the deer? You're okay, babe. Oh, Lena, come here!" He pulled me against him and I clung on like a burr until his skin warmed mine, and that warmth spread inside, calming me.

"Something's wrong with me," I whispered. "I thought Rusty was going to kill us. I can't—get a handle on myself. Nothing's calibrating."

He leaned close to me, and his eyes looked deeply into mine. "I should have realized," he said. "I'll help you, Lena. I'm sorry. About the fireworks, and this ride with Rusty. I—we were just so eager to find out the truth. I forgot your condition."

"I don't want to have a condition. I just want to be Lena again. But I'm not."

"I know. It will come back, it will all come back to you. We'll go to the doctor tomorrow, okay? Just hold on until then."

I nodded. He held out his hand and I took it. We walked to the door, where Rusty waited impatiently. Was it a good idea, I wondered, to go into the empty police station?

But then he opened the door, and I saw that all the lights were on; I spied a receptionist and some uniformed officers. Rusty was their boss; he was the chief of police, and he was trying to help us.

Despite these comforting facts, my trepidation lingered as I followed Rusty and Sam down a hall to a door that said "Chief's Office."

Rusty unlocked it and flicked on a light. A young officer appeared, holding a cup of coffee. "Chief, Marge Bick called. She said she had spoken to you earlier in the day and you told her to call back."

Rusty waved this away. "Yes, I'll call her."

He turned to us. "Have a seat there." We sat on a small couch across from his desk. He pointed toward a little decorative shelf that sat above a small fireplace in the corner of his office. "This place hasn't been redecorated much since my dad was in it. The fireplace is from the days before we had central heating, can you believe it? But those books up there were just part of the decor. Old police manuals and some old law dictionaries. This brown one was his diary." He pulled it down and blew off some dust.

"Do you remember the date?" Sam said. "It would have been around the time she left, which was at the end of August, right?"

"Right. Let's hope he dated these entries. I read some once, when I was in my early twenties, but I found them boring. Little things. A joke his receptionist told, or an anecdote about a deer or raccoon that peered in the window of the station." He sat holding the book for a moment, his face thoughtful and sad as he recalled his dead father, a life long gone. "Anyway. Let's see. Yes, I see dates. Nineteen sixty-eight is where it starts. Wow. Okay, here's '69, and '70. Now '71." He was turning rapidly but gingerly; the pages were obviously yellowed and frail. "August!" he shouted. He scanned some pages and read, his eyes darting. "I don't see any familiar names. August eleventh, August fifteenth . . . Wait a minute. Here we go. I think this is it. Hang on."

He sat and read. A lamp in his office shone down on his still-thick hair and revealed the red beneath the gray and I realized again that a boy still lingered beneath this man, the boy who had lost a father and a girlfriend and his youth . . .

"Oh God," Rusty said. "Oh my God."

"What is it?" Sam asked.

Rusty held up a finger, still reading. Then he sat back, his face slack and pale. "You'd better read it yourselves," he said. He held out the book, and Sam stood up and took it.

Then he came back to the couch, sat beside me, and held the book between us so that I could read it, too. Rusty's father, the former Chief Baxter, had very neat handwriting that was a cross between print and cursive. The entry was dated August 24, 1971. It read:

Some days in this job are real heartbreakers. And even though I believe in something called justice, I realized today that some people never get it, and never will, and it makes me sick, literally sick. I met with the little Wyland girl today, the blonde one called Carrie. I saw instantly why poor Rusty has a crush on her. She's a sweet girl and not at all vain, but of course she was distracted and suffering.

James Graham brought her in. I have always liked and respected James; he's a lot like his father, and that's saying a lot, because old Mr. Graham is one of the last true nobles of Blue Lake. James told Carrie that she was being brave and doing the right thing, and he settled her into a chair and then glared over at me, saying Carrie deserved justice. I told her to tell me the problem, but she couldn't do it. Finally James Graham told me the girl had been raped.

"Oh no," I cried. "Oh God." Sam's face looked grim, but he kept reading, so I went back to the notebook.

I asked about the perpetrator. Young Graham said that Carrie hadn't told him or anyone, not even her family. He wanted me to persuade her to give a name so that the man could be prosecuted. Carrie looked me in the eye and said, "Who would be prosecuted— him or me?" I knew what she meant, and I didn't lie to her. I told her that I could arrest the man, but that he might not be put in jail pending an investigation, and that if she decided to press charges, she might still be interrogated by the man's attorneys, if he hired them. I said I would do my best to keep her name out of the papers, but that in some cases I had not been successful in protecting rape victims. She said she had read horror stories about women who were blamed for their own assaults, women who endured long trials during which they were humiliated, and at the end the rapists somehow evaded prison.

I couldn't lie to that sweet girl. I told her that the Blue Lake police would do their best to put the man behind bars, but that I knew rape victims didn't get the support they needed, as a rule. I said I could refer her to some social service programs.

James Graham stood up then and said, "This is outrageous! She's a human being! She's been brutally attacked!"

She didn't say another word. She stood up, too, regal as a queen, and told James she was leaving. He glared at me and then followed her out. Rusty had been waiting for me in the lobby; he ran in and asked me what had happened, asked why James was furious and Carrie was crying. I said I couldn't divulge that information.

That was the end of August 24, but I read the August 25 entry, which was brief and sad.

I heard that Carrie Wyland left town today. Rusty and all his friends are buzzing with the news. Even Jane Wyland apparently doesn't know why, and she's heartbroken. This anonymous man has a lot to pay for. I wish I could find him. I wish I could wring his neck with my own hands.

I turned to stare at Sam, and then at Rusty Baxter. "Jane was killed because she was looking into an old crime. She didn't know that in trying to expose what she thought was James Graham's crime, she was riling up a man who thought his brutal act was safely buried in the past."

Sam set the book down on Rusty's desk. "And Camilla did the same thing. She said she wouldn't rest until she had sorted this out. Minutes later someone tried to kill you both. This man is desperate."

I pulled out my phone and texted what we had just learned to Camilla, promising her I'd fill her in soon, and assuring her that I was with Sam.

Rusty's face, which had looked sinister to me in the car, now looked vulnerable as a child's. "I wonder how much more Dad could have done for Carrie back then. Let's face it, he was probably right. The world was not kind to victims of rape in the 1970s."

"It often isn't even now," I said.

"But there should have been a way that they could have caught that man and made him pay. A way to save Carrie's life and happiness." He tapped the top of the old book, his face thoughtful. "I hope she found some happiness in Chicago. With her baby. We're looking for the boy. The man, now."

Even now, my suspicions bobbed to the surface. Did Rusty assume Carrie had gotten pregnant as a result of the rape? Did he want to find Carrie's son because the child was Rusty's son, as well?

Sam was studying the side of my face. Suddenly he stood up. "Thank you, Chief. This is important news, and I know you and Doug will pursue it. We'll be on our way."

He helped me out of my chair and accompanied me

into the hall, where Doug Heller was just leading a small group into what looked like an interrogation room. It included a very angry Luke Kelly, a miserable-looking Star, and Belinda.

Instead of going into the room, Star paused and sent me a beseeching look. "Lena," she said. "They've arrested me!"

Luke Kelly looked tired as well as angry. "You're not under arrest, Star. You've been detained for questioning. Now, come in here and answer Detective Heller's questions."

My heart went out to Star. She was obviously guilty, but she hadn't wanted the police to catch her. She had wanted her father to figure out her clues, to come to her and rectify his neglect of their relationship. I'm not sure why I understood this all in an instant—perhaps my own precarious state of mind showed me the fragile state of someone else's thoughts. Star's face looked young and naked in the harsh station lights. A memory came to me: coming home from high school in the fall of my freshman year to find my solemn-faced parents waiting for me. "Lena, your mother saw the doctor today, and we need to talk to you . . ."

Star's eyes were intent upon my face. She sensed that she had an ally in me. "I want Lena in there," she said. "I want her there as my counselor."

Sam stared at me in surprise. "Do you know her, Lena?"

"Yes, of course. Star, I don't think—"

"Miss Kelly, please come sit at the table. We won't keep you long," Doug said.

"I'll tell you everything if Lena can come in," she said.

Her father's face was furious. "You don't get to make demands, Star!"

Doug looked at me. "Lena, would you be willing to sit in?"

"Uh—if I can be of help, sure."

We all traipsed into the room, which held a long table and several chairs. Sam and Belinda sat against the wall. Doug sat on one side of the table, while Star and her father sat on the other. I took a seat at one end, gingerly perching on a chair.

Doug sent Star a stern look. "Miss Kelly, did you damage the law books in the Blue Lake Public Library?"

Luke Kelly stared at his daughter. "Answer him," he said.

"Yes," she whispered.

"And did you have any accomplices in this act?"

"No," Star said.

Doug jotted something on a pad. "Did you also damage the statue in the town square by applying yellow spray paint to its surface?"

Luke hadn't known about this. His eyes grew wide.

"Yes," Star said.

Doug wrote on his pad. "And did you also spray paint on the bus bench on Whitney Street?"

"*My* bench?" her father sputtered.

"Yes," she said, her eyes downcast.

"Why?" Luke cried, his face red and distraught. "Star, why?"

She shrugged. Two large tears worked their way down her cheeks. "I don't know."

"Yes, you do," Doug said. "Because all of those crimes have one uniting theme, don't they?"

Star shook her head, staring down at the table. I could see all of her emotions in her expressive little face: fear, humiliation, regret, hurt.

Luke's face was growing more impatient. His cell phone buzzed, and he glanced at it, then back at Star. "Why, Star?"

Star rustled in her seat, then looked at me, perhaps because I was the only sympathetic face at the table. "Lena knows," she said, and she burst out crying. Belinda crept forward with a tissue and put her arm around Star.

I wasn't sure why Star was convinced that I understood her motives, but I had a suspicion. Her father and Doug looked at me. "I think—Star wanted to come to Blue Lake to be with her father. But Luke is on his own, as a parent and a busy lawyer, and he— neglects her."

Luke started in with a blustery response, then stopped, looking deflated and sad.

I said, "I think Star was lashing out in a way she hoped only her father would see. She was rather short-sighted in that she probably thought these things weren't crimes. More the sort of thing she might get detention for at her school. And now I think she's realizing the seriousness of her actions." I looked at Luke. "And the fact that actions have consequences." To my gratification he looked ashamed.

"Star," Doug said. "Whatever your motives might

have been, you have committed crimes. You have done significant damage to public property."

Luke Kelly raised a finger. "I will take financial responsibility for all the damage. And Star will take responsibility for her infractions, whatever form that might take. I'm hoping that we can agree on community service as a consequence, and a chance to keep this off of her permanent record."

Star's eyes grew wide. "I don't want a record," she said. "I'm not some kind of criminal."

Doug sighed. "Star." He waited until she looked at him. "Until you take responsibility for your actions, we cannot even begin to talk about the consequences. Did you damage anything else in this town? Tell me the truth now."

Star shook her head. Then, in a confessional burst, she said, "I was going to paint something on the side of a barn last night. But some guy showed up to put his car in the barn, and I barely got away. It was scary, and I realized it wasn't worth it. I was there in the middle of the night and this guy freaked me out, creeping up out of nowhere. I learned my lesson."

Doug sat up, arrow straight. "What time was this?"

"Around midnight." She shot a guilty glance at her father. "My dad thought I was asleep."

Sam stood up. "Doug?"

Doug remained calm. "A man was putting his car in a barn at midnight?"

"Yeah."

"What did this man look like?"

Luke Kelly put a hand on Star's arm. "Don't answer, Star."

"What?" She looked confused.

Doug glared at Luke. "What's your problem, Kelly? I need information."

"My daughter will be happy to answer all of your questions in exchange for community service and no permanent record of her misdemeanors."

"Oh, for God's sake," Doug said. He stood up and stormed out of the room. I peered out to see him consulting with Rusty Baxter. They gesticulated at each other for a few minutes, and then Doug was back.

"Fifty hours of community service, and no permanent record," he said. "You will check in regularly with this office until your service is completed and we sign off on it."

Luke nodded. Star looked relieved.

Doug pointed at her. "The barn?"

"Yeah, it was some old guy. He pulled up in his car. Probably not his main car, because it was all squished up. But I thought the barn was deserted; that's why I picked it. I was so surprised when I heard his car coming. I didn't even see it, because the lights were off. It was creepy. But it also kept him from seeing me."

Doug closed his eyes for a moment. "Did you recognize the man?"

"No. It was too dark. Just that he had gray hair. He looked at his phone one time, and I saw the gray glinting in the light."

"But it was a man?"

"Well—yeah. Or I guess a lady in man's clothes."

Sam couldn't take it anymore. "Which barn?" he yelled.

Doug sent him an impatient glance, but Star

answered. "The old Schuler's barn. On Green Glass Highway."

The group stood up, and people began to leave the room. Doug leaned toward Luke Kelly and spoke to him in low tones.

As I walked past the table on my way to the door, Star's hand shot out and squeezed mine. "Thank you, Lena," she said.

Her father looked at me with mournful eyes, but there was something in his face that said he had finally awakened. "Yes, thank you," he said, then turned back to Doug.

A small window was open in the corner of the room, and through it came the sound of a barrage of fireworks, one after the other.

"We missed the finale," Star said in a small voice.

Luke nodded. "Yeah, show's over." I was glad to see, though, that he slung an arm around his daughter's shoulders.

SAM CALLED CLIFF to pick us up, and we followed the police car, at a distance.

Schuler's barn had once belonged to the family who began the Schuler's ice cream empire, but they eventually moved out of Blue Lake and sold their property. The barn, neglected, became one of those lonely skeletal structures that one sees from the highways of the Midwest. Stark and noble against the sky, empty within, made of warped, pockmarked wood that allowed for streams of poetic light when the sun was shining.

Cliff pulled over across from the barn, and we watched as Doug's officers opened the doors and illuminated the vehicle within. An evidence car arrived eventually, and Cliff jogged over to join Doug at the scene. I concentrated on his tall form and his slightly lopsided gait.

"This is it, right?" I said to Sam in Cliff's dark car, watching the endless palette of fireworks over the lake. I wondered how many different towns up and down the lakeshore were providing the exploding array of colors in the July sky.

"I hope so. We seem to get closer and closer. It's a matter of momentum; something has to give," Sam said. "Good—Cliff is coming back."

Cliff climbed in and shut the driver's door. "Not much to learn here right now. The guy scraped off his VINs and removed his license plates. No prints yet, but they're still dusting. He knew what he was doing."

I sighed. "Look at that front end, though. Wouldn't you think that the man might have been injured himself? He crashed right into us without braking. Even if he was wearing a belt—oh my God."

"What?" Sam and Cliff asked in unison.

"If he were injured, he wouldn't want to go to the hospital, right? That would be a matter of record. You guys could find him. You would search there."

"Already have," Cliff agreed.

"So he'd have no option—except to try to find an alternative to the doctor. Like a *vet*."

"Okay," Cliff said, pulling on to the highway.

"Isabelle said that the day she came to town she worked in the clinic for a while. She saw cats and dogs and *a man with a sprained wrist.* She thought he was a local eccentric."

"Where does she live?" Cliff asked.

"Uh—I don't know. She was looking at apartments yesterday, but I don't know if she moved in already. I have to call Allison."

"Do it fast," Cliff said, pulling a Mars light from under his seat and rolling down his window so he could stick it onto his roof. "We're going to visit the lovely Isabelle and nail this guy once and for all."

15

Today was a dark day.
  —From the correspondence of James Graham
                                and Camilla Easton, 1971

ALLISON SHOUTED INTO her cell phone. "Where did you go, Lena? You missed a wonderful fireworks show. We're at Belinda's house, but half of her guests have disappeared! Camilla was worried about you. She and Adam left a while ago; they are so cute together. Camilla was trying to get you on her phone. She figured you were with Sam, though. You left your purse here; I gave it to her to take home."

"Thanks, and yes, I'm with Sam. I texted Camilla not long ago. Is Isabelle still there?" I asked.

"No—she asked Adam and Camilla to drop her at home; I guess she walked over from the vet's office earlier."

"What's home? Is she already in an apartment?"

"No, not yet. She's staying at the Red Cottage. I got Janey Maxwell to give her off-season rates."

"Red Cottage," I said to Cliff, covering the phone.

He sped toward town, and I went back to Allison, feigning normalcy. "Great! I'll fill you in later, but we have to go talk to her."

"Okay." I could hear that she was pouting slightly, but then she brightened. "Hey, Isabelle asked me to help design the decor of her new apartment."

"That's right up your alley! It will be fun."

"Yes! You have to be a part of it, too, and Belinda. Her place is really stylish."

"Great. Ladies' night. Talk to you soon!" I hung up before Allison could ask questions.

THE RED COTTAGE was actually several rental cottages owned by Janey Maxwell. One could go in through the front "red" building and ask for a cottage number or go down a back path and seek out a cottage where someone was staying. We risked the back path, hoping to save time.

"There are only four. Hers would have lights on, and these first two are dark," Cliff said, moving swiftly in front of us.

"That one," I said, pointing to the third cottage. "There's a light, and I can see her purse on that front table. She had it when she visited me in the hospital."

We moved to her stairway and rang the bell. I also texted her so that she wouldn't be nervous. *Isabelle, it's me, Lena. We're at the door—we have a question for you.*

I saw Isabelle peer out the front window, phone in hand, and I waved. She moved away, and moments later her door opened. "Well, hello," she said. "We all wondered where you two went. Hi, Cliff."

"Hey," Cliff said. "Can we come in for a second? I know it's late."

"Sure. I was just making myself a little snack. Would you like anything to eat or drink?"

"No, thanks," I said. "Just a minute of your time."

Sam smiled at her, conveying reassurance. "I know we must look kind of crazy. It's just that Lena mentioned something you said to her, and we thought it could be important."

"Come in, come in." She led us into a tiny sitting room in her cottage, and we sat on the edges of our chairs. "What happened with the guy with the crunched-up car? Anything?" she asked.

"We found it eventually," Cliff said. "He hid it in a barn. But he removed all identifying marks. He's clearly our man, or woman, because this is someone who didn't want that car to be found."

"Oh." Isabelle contemplated her lap for a moment, her dark hair falling over her eyes. "I suppose that's good and bad, then."

Sam leaned forward. "But Lena recalled you telling her about a man at the vet. A man with a sprained wrist."

"Oh yes!" she said, remembering. She started to laugh, then sobered. "Oh my—you think it could have been—oh God. Wow, I just miss all the cues, don't I?"

"You couldn't have known," Cliff said. "You just got here."

"Yeah, I guess so."

"Isabelle, what do you remember about him? What did he look like?" I asked.

She stared at me with wide eyes. "Oh God. Not to sound like a broken record, but I barely looked at him. I just recall he had gray hair."

Sam groaned. Gray hair again.

Isabelle was apologetic. "I know, that's probably a third of the town, right?"

Cliff was thinking like a cop, of course. "Could you pick him out of a lineup?"

She held up her hands. "No, absolutely not. I can't picture him at all. To be honest, I think I was avoiding eye contact because I didn't want him to try to persuade me to look at his hand. I just told him I couldn't do it, that we weren't licensed for it, and that he would have to go to the hospital. I did tell him to keep it on ice."

Cliff scooted his chair slightly closer to hers. "Did you get enough of a glance at the injury to tell how severe it was?"

She nodded. "Not that bad. Enough to cause him pain, obviously, or he wouldn't have been in there. Swollen, bruised, but not broken or he would have been in even more pain."

"Which hand?" I asked.

"His right," she said.

"Good." I took out my phone.

"Lena, what are you doing?" Sam asked. He sounded worried.

I pressed one of my speed dials and Doug Heller answered. "Doug, it's Lena. Are you still at the station?"

"Just finishing my paperwork. What's up?"

"Is Rusty there?"

"Yes. What's happening, Lena?"

"Before he leaves, I want you to go to him and shake his hand. Thank him for being a good boss or something, but squeeze his right hand, hard."

Doug sighed in my ear. "Lena, what is this about? Belinda's waiting for me to help clean up after the party."

"Thanks for that, by the way."

"Lena?"

"Cliff will tell you," I said, handing Cliff the phone. Cliff raised his brows, then spoke tersely to his colleague, telling Doug what we had realized in the car, and what Isabelle told us.

I leaned toward Sam and Isabelle. "That takes care of Rusty. Now we have to check Horace, and Travis, and Paul. Who else?"

"There's just Adam, I guess," Sam said. "And Karina's husband. Have we met him?"

"No—he wasn't at the restaurant, or the fireworks show, as far as I know. But I wasn't concentrating so well there, as you know."

Cliff ended the call and handed my phone back to me. "Doug's got Rusty covered. He and I can check out everyone else tomorrow."

I pondered him for a moment, feeling suspicious. "If you checked everyone's car, then why wasn't this one missing? The one in the barn?"

Cliff shrugged. "We don't know. We got all the records, and everything matches up. Either he didn't drive his own car to the restaurant, or it wasn't one of the people from the restaurant who did this. You and Camilla could be wrong about that, Lena."

I thought about Camilla. Never had I known one of her instincts to be wrong. "No, it was someone at the restaurant. The timing was right, and there was a motive. They heard what Camilla said, and it angered them."

"Then we can't explain it, except that someone must have had two cars. When we came to check, they showed us the intact car and didn't mention the other one. I suppose that works."

Sam nodded. "Makes sense. Could be the car of a spouse or something. How many of them are married, Cliff?"

"I don't think any of them are, except Horace. Adam is a widower, Paul Graves is divorced, and so is Travis Pace."

"Karina, or Key Thibodeau, has a spouse. Or whatever her married name is," I said. "Marge said she married a farmer. What was his name?"

"Ken Fields," Cliff replied. "Chip spoke to him. The man had a number of vehicles in his garage and was happy to show them off, Chip said."

"The car is the key to it all!" I said. "I think we should visit them all tonight. Find a way to shake their hands, or fall into them, make it look like an accident. We can know who this is within an hour."

"It's late, Lena," Sam said.

"So? Cliff is a cop. He can make people get up. Someone is a murderer, and we need to catch him before his hand gets better!"

Cliff stood up. "First thing in the morning, kid.

Meanwhile I think we should all call it a night. Isabelle, thanks so much for the information. Sorry to bother you at this hour. What time is it, anyway?"

"Almost eleven," Isabelle said. "And I don't mind at all. I seem destined to keep meeting you."

It was an ambiguous statement, but Cliff chose to believe it was directed at him. His face grew slightly red and he studied his car keys, then sent her a crooked smile. His eyes met Sam's, and they exchanged a look that I could not read.

Sam said, "Lena, Camilla is going to kill me if I don't get you home to rest. You've only been out of the hospital for a day."

"I can take care of myself," I said. I thanked Isabelle and walked to the door. I could only imagine the secret messages that were being exchanged behind me. I stepped out into the evening air.

WE STILL SAW distant fireworks as Cliff turned off Wentworth Street onto the gravel drive that led up the bluff. I looked at my phone and saw a message from my father. I sent him a quick voice message, saying I was out of the hospital and would contact him soon. "I love you," I said.

I could feel Sam's eyes on me, but he was keeping silent. I understood that he was confused by my erratic behavior, and that made two of us.

Cliff looked at me in his rearview. "Where am I dropping you, kid? Sam House or Graham House?"

I smiled wanly. I had no idea where I wanted to be right now.

Sam touched my hand with one finger. "The kittens are lonely. And I will be, too, if you go to Camilla's."

With a burst of love and gratitude I leaned in and kissed his cheek. "I'm sorry," I whispered. "I know I'm crazy."

"It's been a long day," he said. He leaned forward and tapped Cliff's shoulder. "Let us off here, bro."

Cliff obliged, waiting patiently in the car while Sam helped me out of the backseat. I started to walk toward the path but had a thought and moved to the driver's side window of the car. I tapped on it and Cliff rolled it down. "Isabelle likes you, by the way."

"What? Did she say something to you?" Cliff suddenly looked about eighteen years old.

"No, but she's my friend, and I've seen her before when she likes someone. She likes you."

"Well—I mean—should I ask her out? What's my next move?"

I laughed. A blue firework flowered over the lake. "I don't know. Do you like her back?"

"Yeah. It feels very natural, talking to her."

"That's sweet. Then yes, you should ask her out. Good night."

"Good night, Lena. Feel better."

"Yeah."

Sam murmured a good night, and Cliff's car made a U-turn and drove down the hill.

Inside Sam's quiet house four tiny creatures bounded down the hall, thrilled to see us. Sam and I each scooped up two of them. I had a gray one and Arabella, the black-and-white female. I couldn't do more than crook my arm, but they were happy with that. Arabella curled against me, and the gray boy walked up to my shoulder and sat there. I laughed. "Sam, do you know what I want more than anything in the world?"

"What?" He held Geronimo and Jeeves like little babies, their bellies up.

"A shower. A nice, hot shower. I feel like I haven't been clean for days."

"I can help you with that. Let me feed these guys."

Moments later Sam was helping me strip off my clothes; he draped half of me with a robe but left my cast arm out; soon he was covering the stiff material with plastic garbage bags, taping them with an engineer's precision. Finally, he leaned back and studied it. "You're good to go. Let me go make sure the water is warm."

"Okay." I trailed after him up the stairs, feeling foggy. By the time I got to the bathroom and Sam's lovely blue tile shower, I was half-asleep.

He helped me step into the water and I eyed him blearily. "I want to wash my hair," I said.

"Hang on," he said. He stripped off his own clothes and stood in the shower with me, massaging shampoo into my scalp and helping me rinse it off, then gently using a washcloth to bathe me in areas I couldn't reach. His touch was so light, the water so soothing, I felt a wave of relief pass through me.

"I feel like a new woman," I said.

With a tender finger he wiped some soap from my face, then kissed me. "I don't want a new woman. I liked the Lena I had."

I noticed his past tense, and he realized it, too,

when he saw my expression. "Don't read into that," he said. "You know what I mean."

I avoided his gaze; I was on the verge of humiliating tears. "Okay. Help me out now."

He did, and he found a large T-shirt that I could wear as a nightgown. Feeling fragrant and sleepy, I went to his bed, which he had already turned down. Sam helped me in and then left briefly to turn off lights and check the locks on his doors. There was one rosy lamp still glowing in his room, and by this light I saw the silhouettes of the kittens as they tumbled through the door and used their claws to climb Sherpa-like up the side of the mattress.

"You found me, huh?" I asked them. They walked around like men on the moon, lifting their paws high as they explored the new terrain. Sam returned and stood next to me. "Can I sleep with you? Or will it bother your cast?"

"Yes. And no, you won't bother it. I need to tell you something. I still have pain pills left. Allison said I shouldn't take any more, and that I should see Dr. Salinger tomorrow."

"You think it's the pills, then? Making you feel— off-balance?"

"I hope so. I haven't taken one since three o'clock or so today. And I'm not feeling it as badly now as I did earlier, and yesterday. Basically since the accident."

He sat on the edge of the bed. "Do you have them? We can read the bottle."

"They're in my purse. Camilla has it."

He touched my cast. "Are you in pain?"

"No. I don't think I need them. Even if I did, I wouldn't want to take more."

"We'll throw them away tomorrow. Okay?"

"Yeah. I think that's best."

Sam nodded and he climbed into bed next to me and lay close to my side, facing me. "You look better, Lena. You're getting your color back. And the shower seems to have revitalized you."

"I want my mind back. It's been playing tricks on me. Hey!" Geronimo and Arabella were trying to bite the moisture out of my hair. Sam scooped them up, laughing, and moved them to the bottom of the bed.

"I'll take you to the doctor in the morning."

"Okay."

"You know I love you, don't you?"

I didn't answer him. I had closed my eyes just to rest them, but I found I couldn't open them again.

IN MY DREAM I was once again in the car, and someone was gaining on me. I slammed my foot on the accelerator, determined to outrun him this time. Before I pulled too far away, I remembered that I had to learn his identity. I looked into the rearview mirror and saw him, quite clearly, the shape of his shoulders and the particular style of his hair. His eyes dominated, though, and stayed with me as I sped away. They were full of hatred, and they had been focused right on me.

I sat up, breathing hard, gasping, and Sam woke up, too. "Lena?"

"I saw him. In my dream, I saw him."

"Do you remember who it was?"

"I saw a man at first. But by the end of the dream he had turned into Jane Wyland. That's all I can remember. Her fury, and her hatred. But now I know why she felt so much hate, Sam. Because she thought James Graham took advantage of her sister and made her pregnant, and then paid to get her out of town. And Jane lost that close relationship she'd once had, because Carrie never wanted to return to this place, or to tell people what had happened. She simply cut Jane out of her life."

Sam nodded, stroking my hair. "Do you think you can fall back asleep?"

"I don't know. Something's on me! Something heavy."

Sam pointed to my stomach. "It's two cats. Should I move them?"

I peered into the dark at the curled bodies of two kittens. "Where are the other two?"

"On my side. They seem to like staying together and staying close to us."

"Yeah. They're fine, you can leave them there."

I let my head fall back on the pillow. Sam said, "If you remember, Lena—anything at all—let me know."

"Okay."

I turned briefly and saw, even in the dark, the determined line of his jaw.

·✦· 16 ·✦·

*I know you like mysteries; I fear I find them too
close to reality.*

—From the correspondence of
James Graham and Camilla Easton, 1971

DR. SALINGER'S OFFICE waiting room was almost full,
but I barely had to wait at all before the now-familiar
gray-haired receptionist appeared at the practice door.
"Lena? You can come right through, hon."

I waved to Sam, who sat holding a *People* maga-
zine without really reading it. "Should I come in?" he
asked. "To talk about the medicine?"

"I'm okay. Thanks," I said. I followed the receptionist to the examining room, and she pointed to the table.

"If you sit up there your cast will be just where the
doctor can see it. You can put your purse right here on
this little side chair." I had just reclaimed my purse from
Camilla that morning, but I did as the nurse instructed.
"There we go. The doctor should be in shortly."

"Thank you, uh"—I looked at her name tag, which
said "Sandra Walton"—"Sandra."

"Everyone calls me Sandy, hon."

"Sandy." It took a couple of beats, but then I sat up straighter. "You didn't happen to know a girl named Carrie Wyland when you were a kid, did you?"

Her face changed rapidly over the course of five seconds: it first registered surprise, then confusion, then sadness. "Carrie Wyland? Why in the world would you ask about her?"

"Oh—because her sister was just killed, you know. It was in the papers. And apparently Carrie herself died a couple of months ago."

Sandy Walton faced me in her pale pink smock, her eyes wide. "Carrie Wyland was one of the saddest chapters in my life. One of the happiest, at first. She was my best friend. Two years older than me and my idol in many ways. Oh, we had such fun growing up in Blue Lake!"

"So what made it sad?"

She shook her head. "I don't know. I mean, I don't know why she stopped talking to me, but she did. Just never spoke a word to me again or told me she was leaving town. I tried to find out where she went, so I could call or visit or write a letter, but she was just—gone. I cried myself to sleep for a long time, missing that girl. We were like sisters. And I—to this day, I have to tell you, even as a grandmother—I wonder what I did wrong. How I could have offended her."

Somewhere in her eyes I could see the hurt child she had once been.

"You didn't offend her. That's not why she left," I said.

She took a step closer to me. "How do you know anything about Carrie?"

"They're investigating Jane's death, and I happened to be talking to the chief of police yesterday . . . anyway, we found something out about Carrie. She left because of someone in this town, but it wasn't you. Unfortunately, she left all her friends behind. Her sister, too—her whole family."

"Yes, that's true. What—how do you know that someone made her leave town?"

I shrugged. "I'm sure it will all come out when they finish investigating. When the police have a press conference—her story will come out."

She stiffened suddenly. "You—you broke your arm in a car accident, right?"

"Yes."

"Is it—does it somehow relate to Jane?"

"Why do you ask that?" I asked. The light changed in the room, a shifting of sun to shadow, and she no longer seemed grandmotherly or nurturing. Her eyes, studying me, seemed sinister.

"I—it's silly, I suppose, but you said you had been talking to the police, and Jane's death was a shocking crime in this town, and then here you were with this terribly broken arm—"

I nodded, studying her face. "It may well be related to Jane's death. In fact, the same person may be responsible."

"Oh dear. Oh my, that's terrible." She looked pale; I felt a wild urge to call for Sam, but then the light shifted. The sun filled the room and she seemed again like a friendly receptionist. The door opened and Dr. Salinger came in, tall and attractive.

"Hello, Lena! How is that cast working out?"

Sandy excused herself and went into the hall, shutting the door behind her.

I stared at the closed door while Dr. Salinger studied my arm, saying, "Mmm-hmm," once or twice as she examined her handiwork.

"I'm not actually here about the cast," I said. "Although I did take a shower. I hope I didn't ruin anything."

"Nope. Looks good. What else is on your mind?"

She sat down in her wheeled chair and folded her hands, going into classic physician listening mode. "I had to stop taking the pain pills. I'm not in that much pain, anyway, but I've been—weird. Emotional, like you said, but other things. I'm suspicious of people."

"Suspicious?" Her brows rose.

"Yes. I've felt like there's no one I can trust. Not even my friends, or my boyfriend, sometimes. And yesterday there was a moment that—" I felt on the verge of tears suddenly, with her cool eyes on me. "I hated them."

She lifted my folder from her desk, peered inside. "Do you still have the pills?"

"Yes, in my purse. Unless my boyfriend threw them out this morning."

"Why would he throw out your medication?" Brows raised again.

"No, I mean—I told him to. I felt bad, the worst I've felt since I left here. But I've been pretty uneven emotionally. I know that, I can see it now, but when I'm having those emotions I can't see any other view. I've been wondering who did this to me and I've suspected almost everyone. To be honest, I was suspecting your receptionist a minute ago."

"Sandy?" she asked. She didn't laugh or mock me, much to my relief. She snapped the folder shut. "I definitely want you off the pills. You said you're not feeling much pain? You shouldn't be."

"No, I'm good. But I want to know how long I'll feel like this."

She frowned. "It's not a common side effect, but you seem to be experiencing some paranoia. If you stopped taking the drug yesterday, you shouldn't have too many more unpleasant reactions, although there can be withdrawal symptoms with the abrupt cessation of opioids."

"Meaning what?"

"Well, there can still be some anxiety or depression. Considering the fact that you just had a traumatic incident and that you've been experiencing the paranoia, I'm thinking that you won't be fully yourself again for a couple of days. You weren't on the pills long, but there are other factors that can affect your overall emotional and psychological health. You're a victim of trauma. Your body underwent a severe injury. And you need to process all of that emotionally; even after you get rid of the pills. I can give you a referral to a wonderful therapist, if you'd like to work through some of the emotions with her. It makes sense, anyway, post-trauma."

"Uh—I'll think about it," I said.

"I can at least write down her name." She patted her pockets. "I left my pad at the front desk. How about if you follow me there now? Unless you had any other questions?"

I was disappointed; I had hoped she would tell me a way that I could flip a switch and feel normal again, ready to sit with Camilla and dream up a suspense tale while we drank tea and laughed together. Ready to sit with Sam and not see his eyes creased with worry. Ready to reclaim my life . . . "No, I guess not."

She assessed me with a shrewd glance. "You have to be patient, Lena. And when you feel those strange feelings creeping in, tell yourself that you're imagining them. It helps to push back against them."

"Okay. Thanks, Doctor." I followed her to the front desk, where she jotted a name on a pad. Sandy was back in front of her computer, typing while she talked to someone on the phone, murmuring about the doctor's availability. Before I walked toward Sam she gave me a friendly wave.

I handed Sam the referral in the hallway. "What's this?" he said.

"A shrink. In case I want to go that way."

"What did she say?" he asked, taking my free hand.

I told him the gist of our meeting, and he nodded. "We can get through this, babe. Okay?"

"Okay."

I knew he was studying my face; I had no idea what expression I wore. He didn't say anything until we got to the car. Then he turned to me. "Something was wrong, even before the accident. Something about you and me. Tell me, Lena. Maybe it will help to talk."

"What do you mean? Nothing's wrong."

He shook his head. "Belinda told me that you were sad before the accident. Almost crying, she said."

"I was just emotional that day. Marge had told me this story about the bear, the grizzly in the lobby of Bick's. Did I tell you?"

"You can tell me later. What else was making you sad?"

I shrugged. "I think it was the letters. The ones from James to Camilla. I had started reading them, and Camilla told me about him. How they met and fell in love. It was—very romantic."

"I think the way we met is very romantic."

"It is!" I reached across my lap with my right hand to touch his arm. "I just—I got this weird thought in my head that you never really had the option to choose me. I was—sort of thrust into your life and you felt grateful to me, and things just progressed from there."

"That's nonsense." His mouth thinned into a line.

"The reality is that our relationship was forged under stressful circumstances. They say those don't last."

He stiffened. "Are you saying you're unhappy with me?"

"No! I love you."

"Then why are you manufacturing all this—drama?"

"I just wondered what it would be like if we had to be separated for months, the way James and Camilla were."

Sam's mouth hung open slightly. "You think I would lose *interest* in you?"

"I don't know. I'm just telling you how I felt—you asked me to tell you."

He snapped his mouth shut and looked out the windshield at the side of the hospital. "I didn't expect you to say *that*."

"Sometimes you seem restless. Even Camilla said so."

"What? What do you mean, 'restless'?"

"Like you would rather be somewhere else."

His blue eyes were wide as he studied me. Emotions warred on his face while I sat in silence. "Lena—I don't know what to say to you. This is the trauma talking, and the pills. I think I was wrong. I don't think we should talk about this right now."

"Okay." I turned to look out the window. There were ridiculous tears in my eyes once again.

SAM DIDN'T EVEN ask if I wanted to be dropped at Camilla's. He drove straight to his house and helped me out of the car. "I'm going to make you some lunch," he said. "You didn't eat breakfast, did you?"

"No. Thanks," I said. I was trying to scoop up kittens, but I could get only one. "Miss Arabella, I have caught you," I said. I set her on Sam's kitchen island and starting snapping pictures of her on my phone. I sent one to Camilla and said, *I'm having lunch at Sam's, but I'll come to see you soon.*

Then I dialed the phone. "Doug Heller here."

"Doug. Did you find all of our friends and squeeze their hands?"

Sam had been peering into his refrigerator, but he turned his head swiftly, looking alarmed.

Doug's voice was calm in my ear—too calm, as though he were speaking to a child. "Lena, we'll be seeing everyone today. The sun will not go down without us apprehending the man who put that car in the barn. You can relax. Have a cup of tea with Camilla and let Cliff and me do our jobs."

"Right. Fine. Thanks," I said, and I ended the call.

Sam closed the fridge and looked at me. He seemed to be choosing his words with care. "I know it feels terrible to not have control over the situation."

"You're right. It does."

He walked toward me and kissed my cheek. "Let me get started on lunch."

"I think I'll lie down for a couple minutes."

"Good idea. I'll call you when it's ready, okay?"

"Sure." I went upstairs and sat on Sam's bed. The two gray kittens were sleeping on it in a pile. "Hi, Jeeves and Wooster," I said, petting their silky soft fur. They lay, seemingly comatose, their tiny tummies going up and down. I took my phone from my pocket once more; it was almost out of battery power, but I risked dialing a familiar number.

"Lena?"

"Hi, Camilla. I'm sorry I've been AWOL for a while."

"Are you all right?"

"Not really. I'm moody and alienating everyone. I was just rude to Doug and made Sam feel bad."

"Lena, it's been four days since your arm was almost snapped off. No one is judging you."

I wiped my eyes. "I know. I guess. I just—I want

this to be over, Camilla. Doug says they'll have him, one way or the other, by tonight. But I need to go over it in my mind."

"Let's go over it together."

"I'm trying to see him. The way I saw him that afternoon before the crash. The way I've seen him in dreams and in a couple of visions that disappeared. I know he's there, right behind my consciousness."

"So we'll bring him out. Let's think of the clues. All the things James has told us, in his letters, about Carrie. Rusty called me this morning, adding to what you told me last night. I missed quite a series of events."

"I'm guessing you wish you had been there to hear it all firsthand."

"I do. But I'm glad that you got information. So our perpetrator might have a swollen wrist. But we know something else. Remember what you told us about your time in the recovery room? If you called out his name in the hospital, it was a strange name. Isn't that what the night nurse said? Doug was going to talk to her, wasn't he?"

"If he did, he never got back to us."

"Perhaps we should call her. But let's think: whose name would be considered strange?"

"Not Paul Graves. Unless she thought 'Graves' was weird," I said.

"Travis Pace?"

"Is that a weird name? I guess it might have sounded odd to her, especially if I slurred the first and last names together." I tried to imagine myself, asleep in that blue-walled recovery room, calling out the name of a murderer.

"Hmm. And what about Thibodeau? That's a remarkable name."

"Yes. So is 'Key.' I was actually feeling very suspicious of her, last night in the dark. I wondered if she were staring at me, wanting me dead. You see how weird I am?"

"It's not weird at all, Lena. One of those people *did* try to hurt you."

"So she's a suspect. Her name is unusual."

"But are we thinking about a woman at all?" Camilla asked.

I sighed. "I don't think so. Not if we're looking for a rapist. Assuming that the rapist is also the murderer, and the attempted murderer."

"Maybe Key's husband?"

"But would I have been thinking about her husband in the hospital? Even if I saw him in the rearview mirror, I wouldn't have recognized him. So how could I link that to his name?"

"Hmm. Yes."

"What about Rusty? What if I said his name? But he seemed genuinely surprised when he read his father's journal." And yet, hadn't I been truly afraid of him in the car? Hadn't I feared for my life?

"Let's look at it this way. If one of those men is a rapist and a killer, and we stood in front of him and said we would find the truth about Carrie, wouldn't it be hard for him to hide his dislike?"

"So we're taking the psychological view here. Okay, who seemed mean or aggressive at the restaurant?"

"They all looked a bit annoyed, even Marge and Karina. Well, maybe not Marge. She invited us over, after all. But you know what, Lena? Now that I think of it, most people had kind things to say about both Carrie and Jane. Except one person: do you remember?"

I thought back. "Someone said that they were grasping. That they were always grasping around for men or attention or something."

"Yes. Has anyone else ever said that about those women? James certainly never said a word against either of them."

"And who said that? Was it Travis?"

"Yes." Camilla's voice grew thoughtful. "Travis Pace. Really, when I think of it, wasn't it most inappropriate for him to speak ill of the dead? Of *two* dead women? Or was it perhaps that he couldn't resist trying to blame them for their own fates? Blaming the victim has always been popular among criminal types, hasn't it?"

"Travis," I said, mulling it over. "I'm going to call the hospital and ask Nurse Annie."

"You do that. I'm going to scour some letters to see if James mentions Travis's name. I know we certainly didn't see much of him when I got here. But, of course, James didn't know who was responsible, did he? I've been thinking about this since Rusty called. Poor James was in quite a dilemma, trying to protect Carrie and to get justice for her at the same time. And it turned out he could only do one of those things."

"Camilla, let me call you back. I want to call the hospital."

"All right. Call me soon."

I agreed and ended the call. My phone rang in my hand. I slid my finger across the screen. "Hello?"

"Lena? This is Sandy from Dr. Salinger's office. You left your purse here, dear."

"Oh, darn. How did I not notice? This is the second time I've done that." Dr. Salinger had told me to follow her to the front desk where she would write down the name of a therapist. I had done so, apparently leaving my purse behind . . .

"Rather than come back out, would you like me to have someone drop it off? I see you live off of Wentworth; I was just talking to my brother, and he's going that way. Shall I have him drop it off to you? He can be there in ten minutes."

"That would be wonderful, thanks. But I'm at a different address, right next to the other one." I gave her Sam's address. "Thanks again. And Sandy? Can you transfer me to another department?"

"Of course. What do you need?"

"I want to talk to Nurse Annie from recovery. Or at least she was working recovery a few days ago."

"I'll transfer you."

"Thanks, Sandy!"

A recovery nurse answered after three rings but told me that Annie wouldn't be on duty until four o'clock. I thanked her and ended the call. My hands itched, and I felt restless. I paced around the room, noticing that my little gray friends hadn't awakened through any of my phone conversations.

I found a charger in a drawer of Sam's bedside table and plugged in my phone. I looked up to see Arabella strolling past, with the mien of feline royalty. She certainly had settled in to her new house. I laughed and left the room.

Downstairs the table had been set with a lovely blue cloth; Sam had lit a fat white candle and set out colorful plates. I thought of the first meal we'd ever shared in his kitchen, when he'd made waffles for me and I realized that I was attracted to him. He waved from his spot at the counter and said, "I'm almost ready, Lena. Let me just toss out some bread for Eager." That was the name of Sam's chipmunk, who visited regularly in hopes of food.

"Okay. Someone's going to come to the door. I left my purse at the doctor's office and Sandy is sending her brother to drop it off."

"Sandy?"

"The receptionist." I realized I hadn't told him what Sandy said about Carrie. I could do that over lunch, assuming we could get over the new constraint that seemed to mark our dialogues.

Sam carried some crumbled bread to the glass door that led onto his patio and slung open the door. Little Geronimo appeared from nowhere and hurtled through the opening.

"Oh no!" I said. "Isabelle says to be sure to keep them indoors. It's safer, she says."

"Shoot," Sam said, and gave chase.

The doorbell rang. I stiffened, then realized it was probably Sandy's brother with my purse. I walked to the door. In retrospect it seems that I did it all in slow motion: moving toward the frosted glass–paneled door and seeing the silhouette of a man. The shape of my purse was visible in his hand, and I was already turning the knob when I realized something else: his hair made an odd halo around his head, just as it had in the gray light on Juniper Road. I paused, the knob turned to the right, but I stopped short of opening the door. *Travis Pace.* These thoughts went tumbling through my head:

If Travis Pace was on my doorstep, that meant he was Sandy's brother. No one had ever mentioned that Travis had a sister, or that she hung around with the group. But of course she hadn't, because "Sandy" had been two years younger than Carrie. Still a schoolgirl.

Sandy said that Carrie had never spoken to her again. If Travis Pace had raped Carrie, she wouldn't want to look at Travis or his sister or anyone who reminded her of him.

Travis Pace had a sister *who worked at the hospital*. He could have borrowed scrubs from her. He could have walked around undetected because everyone knew he was Sandy's brother.

Perhaps it was Sandy's car that had struck us?

It hadn't dawned on me that the door was essentially open because I had frozen after turning the knob. He pushed on it from his side and the door swung back.

Travis Pace forced a smile. "Lena? I think this is yours."

I couldn't hide my horror, or my recognition of his face as I had seen it just before the terrible impact. He saw my expression and knew everything in an instant. He threw my purse past me on the floor and pulled something out of his pocket with a hand that was weirdly swollen. I managed one short scream before I felt a pricking pain on my good arm and turned to see the syringe sticking out of it, then looked up in shock.

"What did you do?" I managed, my words slurred.

His face, filled with hatred and a weird triumph, was the last thing I saw before I fell.

✦──·✦ 17 ✦·──✦

I think you are brave and strong, Camilla. I
think women in general are braver than men.
—From the correspondence of
James Graham and Camilla Easton, 1971

FOR THE SECOND time in a few days I found myself
gradually returning to consciousness. Something
darted past my eyes, again and again, like a persistent
bird. After a few minutes I realized it was the flashing
of scenery—mainly trees—as we sped past them. We
were in a forested area.

My mind became lucid enough to panic. How long
had I been out? Were we still in Blue Lake? What if
he had taken me hours away? And what exactly did he
intend to do with me? I was lying on the backseat of
a car; I could see the back of Travis Pace's head as he
sat in the driver's seat. There was no one else in the
car. Surreptitiously, I readjusted myself so that I could
look directly out the window. The trees we flew past
did not look particularly familiar; I waited, hoping to
see a billboard, a road sign, anything that would give
me a sense of my location.

Finally, I spied a rustic wooden sign that said, "Entrance to Emerson Woods." The car slowed, then turned into the driveway.

My insides grew cold. The Emerson Woods Nature Preserve was in Canfield, which was several towns away from Blue Lake. I moved my good hand slowly and carefully over my pockets. My phone wasn't there. With a pang I remembered that I had been charging it at Sam's house. This was a desolate reality. The last time I had been in trouble, my phone had given me access to the outside world. I had called Doug and Cliff, and they had come to help me confront a madman.

How had Travis gotten me into the car? He had a sprained wrist; but adrenaline, I knew, could achieve wonders.

So here was another madman, driving me into a forest. What did they always say in self-defense presentations? Never let them take you to an isolated location. Never walk willingly into the woods with an abductor. I assumed Travis wanted to take me somewhere private before he did away with me. My thoughts pinballed crazily in my head as I tried to work out a solution. I needed to get away, to separate myself from Travis Pace. Perhaps if I held very still he would leave me alone; there was no way he could carry me far, and surely there would be other people here?

My main concern was that, while my thoughts seemed lucid, my fear impulse was dulled. I knew I should be afraid, but there was a distance between me and my terror. In a vague way I knew this was probably the residual effect of whatever drug he had given me, so I lay there in the backseat, almost peaceful, watching the trees flash by and wondering what to do.

When Travis finally pulled into a parking space just across from an opening in the trees, I saw that there were no other cars in the lot. This was not good. A remembrance of fear glimmered beneath my drug-induced calm.

Pace turned off his engine and stared out the front windshield for a while.

I lay still and silent.

"I know you're awake," he said, still facing forward. "I saw you squirming around back there."

I said nothing.

He said, "I'm not some kind of monster, you know. I just want to stay out of jail. If you and your friend Camilla had kept your noses out of things I wouldn't have to do this now."

My voice sounded weirdly serene to me. "That's called 'blaming the victim.' People do it when they're not capable of taking responsibility for their own actions. That's you in a nutshell, Travis. I have you figured out."

"Do you?" He sounded bored now.

I sat up, struggling against my cast. "Yeah. A spoiled, indulged, self-centered kid who couldn't believe someone would reject you. When Carrie did, you took what you wanted anyway, figuring somehow you wouldn't have to face any consequences. And I guess you were right. Only Carrie had to face them. She endured a traumatic experience and self-banishment from the town she loved. All because she knew society wouldn't punish *you*."

"You don't know anything about it. You weren't even alive."

"I know your type. Camilla and I write about them all the time. They're called the villains."

He tapped his hands on the steering wheel. "You're a lot like Carrie. She was very spirited. I loved her; I'm not some demon. I cared about her."

I snorted.

His eyes met mine in the rearview mirror, and there was a terrible moment of déjà vu: his eyes, angry as they were now, looking into mine before the giant impact, before the loss of control, before my world spun away while Camilla screamed my name . . .

"Why did you kill Jane?" I whispered.

"She wanted to dig it all up again. I have a career, a family. I couldn't have her maligning me with accusations from the past."

"It's not maligning if it's true." I suddenly remembered the hospital, the man in scrubs. "Why did you come to the hospital? My hospital room?"

He shrugged. "You saw me, huh? You said something, but I wasn't sure if you were talking in your sleep. I wanted to find out your condition. And to see if you recognized me. But some nurse was coming, so I couldn't."

"What if I had recognized you?"

He shrugged again.

In a tiny burst of heat, I said, "You still won't take responsibility. And look at you now: a man with a prisoner in your backseat. Look at your horrible life."

A part of my brain said it was a bad idea to anger him, to rile his violent tendencies, but it didn't matter.

My fear was emerging as fury, and I was flinging everything I could at him while we sat in our surreal tableau—he immobile in the front seat, I in the back. I didn't even consider running because I knew that my cast would slow me down and that despite his age he would catch me. Yet I saw no sign of a weapon . . . did he still have the gun which had killed Jane?

He turned toward me. "My life is just fine. You're the one who made this happen. Always digging into people's lives, disrupting them. You ruined that Greek tycoon—he had everything until he met you."

My mouth hung open. What was wrong with this man? "That *tycoon* held his wife prisoner and then kidnapped his own daughter. He eluded police and protected his sister when she committed murder. But wait, that probably all sounds okay to you, right?"

He threw his door open with a sudden violent movement that made me scream. He leaped out and flung open the door to the backseat. "Get out," he said. "We're going for a walk."

"No." My eyes darted around the parking lot, looking for any other vehicle. Why were beautiful places like this so often deserted?

His eyes lingered on my cast. "Get out, or I will come in and get you, and I won't be gentle."

My mind raced. I thought of Camilla's character, Prudy Penrette, who realized that her cousin had attempted to kill her and would come back again to kill her while she lay helpless in bed. When he crept into her room one night, she was awake and waiting for him, and she used the only weapon she had . . .

"Okay," I said, and I edged toward the door. "Move

away from the door so I can get out. It's harder with my cast."

He inched back and I swung my feet out of the car, stepping on the hard ground and straightening up to look into his face. I flexed the fingers of my one good hand. "Just one thing," I said.

"What?"

His face looked old, but I still saw the youthful defiance of a boy who felt he could claim everything as his own. He squinted slightly; he was facing the sun and I was facing away from it, and I prayed that would be an advantage.

"This," I said. I lunged forward, my right hand stiffened into a defensive claw, and thrust two fingers into his eyes. I jabbed hard, knowing I had only one chance. I felt moisture and a strange slick resistance, and he screamed in anger and pain.

Then I was running back the way we had come, my feet transformed to wings by adrenaline and terror. I heard nothing behind me at first, but gradually I heard rumblings—the noises of what could have been an angry bear. I moved off the long, wooded driveway and hurled myself into the trees, where I could potentially find a hiding place. Oh, for a phone, a phone, a phone . . . What must Sam have thought when he came back in from feeding Eager and chasing Geronimo? He probably hadn't been out there for more than a minute or two. He would have seen the door open, my purse on the floor, signs of a struggle. He would feel guilty. I didn't want him to have any more grief in his life. I thought of him as my feet hit the ground: poor Sam, poor Sam, poor Sam.

18

I read the suspense novel you recommended.
The last chapter was excruciating; how was it
that I felt so much fear for someone entirely
fictional?

—From the correspondence of
James Graham and Camilla Easton, 1971

THEY WOULD BE looking for me, of course. But how
would they know where to look? Doug and Cliff were
probably out scouring the roads, scanning for any
sign . . . but did they know who they were searching
for? What if no one even knew I was with Travis?
Would Sam remember what I had said about my
purse, about the receptionist? Surely they would be
able to trace that to him. Surely Camilla would tell
them what we had been discussing just before I went
downstairs?

I found a tight copse of trees and wedged my way
into it, breathing hard, trying not to groan as the sharp
branches cut my skin. I could barely see out, so I
doubted he would see in. I knelt down and tried to
silence my gasping breaths. I could hear him lurching
down the path, saying, "Where are you?" in a low,
ominous way.

He was coming closer; sweat ran down my face, and I realized for the first time how hot it was. My right hand started shaking, a tremor I couldn't control, and the branches around me rustled slightly. Would he notice it? If so, might he think it was caused by a passing breeze?

There is no breeze, my brain said, and I wished my left hand were free so that I could clasp my right one and hold it still. I was nearly weeping aloud when I heard footsteps on the path—new footsteps. Then a voice that said, "Travis." It was Adam.

I heard a sudden swirl of gravel and dirt—Travis had spun around. "What are you doing here?"

"I might ask you the same thing. Where's the girl, Travis?"

"What? What girl? What are you talking about?" Travis was a terrible actor. He may as well have admitted his guilt.

Then he sighed. "I don't have any girl. I'm taking a hike. It's a beautiful day. The question is, why are you here? Why would you even think to look for me here?"

Adam seemed to move closer. "A long time ago you said something about Emerson Woods. You were joking, supposedly. You said if you ever had a captive you would take them here. I never forgot it because I found it disturbing. And now here we are."

"You're obsessing over something I said as a kid? Get over yourself, Adam."

Silence.

Travis went for a lighthearted tone. "Well, feel free to join me. I'm hoping to get in a mile or two."

Adam made a sound, a snort of disbelief. "They know what you *did*. You attacked a woman right in front of a security camera. The police are after you. I wouldn't be surprised if they killed you on sight." His voice shook slightly.

Travis tried a different tack. "Adam, you have to help me. This is all a big misunderstanding. In the name of friendship, I'm asking you—"

"What? In the name of *what*? Carrie was your friend. Jane was your friend!" His outrage was audible. "Do you know, I think James knew it was you. Or at least he suspected. He broke away from everyone, but it was you that he avoided most of all. He never burdened me with that knowledge, though. Fool that I was, I went on being your friend. Shared meals with you, worked with you, never knowing what kind of man you were."

Travis's voice changed again. "Yeah, I know, I'm a monster. I already heard this speech."

A pause, and then Adam's voice, near tears. "You're out of breath, and sweating, and Lena is nowhere in sight. I am afraid to ask this question: what did you do with that girl, Travis? If you killed her, I will kill you."

A gasping sound. "Whoa, Adam, put the gun down. Let's not get crazy now. I don't know where she is. She ran away."

I sat frozen in my bushes. If I made a sound, it might distract Adam and give Travis an advantage. I didn't dare risk it.

Adam's voice again. "I don't believe you." The sound of a pistol being cocked. "I don't believe you, and I don't trust you. Camilla never did, either. I should have listened to her long ago. She told me there was something wrong about you, not long after she arrived."

Travis's voice, sneering despite his predicament. "We all know you were in love with Camilla. Did James know, I wonder? Did your wife know?"

"Don't speak about Camilla, or Judy. You're not worth the little finger of either of those fine women. I never knew what it was to hate someone, Travis, but I hate you."

Travis sounded panicked. "Put down that gun. I know you can't use it. You're not the type. You and James—you were always weak."

The cool fury in Adam's tone made me afraid. "If by 'weak' you mean we felt compassion for other human beings, then yes, Travis, we were weak. And I am disgusted I never saw before that you don't possess this particular *weakness*. Put your hands behind your head. Do it!"

A rushing, scrabbling sound, and then a sharp percussion, ringing in my ears. Adam had fired the gun. I gasped, but the sound was drowned out by what sounded like the scuffling of the two men. I stood up in place and saw that Travis had lunged forward and knocked Adam back, and they were fighting over the weapon.

I don't remember leaving the safety of the scraping bushes, nor do I remember walking toward the men. I know that I feared Adam would lose the struggle; Travis had an advantageous position, kneeling over him and grasping Adam's wrist.

Again, the drug in my blood seemed to have a

cloaking, dulling effect. I knew I had to help, but I felt little else, including fear. I moved forward, and Adam spied me over Travis's shoulder. His eyes widened. Later he told me that I looked like the madwoman from Rochester's attic—frantic hair; bloody, scratched skin; and wide, dark eyes.

I lifted my right foot and swung it back, then kicked Travis Pace so hard in the flesh of his side that he lost his grip on Adam and tipped over, howling in pain. Adam was saying something, thanking me, but I moved toward Travis again. He had rolled over and was moaning, asking me for help, and I lifted my foot again.

"Lena—" Adam said, but then stopped. Perhaps he realized the irony of trying to prevent me from causing pain to the man he had just threatened to kill.

I kicked Travis, hard, in the groin. "That's for Carrie," I said as he howled again. "And I have another one ready for Jane if you move again. And another for your poor sister. You took away her best friend, you loathsome monster!"

Adam kicked the gun down the path and glanced at Travis, curled into a fetal position, before he walked to me and folded me in his arms, and only then did feeling seem to return to my body.

"You're all right, Lena. I'm so *glad* you're all right!"

"And I'm glad you found me. How did you know?"

"Just a minute. Let me make a phone call." He dialed the phone and called Doug, then Camilla. I heard him say, "I know, sweetheart. I know. It's over now; she's safe." Vaguely I thought I heard Camilla crying.

"Will someone tell Sam?" I asked, still clinging to Adam.

"He was with Camilla. They—needed each other. I suppose they love you best."

I pulled back to look into his eyes. "But they're not the only ones who love me. And I love you, Adam. Thank you for being a good man."

Travis rustled on the ground and I glanced at him. He held up a hand and looked at Adam. "Don't let her near me again!" he said.

SEVERAL POLICE CARS were parked in the forest preserve lot, their lights flashing. Travis Pace had been read his rights and sat handcuffed in one of those cars. Doug and Cliff both left their duties briefly to give me bear hugs. "Stop trying to get attention," Doug said. He was aiming for a lighthearted tone, but it was belied by the tears that he quickly dashed away with one hand.

Cliff kissed my head. "Sam's been in agony, as you can imagine. I'm surprised he and Camilla aren't here yet. Hey, let's take a look at those scratches!"

He jogged to his car, then returned with a first aid kit and started putting ointment on my wounds. "Is the arm okay?" he asked.

I nodded. "Yeah. Thanks, that feels better. I probably look like a wild animal."

"You are the best sight I've ever seen in my life," Cliff said. "Doug cried like a baby when Adam called. He couldn't believe Pace scooped you up right on

Sam's doorstep. Do you know we had showed up at Pace's house to arrest him?"

"What?"

"Yeah. Marge Bick had been calling the station, saying she remembered something. She told Rusty that Travis had told her once that he liked Carrie. On top of that one of our techs ended up finding a fingerprint on the car in the barn. It belonged to Pace's sister, who was in our system because of a vandalism arrest, back when she was in high school. She told us she had lent the car to her brother, Travis, and he told her he had brought it in for some mechanical work. We headed straight to his place, only to find him gone. Then Sam called."

I processed this for a moment. "Travis was desperate. That's the only thing that would make him think he could get away with what he did. I'm so grateful that Adam had the idea to check Emerson Woods. All because Travis had said something creepy a long time ago, and Adam never forgot it. Hey, why are they examining him? Is he okay?"

A technician was looking into Adam's eyes with a penlight.

Cliff patted my shoulder. "He had a fall when Pace attacked him. Landed on his head, but he said he hit his tailbone first, so his head didn't bear the full force of the impact. He doesn't look like a guy with a concussion."

"Still," I said. "He should go to the hospital. Get it checked—"

A car tore into the parking lot and drove right up to

the place where Cliff and I stood. Camilla emerged first, looking frail. She held out her hands to me and I took them. "Oh, Lena," she said. "We really must draw the line between fiction and reality." She began to cry.

I embraced her with my good arm. "Camilla, thanks to fiction, I was able to get away from him. Prudy Penrette to the rescue!"

She snuffled in my ear, and Adam broke away from his attendant to walk toward Camilla and, in a knightly gesture, offer her a handkerchief. I pulled away from her slightly and patted her cheek, then leaned in to look at her in the sun. "Camilla, what color are your eyes?"

"They're violet," Adam said. "Dark violet, like Elizabeth Taylor's."

"I always thought they were brown. They're quite remarkable," I said. "I've never seen them in the sunshine like this, without your glasses."

Camilla sniffed and shrugged, but I studied Adam's face as he smiled down at her. What must it have been like for him, forty years ago, to fall in love with a woman who had come to America to marry his best friend?

I had been vaguely aware of Sam parking the car and coming to join us; he stood now at my shoulder. I turned and leaned into his embrace, then looked up into his face, which seemed to have aged a hundred years. My heart welled in my chest.

"Did you find Geronimo? Is he all right?"

He closed his eyes. "Yes, he's fine. God, Lena—"

"Don't feel bad," I said. "You were feeding Eager.

That makes you good. A horrible man attacked me; that makes him bad. Don't confuse those two."

He nodded. "But I am bad. If I had found him, Lena, I would have killed him." His eyes were on the car that held Travis Pace.

"No, you wouldn't. Adam felt the same way, and he couldn't do it."

"What's that?" Doug asked, with a surprised look at Adam.

Adam pointed toward the trail. "The gun is back there. I was going to tell you." Doug signaled to Chip Johnson, who ran back toward the path.

Travis shouted something from inside the car about a phone call and a lawyer. His voice made me stiffen, and the tremor returned to my right hand.

Sam's arms tightened around me. "You're shaking again. This is all too much."

"It might be," I agreed.

Sam spoke to Doug and the others over my head. "Are you finished with her for the time being?"

Doug must have nodded, or gestured, because Sam pulled me gently toward the car. "Come on."

"Gladly."

I turned to see whether Camilla was all right, but Adam was studying her violet eyes up close, and she was speaking earnestly to him.

Sam tucked me into the passenger seat and started the car again. "Camilla can go with Adam. I'm getting you out of this place."

"Good. Farewell, Emerson Woods. I shall not return."

"I don't mean the forest preserve," Sam said. "I mean Blue Lake."

I swiveled my head in surprise; Sam's profile was hard and determined. He looked like a man carved from stone.

❧ 19 ☙

Life is ugly sometimes; there are things that have made me question the compassion of God. But then, in the midst of a rotten reality, something beautiful can emerge. You are the beautiful thing in my life. And you have given me back my hope.

—From the correspondence of
James Graham and Camilla Easton, 1971

TWO WEEKS LATER I lay on a lounge chair, contemplating the blue sky above a turquoise ocean while gulls flew lazily above me. Tabitha, my father's wife, fussed around me as though I were a child. "Here's your piña colada, hon. I went light on the rum, the way you like it."

"I just like the coconut," I said, sipping it and smiling at her. "Thank you."

"And here's your book. I love this old hardback of Camilla's—where did you find this nice old-fashioned cover?"

"A friend of mine saved them for me when the library gave them away. I thought I'd bring some with me."

Tabitha plopped down beside me, adjusting the

umbrella she had poked into the sand. "I'm so glad Sam brought you here. And it was lovely to have him for a couple of days. I wish he could have stayed longer."

"Yes." I slung my leg over the side of my chair and made a pattern in the sand with my toe. It *had* been nice, watching Sam sit with my father at the dining room table, chatting about sports and politics and movies. It had been hilarious watching him bake cookies with Tabitha, wearing a frilly, bedazzled apron she had made herself and which she had placed upon him so proudly that he couldn't refuse. It had been lovely walking with him on the beach at midnight, the sand cool under our feet and his eyes mysterious in the moonlight.

He'd left after three days, telling me that I needed time to recuperate and time to be with my father. And only I would know how long a time it should be, he'd said before he kissed me good-bye.

I was furious, not only because Sam was leaving again, but because I knew he was right. Florida, and my father, and an escape from Blue Lake, had been just what I needed, and still needed.

"What else can I get you, sweetie?" Tabitha asked.

"Oh, please. Just rest, Tabby. You've been slaving over me since I got here. I'm doing fine. But I can't wait to get this cast off. It's been the only part of this visit that isn't perfect."

"It must be just murder," she said, her voice sympathetic. "But only about one more week, right? Then they'll remove that filthy thing, and life will go back to normal."

I studied the cast. The well-wishes people had scrawled in marker were beginning to fade. I could still make out Doug's name, and his faded message, "Don't ever do this again." I smiled. I saw Sam's name and the heart he had scrawled while wearing his perpetually distracted expression. Allison's "I will always take care of you" had degenerated to something like a warning: "take care." Still, it made me feel good to see the names on the red plaster: Doug, Sam, Adam, Camilla, Allison, Belinda. "I hope so. I am looking forward to getting it off. But a part of me doesn't want to leave Jupiter beach. It's like paradise. If paradise were on fire. Geez, I thought Blue Lake was hot."

Her laugh was like a little tinkling bell. "You're so funny, Lena."

I really wasn't, but Tabitha had always thought so. Maybe, to her, I was.

My father appeared, wearing white shorts and a coral polo shirt. "Mail call," he said cheerily, kissing me on top of my head. "Yes, my eager child, you got some." He handed me a stack of mail, and I flipped through it greedily.

"Thanks, Dad."

"You would think that whole town was in love with you," my father said indulgently, bending to kiss Tabitha's cheek. "Did you both put on enough sunblock?"

"Yes, I made sure," Tabitha said.

They kept talking, but I was distracted by my mail. Doug had sent me a postcard—the third from him in the last two weeks—on which was a picture of Blue Lake at sunset. On the back he had scrawled, "Enough vacation already. Belinda misses you. And I need to beat you at Trivial Pursuit."

Doug had called me once, as well, to fill me in on what he had learned about Carrie. They found her son, William Guthrie. Carrie had in fact married her employer, now an eighty-year-old man, named Cal Guthrie. Carrie and Cal had another child five years after William was born—a girl named Jane, most likely named after Carrie's sister. "William told us that his mother was a generally happy woman. She told him she had family in Blue Lake, and someday when he was older he should look them up. But she said she herself was never going back. Carrie died a few months before her sister Jane was killed; she had been battling cancer."

"It's sad that she felt banished from her town," I said. "But I'm glad to hear that she was happy."

"William said she was an ideal mother. He was clearly under the impression that Cal Guthrie was his father, and I did not tell him otherwise. I did say that there are records here in Blue Lake relating to his mother, and to her sister's murder, if he or his sister, Jane, ever want to look at them."

"What else is happening in Blue Lake?" I had asked.

"Nothing. You're on information lockdown until further notice. Sam wants you relaxing, not finding things to worry over. Go play in the sand."

Grinning at this memory, I opened Camilla's letter, which shared some of her latest ideas for our book and was signed with Lestrade's paw print—a sweet touch that made me feel rather tearful.

Finally, I opened Sam's letter. He had written me one almost every day, and I knew that he was feeling pressured to be like James Graham, to give me the sort of correspondence that I had so admired in Camilla's relationship, although it wasn't the letters themselves that had been compelling.

Still, the fact that Sam wanted to provide them made me feel weak inside, as did the first line of today's letter: "I know Blue Lake has been rough on you, but it also isn't Blue Lake without you."

I paused, thinking about this, and saw my father watching me. "Your color is much better," he said. "You were like a ghost when you got here."

"I feel better. Very good, actually. Just a few more days ought to do me," I said.

He brushed some sand from his knee and said, "A part of me wishes you would move here permanently. There are some nice condos right down the road. You and Sam could buy one, and we could be neighbors."

"That sounds nice."

"But another part of me thinks I need to push you out of this little comfort zone before you convince yourself you can never go back to Blue Lake. It's been a complicated place for you, but everything that makes you happy is there."

"Except you and Tabitha."

"And we'll always welcome you here."

I sat and thought about this. Even my father, who generally begged for my visits, was suggesting that I should go home.

"Maybe we'll buy a condo anyway. Then we have an excuse to come here more often."

My father's handsome face lit up. "Now you're talking!" he said.

"And when I say 'we,' I mean Sam. He's the one with all the money."

Tabitha giggled and gently slapped my knee. "Oh, Lena, you are so funny!"

On the night we met, my face was the first you saw when you entered the room. And when your plane lands, and you finally come home to Blue Lake, my face will be the first you see in the crowd waiting at the gate.

—From the final letter sent by
James Graham to Camilla Easton, 1971

MY TAXI PULLED up outside Graham House at eight in the evening. I had told Camilla I was coming back, but no one else. I wanted one evening to myself to get my bearings.

Just before the driver flipped off his radio, I heard the start of a story on the local news: "After more than a week's incarceration at the county courthouse, a Blue Lake man was transferred to an Indianapolis jail today for his arraignment on charges of murder and attempted murder. He is also allegedly the perpetrator in a forty-year-old rape case. At the advice of his counsel, he has pleaded guilty to the two charges. His attorney will ask for a reduced sentence in exchange for his client's cooperation . . ."

I trudged up the steps, feeling a bit weary after a flight and a cab ride. My driver kindly put my bags on the porch for me, and Adam appeared to tip the man. "Welcome back, my sweet," he said, kissing my cheek. "You would not believe how much you were missed."

My father had said something similar when I arrived in Florida, and I stood on the porch for a moment, reveling in the knowledge that I was loved—and longed for—by two different families.

Camilla appeared at the door, wearing a pair of white pants and a peach linen shirt. "You look like a dreamsicle," I said, and she darted forward to hug me. Rochester and Heathcliff, like busy river barges, milled around us and tripped us repeatedly as we tried to walk to the kitchen.

My cat, Lestrade, who normally gave me the silent treatment after one of my absences, strolled into the kitchen just as we did and stropped around my legs. "Wow! Lestrade isn't mad at me!"

Camilla bent to pet him. "As you requested, we gave him lots of extra attention so that he wouldn't feel neglected. It seems to have worked."

"I think it's because he sees you as his family now," I told her. "We both do."

She smiled at me, then at Adam. "We are both very glad to see you."

"I believe you and I have work to do," I said.

Adam yawned. "Well, now that you ladies have been reunited, I will leave you to your catching up. I have an appointment with my pillow."

I frowned. "Adam, it's only eight o'clock."

He smiled absently. "Oh? Oh yes. Well, we've been

very busy around here. Camilla's garden, and her book notes, and doing Rhonda's work—Rhonda's back, by the way—and it's just been a very busy time."

"Fair enough." I hugged him. "Adam? I was wondering something on the plane as I came back. Do you mind if I ask you something kind of personal?"

"What's that, dear?"

Camilla moved closer, curious. "Remember when we were all looking through photos, trying to figure out what could have made Carrie leave? And Sam found that letter in your photo album. You acted so strange about it . . . and you put it away. I just wondered what it was. Who it was from. I know it's none of my business, but it had me curious."

Adam smiled at Camilla, who smiled back. Ever since I had realized her true eye color I couldn't seem to focus on anything except that alluring purple.

Adam said, "It's funny you should ask. Camilla and I discussed that letter just a couple of days ago. It was from James. I decided that she should read it."

"Oh, okay. If it was too personal—"

He slid an arm around Camilla's shoulders. "James told me, in the note, that he knew I was in love with Camilla. This was just before their wedding. He said he understood. He couldn't believe that every man who saw her didn't fall in love with her. That's how generous my friend James was—he knew I loved his fiancée and he said he understood." Adam shook his head. "Anyway, he wanted me to know that he knew because he didn't want it to cause estrangement between us, and because he believed that I could still have a good relationship with Judy; we were going steady at that point. He was right. We had a wonderful marriage."

"I wish I had met him," I said. "But in this last month—I feel as if I did."

Camilla touched my hair, then said, "Adam, I'll walk you to your car."

I kissed Adam good-bye, and they moved toward the front door. Adam called back, "Lena, I already moved your bags upstairs."

I climbed the familiar staircase of Graham House and found my room was cool and lovely; Camilla had flipped on a lamp and turned back a corner of my coverlet. There were roses in a vase on my side table, a sure sign that Rhonda was back in town, and my curtains were thrown open so that I could see the lake, just a moving shadow now in the waning light. Lestrade leaped up on the bed and began to take one of his elaborate baths.

I sat down and said, "I'm home, boy. This is home, now and forever."

Lestrade stopped his toilette momentarily to twitch a whisker at me. He did not seem impressed by my decision. That's what made him my Lestrade.

By ten o'clock Camilla and I were talked out and ready to sleep. "I must confess I think that the anticipation of your arrival used up some of my energy," she said, yawning. "I don't normally feel this tired."

"Me either. Must be something in the Blue Lake air. Well, I'm off to bed."

"Good night, dear. I'm so glad to have you back in your room. This house isn't the same without you."

"Thank you. I am glad to be back, Camilla. You've made this my home, and I missed it."

I gave her a hug and trudged up the stairs. I washed up in the bathroom and donned the long Sherlock Holmes T-shirt that served as my pajamas. My window curtains were still open. Hadn't I shut them? Clearly, I was as tired as Camilla was.

I moved to the window and realized that now it was so dark I could not see the lake at all, but merely the shadowy, wide expanse of Camilla's yard before it led to the sand below. This, too, was dark, except for a strange, dancing light. People walking with flashlights? I leaned closer to the pane. The light was brighter now, and leaping, jumping, as if it were—flame.

Fire.

The first thought in my head was that Travis Pace had escaped and was back, furious and vengeful. These flames were the revenge that ended *Jane Eyre*, that ended *Rebecca*. Didn't everyone get revenge through fire?

I tore into the hallway, where Camilla was wandering past in her robe, clutching a novel and a book light. "Camilla, something's on fire on the lawn! I think we need to call the fire department!"

Her eyes grew wide and the book fell from her hand. "Oh dear. Oh my. I'll call now." She moved toward her room, where one of her two landlines sat on a table. "Lena, peek out the kitchen window and see how bad it is," she called.

I ran down the hall and tore down the stairs.

Heathcliff and Rochester were at my heels, and they gave me courage. In the dark kitchen the flames were more visible, but they were strangely contained—I saw what looked like several separate fires burning on Camilla's back lawn. "We're going out there," I said to the dogs. I grabbed Camilla's fire extinguisher from under the sink and opened the door.

"Who's there?" I called. There was no sound except the rustling of trees and the lapping of the lake.

I moved forward and saw that there were three barrels set at intervals of three feet or so; each one was on fire, or at least contained fire. The grass wasn't on fire, nor were the trees, and there seemed to be no danger of it spreading. It looked like a weird nighttime barbecue.

"Travis?" I called. He couldn't be out of jail, could he?

I moved closer, emboldened by the dogs, who stayed near my feet. Only then did I notice that something had been painted on each barrel. *Star Kelly!* said my brain, and I felt bitter disappointment at the idea that she might be vandalizing again. But what grudge could she have against me, or Camilla?

I inched forward and leaned toward the barrels until I could feel the heat of the crackling flames. The words were written in some sparkly substance that made them glow in the darkness, one on each barrel. The message, I now saw, said:

Marry Me Lena

I'm not sure how long I stared, but then I spun around and saw a shape in the darkness. It moved forward and resolved into Sam. I hadn't seen him in weeks, and he had never looked more handsome to me than he did then, with his hands thrust in the pockets of his jeans and his hair blowing in the breeze. "Sam."

"I'm sorry I frightened you. I was going for dramatic," he said.

A light went on in Graham House, and I saw Camilla and Adam standing at the window, fully dressed. "What is going on? She lied to me! She was dressed under that robe! She is a *conspirator*!"

Sam waited until I looked back at him. "Lena. It's time for us to talk."

"How did you even know I was back?"

"Your father called the minute you got on the plane. Another conspirator, I'm afraid."

"Unbelievable."

He edged slightly closer. "Did you like my letters?"

"I loved them."

"Did you believe what I wrote in them?"

"Yes, mostly. I didn't believe the stories you made up about Geronimo. I think he's a little too small to fight off intruders."

"Those might have been exaggerated. Although he did climb all the way up the living room curtains. I think Arabella was egging him on. She's a troublemaker."

"I see." I smiled down at the dogs.

"Lena? If I had a thousand chances I would always choose you."

"Sam—"

"No, listen. There's a reason I wanted to light fires in your backyard. Look up at the stars."

I did, appreciating the speckled, glittering sky.

"Now imagine if they were all gone, along with the moon."

I closed my eyes and pictured the void of blackness, the sad emptiness of space without light.

"Lena, you are my light in the darkness. You have been, from the first day. If I try to imagine a life without you—and believe me, over the last couple of weeks, I had some very dark moments when I thought that might be possible—it's dark and empty and dismal." He took another step forward. "I love you. Not because I have to. Not because I'm grateful. But because you're Lena and I fell in love with you practically the moment you entered this town. I want you to marry me and be in my life forever. Now tell me what you want."

I looked up at the stars again. The wind was back, more gently, and it caressed my face. My eyes moved to the barrels and the glittering words. I wiped away some tears. Sam moved closer. "Lena?"

I took a deep breath. "I would love to marry you, Sam West. I would marry you tonight if I could."

He held out his arms and I dove into them, careful of the cast that would soon be a thing of the past. I leaned my head against his chest and felt his heart beating. "This is very beautiful and romantic, and I'll remember it my whole life. Thank you for that."

"I bought a ring. I left it with Adam because I didn't want to lose it out here in the dark."

I smiled and looked up into his blue eyes. "I don't need a ring, but I'm sure it's beautiful and I will love it."

He pressed his mouth against mine, and I didn't pull away until I heard footsteps marching toward us across the grass: Doug and Cliff, wielding their own fire extinguishers. "Take it inside," Doug said, grinning at us.

Suddenly Graham House was filled with light. I heard a hint of music and saw people moving around. "I'm in pajamas," I said. "Are they throwing an engagement party in there? And if so, what if I had said no?"

"We all would have gone home," Cliff said, dousing the fire in the first barrel.

"Don't destroy the lettering," I said. "I'm going to turn those into planters or something. I want to save them forever."

Sam kissed my hair. "I am a happy, happy man."

The scent of the lake reached us on a fresh breeze. Somehow the stars seemed to glow even more brightly once Sam's firelight was extinguished. They hung above us like diamonds that had spilled out of the waxing gibbous moon. I lifted my fiancé's hand and kissed it. "And I'm a happy woman. Let's go in so I can put on some clothes to attend my own engagement party."

We began to walk across the grass, accompanied by two jocular policemen and two excited dogs.

In the doorway of the house I saw Camilla Graham, watching and waiting to celebrate with us. My free hand was in Sam's, so I nodded at her.

She waved, and I remembered with a new burst of joy that we had a novel to finish writing, and that we would most likely get back to it in the morning.

Keep reading for a sneak peek of

DEATH WITH A DARK RED ROSE

the next Writer's Apprentice Mystery . . .

*A reader wants a heroine she can understand,
admire, aspire to be. But a reader also wants to
see that main character as an extension of herself. If the heroine confronts a murderer, the
reader does so as well, as the heroine's loyal
companion in that story. The average reader is
just as good and clever and brave as the person
she chooses to follow into a literary adventure,
and a good book helps her (or him) come to that
realization.*

—From the notebooks of Camilla Graham

NOSTALGIA ISN'T A phenomenon reserved exclusively
for those in later life; it can take a person of any age
by surprise, simply by reminding them of what once
was, and is no more. Walking through Blue Lake, Indiana, on a crisp October morning made me feel nos-
talgic for a Lena London of the past, a Lena who
would never exist again. That Lena had entered town
under a dark cloud, full of fear and wonder at the idea
of meeting her new employer (and idol) Camilla Graham. That Lena had been surprised to meet a young
police detective on the side of the road, and then later
at the site of a murder, and had been initially suspicious

of his charm. She had disliked the local recluse, Sam West, on sight, but grew troubled when she learned his tragic story. And she had been glad to know that at least one person in town, her best friend from high school, Allison Branch, would always love and protect her.

Now, almost a year later, standing on a scenic overlook that let me admire the sun-dappled town and the glorious lake (which did in fact look very blue today), I realized how different my life had become—drastically, irrevocably different. Camilla Graham, my unknown employer, had become my family, my dear friend and confidant. Doug West, too, that wonderful police detective who had solved several mysteries in town since my arrival, was like my brother, and his girlfriend, Belinda, a genius of a research librarian who had helped me solve two very personal mysteries, was like a sister. Allison had proven her friendship to me time and again, most recently when I was recovering from a terrible injury, and she had nursed me both physically and emotionally. All of my Blue Lake friends had become a sort of family in one way or another. Most significant of all, Sam West, the scowling, unfriendly neighbor of one year ago—the man who had been accused of murdering his own wife, and later of murdering his wife's friend—was in fact a sweet, kind, gentle, generous, and sexy man. He stood beside me now, not as a friend or a neighbor, but as my fiancé. I glanced down at the ring on my left hand, and at the scar on my left arm, partly visible now that I had pushed up the sleeve of my sweatshirt; it was more than six inches long when totally uncovered. Some memories stayed with you, imprinted on your very skin . . .

"Are you having one of your deep-thoughts meditations?" asked Sam, studying me with his lovely blue eyes. "Because you've been awfully quiet, and I thought we were going to make some wedding plans while we walked."

"Sorry. It's been almost a year, did you realize that? It struck me this morning when I put Lestrade's vet appointment on the calendar. Almost a full year in this town, and a lot of turbulent water under the bridge."

"Very true." Sam looked out at the lake, but reached out his right arm and pulled me against his side. "But it's true that sometimes you can come through adversity and find life even better on the other side. How can I complain when I have you? And Cliff? And all these new friends?"

"You can't," I said.

"Then I won't." He leaned over and kissed the top of my head. "Do you want to get married here? Or in Chicago, where you grew up? Or in Florida, near your dad? Or in Indianapolis, where we've escaped for some very romantic dates? Or on some far-flung island, like all those trendy people who have 'destination weddings'?"

"How do you know about destination weddings?"

"I've done my research. I'm a very thorough person." He looked at me, all windblown brown hair, deep smile lines, and intense blue eyes, and his second statement seemed somehow suggestive. I blushed, and he smiled.

I shook my head and looked back at the lake, taking a deep breath of fall air. "Mmm. Someone is burning leaves. I have to tell you—despite everything we've been through in this town, I can't imagine getting married anywhere but here, can you?" I glanced back his way.

He shrugged and smiled. "Not really."

"Okay. One wedding plan decided. It will happen in Blue Lake."

"Actually two plans. The first was that we decided who to marry."

"That goes without saying."

"I just like to say it," said Sam. "I'm going to marry Lena London."

I hugged him and kissed his newly shaved cheek. "I like it when you say it, too."

"It's a good thing Cliff and Doug aren't here. They would find our dialogue disgusting."

"Only because they're jealous. Though God knows why. They both have amazing women in their lives. At least Doug does. Is Cliff still dating Isabelle?"

"I think so. Or at least they've gone on a few dates. They both work weird shifts, which makes it harder."

"Love conquers all," I said.

"Ours did."

I squeezed him more tightly. "That should be in our vows, don't you think?"

"Absolutely. Along with something about not believing in first impressions, and the importance of cats and dogs in forming a strong relationship."

I giggled. Sam had recently become the adoptive parent of four cats, two of whom he gave to his half brother, Cliff (another new addition to his life). Now, between his two cats, my spoiled feline Lestrade, and Camilla's two dogs, we had been forced to make animals a big part of our daily routine.

Sam's phone buzzed in his pocket, and he pulled it out and answered, after kissing my cheek. "This is Sam . . . Hey, Doug, we were just talking about you! What? Okay—yeah, we can do that. No, that's fine. We'll be there in ten minutes." He ended the call, his expression suddenly sober.

"What's wrong?"

"I'm not sure. He said he needs our help, and he wants us to come to Belinda's house."

"What? That's weird. Is he on duty?"

"I don't know—wait, yes I do. Cliff told me last night that he, Cliff, was on duty today because Doug had the day off and was going to take Belinda to Daleville for their Oktoberfest."

"Okay, let's go. We can take my new car—it's closest." We moved quickly back down the path until we reached the pebbled driveway of Graham House, where Camilla lived. She was outside now, throwing tennis balls for her German shepherds, Heathcliff and Rochester, who cavorted in the fall air like happy lambs. Camilla looked good. She had new glasses that accentuated her lovely bone structure, and she had been taking daily walks with her devoted boyfriend, Adam, leaving her looking fit and content. She was about to embark on a two-day escape with Adam, in search of togetherness and fall color.

"Hello," she said. Then, ever attuned to our feelings, she said, "Something's up?"

Sam shrugged. "Doug called and asked us to come to Belinda's. He sounded a little . . . out of sorts."

The dogs were back; they laid slobbery balls at Camilla's feet, and she picked them up and threw them again. "Go, by all means. Lena knows I was going to have lunch with Adam, anyway. But please do keep me apprised, if anything is going on."

I think Camilla saw us all as her Blue Lake children—me and Sam, and Doug Heller and Belinda, and my best friend Allison and her husband, John. We were all around the same age, and we all looked up to Camilla and Adam. If Blue Lake was a kingdom, then they were the king and queen, with their castle at the top of the bluff. "We will, of course," I said. "And I know we're back on our writing schedule on Friday, correct? Meanwhile Sam and I will keep an eye on things here."

"Thank you. It's a lovely time to go see the fall color, isn't it? I think Adam wants to leave by noon. But I'll have my phone on, and I want to hear everything."

"Yes, all right. Have a great time." I gave her a quick hug, then ran inside to get my keys and purse, and then Sam and I climbed into my new car—a green Dodge Caravan. My father had approved its safety rating (since my last car had been totaled in an accident) and my insurance company had approved the price. I waved to Camilla as we pulled away; the dogs stood at her feet, staring at me with wide, panting mouths.

Navigating the pebbly downward road, lined with trees dressed in yellow and rust-colored leaves, I stole a glance at Sam. "Any guesses what this could be about?"

He shook his head. "Truly not a clue. Everything seemed fine last night, didn't it?"

We had dined with Doug and Belinda the evening before; Sam had barbecued steaks on his back patio and we ate them in his large kitchen. Belinda had been proud of the potato salad she'd made from scratch, and Doug's eyes had drifted to her often, just as his hand often found its way into her long blonde hair. He smiled at her whenever she addressed him. It had been very sweet and comforting to see them so happy together.

I knew the way to Belinda's house well now; I had visited it first at a July 4th celebration (not a happy evening), but had been back several times since, sometimes in a joining of couples, sometimes just when Belinda and I wanted to chat. On those latter occasions, my friend Allison occasionally joined us. We all had different work schedules, so our social meetings had to be carefully timed. We did a lot of texting.

By the time we reached Belinda's subdivision the sky had become slightly overcast. I waited until Sam met my eyes. "Why am I nervous?" I said.

"It's fine." He brooded for a moment before he said, "Although it's very unusual behavior for Doug."

I pulled into Belinda's driveway; it was covered in yellow leaves from a tulip tree in her front yard. I wondered why the meticulous Belinda hadn't been out raking them. They were even scattered across the windshield of her car, which sat just in front of the closed garage.

We got out and went to the door, only to find it ajar. "Doug?" I called, pushing the door open. We entered Belinda's familiar, airy living room and moved toward the kitchen, where we heard rustling. Doug stood at

Belinda's kitchen island, opening drawers and rifling through the contents. The room was in disarray. Sam looked as surprised as I felt. "Doug?" he said.

Doug looked up at us, his brown eyes troubled. "Hey—thanks for coming. I need your help."

"What's going on?" I said, setting down my purse and giving him a quick hug.

"I came here to pick up Belinda. Her car is there, and her door was unlocked."

"Maybe she ran a quick errand with a friend?"

He frowned. "I tried to text her, ask her where she was. That's when I realized her phone is still here, along with her purse." He pointed to a little side table which held those items. "And this." He went to her counter and held up a single long-stemmed dark red rose, fresh and perfect. "This wasn't here last night when I dropped her off," he said. "And if Belinda had bought it, she would have put it in a vase."

That was true. We all knew Belinda.

"So if she's gone on an errand, she's doing it without money or identification?" Sam asked.

"Something's not right," Doug said. "Nothing's been ransacked—I made this mess. The house was perfectly clean when I got here, just with a rose on the counter. But she hasn't been in touch. We should have been in Daleville now, looking at fall color." He glanced out at some autumn trees rustling near Belinda's kitchen window, his eyes creased with concern. Then he looked back at us. "I think someone took her."